VIPER

Fallen Angel Series #2

BROOKE BLAINE
ELLA FRANK

Also by Brooke Blaine

South Haven Series
A Little Bit Like Love

A Little Bit Like Desire

The Unforgettable Duet
Forget Me Not

Remember Me When

L.A. Liaisons Series
Licked

Hooker

P.I.T.A.

Romantic Suspense
Flash Point

PresLocke Series
*Co-Authored with *Ella Frank
Aced

Locked

Wedlocked

Fallen Angel Series
*Co-Authored with *Ella Frank
HALO

VIPER

ANGEL

Also by Ella Frank

ONE

Viper

FUCK. I FEEL amazing...

The distant sound of crashing waves woke me from one of the best night's sleep I'd had in months. It was a lazy sound, relaxed, a direct contrast to the hot-as-hell sounds that had come from Halo last night when I'd been deep inside him, making him shout my name.

I stretched beneath the tangle of sheets, burrowing my face into the pillow, and as the smell of Halo's shampoo hit me, I ground up against the mattress. I groaned, that scent making my blood hum through my veins as my body revved up for round two, and suddenly, the mattress wasn't good enough. I wanted Halo under me, I wanted his legs wrapped around my waist, and I wanted to watch that flawless face of his when we came all over each other. And with that delicious thought in mind, I turned my head, searching for the angel who had weaved a spell over my throbbing cock.

The room had been swallowed up by shadows, and as I reached across the wide expanse of the California king to get my hands back on the body mine seemed to crave, my hips stilled, as I felt around the empty space beside me.

Putting my hands on the mattress, I shoved up so I could look over to the other side of the bed, and when I found it empty, I glanced over my shoulder, to see if Halo was somewhere else in the guesthouse. When all that met my eyes was darkness, I cursed and shifted over to the nightstand so I could flick on the bedside lamp. I winced against the brightness of it as I turned to sit up, and as I scanned the living space, taking in my duffel bags and guitar, it became crystal clear that the only thing missing from the room was Halo.

What the fuck? He left? When? I shoved my fingers through my hair and pressed the heel of my hand against my dick, trying to get it to calm down now that I knew it wasn't about to get any kind of fucking action. My mind was busy trying to play catch-up, but with the fog of sleep still lingering, I was finding it difficult to put two and two together.

Halo had left my bed. Crept out like a thief in the goddamn night. And while I'd usually be ecstatic if one of my casual hookups took such initiative, the fact that Halo was gone and I wasn't done with him yet had me swinging my legs over the edge of the mattress to hunt down a pair of sweats.

As I rounded the end of the bed for the duffels, I spotted my phone over on one of the recliners and made a beeline for it. Picking it up, I checked to see if Halo had left a text or a voice message, and when nothing came up, I tossed it back on the cushion and grabbed some sweats from my bag.

After pulling them on, I picked the phone back up and reached for the packet of cigarettes on the coffee table. I made my way to the French doors, unlocked them, and pushed them open, still trying to think of a logical reason as to why Halo had ghosted. That had never happened to me before, ever. Usually, it was the other way around.

Planting my ass on one of the Adirondack chairs, I stared at my phone, trying to decide what the fuck to do next, because this... this was so far outside the norm for me that I had no clue what was expected of me right now. Was anything?

Fuckin' Halo. I swear, ever since he'd shown up, he'd had me all kinds of messed up. I wasn't the insecure type, but here I was before the ass crack of dawn staring at my phone like a schmuck and wondering if he'd run away because I'd done something to upset him.

Had I hurt him? *No.* I *knew* Halo had enjoyed himself. Hell, I'd made sure he got off before I even thought about it, and when he came all over my hand and his ass had tightened around me, I'd had a difficult time holding back to give him what he'd asked for.

But I did. I gave him exactly what he'd asked for. He used me, I used him, and there was no reason I should be sitting out here feeling— *Shit*, I didn't know what I was feeling. But it was nothing good.

Opening up a new thread on my phone, I shot off a quick text to the angel. Correction, I shot off a quick *lame* text. **You okay?**

I wasn't sure how long I stared at the phone, three, five, ten minutes. But when I got no reply, I shook my head and reached for my pack of cigarettes. As I lit up, I stared out at the white wash crashing onto the sand and couldn't stop my mind from replaying in vivid detail the words, the images, the sublime feeling of finally having Halo in my bed, and I knew I was screwed. Once hadn't been enough for me; I'd woken up wanting the unthinkable— more. But judging by the angel's vanishing routine and my unsatisfied cock, it seemed like once was all I was going to get.

Fuckin' Halo...

TWO

Halo

_____

I WRAPPED A towel around my waist as I stepped out of the shower the next morning, still feeling the ache in my muscles even after soaking them under the hot water. But I wasn't sad about that. Not at all. The soreness I felt was a reminder of my night in Viper's bed, and I wanted to hold on to it for as long as I could.

As I brushed my teeth, I looked at myself in the mirror, expecting to see some kind of physical change, one that would blast to everyone what I'd done last night. *I had sex with Viper,* it would say. *And I fucking loved it.*

But, of course, there was nothing there, no words written across my forehead, no markings anywhere someone would be able to see. My eyes dropped down to the barely there bruises along my hips from where Viper's fingers had gripped me as he drove into me from behind.

God, he'd made me so crazy, so delirious with lust that I thought I'd known what to expect when it finally happened, but nothing, and I mean nothing, could've prepared me for the force that was Viper. The sheer control he wielded over my body, playing it the same way he dominated his guitar, had been like nothing I'd ever experienced. Had I known how fucking good it would feel to have Viper inside me, I would've let my guard down a hell of a lot earlier.

But then I'd still be in the same situation I found myself in now, wouldn't I? Creeping out of the guesthouse in the middle of the night to avoid an awkward morning after that I had a strong feeling Viper usually did his best to avoid. Knowing him, he'd wake up grateful I'd given him an out, though I wouldn't have minded staying, stealing more time with him.

And that was the problem, wasn't it? What had he called me last night? A "romantic"? I could already see the way this thing would go, and I needed to stick to what I'd told myself would happen from the first moment I found myself being tempted by Viper. He was a one-and-done kind of guy, he didn't do relationships, and while whatever this thing was between us had exploded in something seriously hot last night, that was all it would ever be, and it had to be enough to get him out of my system. I couldn't afford to be stupid about this or let emotions get involved. We were bandmates, for fuck's sake, and that needed to take priority over everything.

After rinsing my mouth and tying my hair back so I wouldn't have to deal with it today, I threw on a pair of shorts and a T-shirt and then grabbed my phone from the jeans I'd been wearing last night. As I turned on the cell, a message from Viper, sent around three a.m., popped up.

You okay?

I sat down on the edge of the bed, my eyes still on the two simple words. So Viper had woken up after I left to realize I wasn't there, and shot off a text to check on me? I doubted he sent a message like that to his other one-night stands, and for some reason, that made something in my chest lurch.

I started to text him back but got a look at the time and jumped up, shoving my cell into my shorts pocket. It was closing in on ten a.m., and the producers we'd be meeting with today were apparently sticklers about starting studio sessions on time. I needed some coffee if I was gonna be able to function on all cylinders today.

The kitchen was empty when I walked in, but I could smell the freshly brewed coffee, so I wasn't the first one down. Grabbing a travel mug, I headed over to the coffee station and dumped a spoonful of sugar into the mug before pouring in the hot brew. I gave it a stir, took a sip, then capped it, just as Viper's voice came from behind me.

"Mornin'," he said, as I turned around to face him. Damn. Viper's dark hair was still wet and combed back from his face, showcasing his strong jaw and those lips that had worked me over last night. In the light of day, it was hard to remember why I thought leaving him had been a good idea. I should've stayed and woken up to that face...

Before I could give any more thought to that, I set my mug on the large granite island between us. "Hey."

"Hey." He leaned his elbows on the counter, mimicking my position. "Where'd you run off to last night?"

"Hmm. What makes you think I was able to run?"

Viper's lips quirked. "You sayin' you crawled? 'Cause that would be a real stroke to my ego."

I laughed and took a sip of my coffee. "Like you need your ego stroked any more. But yeah, running would've been...difficult."

"Uh huh." Viper smoothed the stubble on his jaw. He hadn't shaved the past couple of days, but the look suited him. Made him look even more dangerous than I now knew he was. "So. I thought you had a good time last night."

Good was an understatement, and as the images from the night before flashed through my mind, a small smile turned my mouth up. "I had a great time. Pretty sure you know that."

"Oh yeah? What was with the vanishing act? I woke up lookin' for you, but you'd ghosted."

"Maybe I didn't want you to see me crawl," I teased. "Or maybe I was saving you the awkward morning after." When Viper's brows pulled together, I said, "You're not the cuddling type, and I get that. So don't worry; I'm not gonna pull a stage-five clinger act."

"Huh." Viper cocked his head to the side, studying me, but when he didn't say anything else, I picked up my coffee.

"See you down there," I said, walking by him out of the kitchen and heading to the studio.

There. Now he wouldn't have to stress about whether I'd be cool about things. We could go back to working on music, and if something happened again between us, it happened again, and if not...well, at least things would stay amicable. Right?

THREE

Viper

TODAY WAS GOING down the shitter, that was for damn sure. For the past eight hours we'd been locked up in the studio with the producers, and what did we have to show for it? Absolutely fucking nothing. Every song we'd attempted to lay down sounded jacked, and the more we reworked it, the more it tanked.

I'd like to say it was everyone's fault, because that would be the easy out, but that would be a total lie. It was me, and only me. I was annoyed, irritated, and distracted as hell, and all because of the man sitting behind the piano on the opposite side of the room to me—Halo.

"Stop, stop, stop," Killian called out for the umpteenth time, and aimed a glare my way that spoke volumes—volumes on how much he thought I sucked. "V, you totally missed your cue. What the hell is going on with you today? The concert last night make you deaf or something?"

I narrowed my eyes on Killian, who was waiting for some kind of explanation as to why I couldn't seem to get my shit together today, but when nothing logical sprang to mind, I said, "How about you get off my ass?"

Killian walked over to me, his eyes blazing, an argument swirling in their depths even as he tried to bank it. "Maybe if you had someone *on* your ass you'd be in a better mood. Jesus, V. I can't remember the last time you sounded so off."

I could. It was right after Trent Knox had walked out on the band. My concentration had gone to shit for about three months after that. Actually, it hadn't gone to shit—it had found its way down to the bottom of every bottle of whiskey I could get my hands on. And as I stood there facing off with Killian, I tried to pinpoint what exactly it was about my exchange with Halo in the kitchen that had me so...so...pissed the fuck off.

"Sorry I can't always be perfect. Maybe you bunch of losers should start pulling your weight."

Killian grabbed hold of my arm, his fingers digging in tight, as he turned me away from the rest of the band members. "Seriously, V? What's going on with you?"

Aiming my eyes at the hand Killian had on me made him let go. "Nothin'," I said, knowing that was a total lie. But considering *I* didn't even know why I was so prickly, I couldn't exactly explain it to Killian. Could I? "I'm just having an off day, and I don't appreciate *you* getting all up on me about it."

"I thought I'd been pretty good about keeping my mouth shut, considering this mood of yours has been lingering like a dark cloud from the second you stepped inside the studio this morning."

After shoving my hand through my hair, I shook my head and reached for the strap of my guitar, pulling it up and over my head. "Well how about I do you all a favor, then, and leave. That way, you can all play with yourfuckingselves without me."

I turned away from Killian to put my guitar in its case, and as I did, my eyes caught on Halo's, which were locked on the two of us, a frown marring his forehead. I could see the concern in those light eyes of his, the confusion. But whatever. He was the one who'd decided to walk last night without bothering to say a word, so it wasn't like I owed him any kind of explanation as to why I suddenly wanted to put my fist through a wall—even if he was the reason.

Tearing my eyes away from Halo, I slammed the case shut and straightened.

"Viper. Come on, man," Jagger said from behind his keyboards. "Kill didn't mean anything by it. We all have off days."

Yeah, we did. But mine were few and far between, and Killian knew it. For me to play like utter shit—which I was man enough to admit I'd been doing today—something was usually off.

"Don't care. I'm out," I said as I headed toward the door, not bothering with any other kind of back-and-forth. I was ready to get out of that room, to get away from Killian and the rest of the guys. I wanted to track down a goddamn drink, and try to block out the way Halo's face had looked when he'd lain naked under me and told me he could watch me fuck all night. I *also* wanted to forget how cool and collected he'd been this morning telling me how he was saving me from an awkward morning after, because as far as I was concerned, this was feeling pretty fucking awkward.

As I slammed out of the studio, I stormed down the hall in the direction of the stairs, my goal and intention crystal clear. I was about halfway up them when I heard my name, and there was no mistaking the voice that had called it. After hearing Halo shout it, curse it, and moan it in my ear the night before, I didn't think I'd ever be able to get the sound out of my head. But as I came to a stop, three stairs from the top, I shut my eyes and shoved those thoughts aside.

"Viper? Wait up, would you?"

I told myself I should just keep going, but my annoyance only increased when I ignored my stupid self and turned around to see Halo coming up the stairs after me. He was wearing a pair of shorts and a tight-fitting shirt that showed off all his lean muscles, and with his hair tied back off his face, I could see the light stubble lining his angular jaw. I had the insane urge to take the couple of steps down, grab hold of his shirt, and yank him in close enough that I could scrape my teeth along his jaw. But with the mood that was riding me, I knew I couldn't temper whatever would happen after that, and since I didn't know what was going through the angel's head today, I kept my distance.

"What's the problem, Halo?" I wasn't sure when I'd consciously decided to revert to using Halo's name instead of the nickname I'd used from day one. But the change wasn't lost on him, judging by the sting of dismissal that flashed through his eyes.

"Um, I..." Halo blinked as his words trailed off, then he glanced over his shoulder, and when he saw we were still alone, he seemed to find that good enough to move up the stairs closer to me. "Are you okay?"

Deciding to play this his way, I slipped my hands into my pockets and eyed him for a beat. "I'm just peachy. You?"

Halo swallowed, his tongue coming out to worry his lower lip as he nodded. "Yeah, I'm good. You just seem—"

"What?" I said, and took the final step down so Halo had to angle his head up to look me in the eye. "What do I seem to you, Halo?"

Halo's lips parted, his eyes narrowing a fraction as though he were trying to work out what was going through my head. "Why do you keep calling me that?"

I knew exactly what he was talking about. But since he'd been the one to put me in this fabulous mood, the last thing I would do was make this easy on him. "What?"

"Halo."

I chuckled, the sound strained even to my own ears. What the fuck was the matter with me? *Oh, that's right, I'm an asshole.* But then I reminded myself that Halo had started this.

I shrugged. "That's your name, isn't it?"

"Well, yeah. But you never—"

The sound of the doorbell pealing through the mansion cut off Halo's words, but it wasn't hard to see where he'd been going with them. *You never call me that*—that was where he'd been going, and thank fuck for the doorbell, because if he'd actually said those words to me, I would've grabbed him, shoved him up against the wall of this staircase, and damn the consequences.

As it was, the sound of the bell had the others exiting the studio, judging by the slamming door and chatter that followed. I took a step back from Halo and said, "I'm gonna go see who's here," and before he could say another word, I turned and took the rest of the stairs away from him as though there was a fire burning my ass—and considering what I'd just been about to do, I'd say that was a pretty accurate description.

FOUR

Halo

———

I STARED ACROSS the long dining room table at the man who'd claimed the seat beside Viper. Ever since the guy had come barreling in, along with a handful of others, all of whom the band seemed to know, he'd been plastered to Viper's side.

Even now, while the rest of us dug into the steak and potatoes we'd had delivered, the shaggy-haired guy—Ansel or some stupid name like that—wouldn't stop whispering in Viper's ear. Ten bucks said the hand he had under the table wasn't on his own leg.

"Halo, tell everyone what Carly Wilde said to you after we did her show," Killian called out from the head of the table.

Viper's head lifted, his eyes meeting mine before I forced my gaze away.

"Sorry, what?" I said.

"Carly Wilde," Killian repeated. "What was it she said to you?"

"Oh. Uh..." I remembered exactly what she said, but I wasn't self-indulgent enough to repeat it, and not to a bunch of people I'd just met. "I must've forgotten."

Killian frowned like he knew I was lying. "She called him an angel and told him if he ever wanted to fall to the dark side..." Then he waggled his brows, and I flushed.

"She said that shit to you?" Viper's voice was like a freshly sharpened blade, and when I looked his way, his eyes narrowed.

I could feel everyone else staring, and the last thing I wanted to do was turn the focus on me, so I shrugged. "She was joking."

"Bullshit," Jagger said. "I was there, and the woman was practically drooling. She slip you her number?"

I recoiled. "No, she didn't give me her number. Jesus."

"Dude, you could've fucked Carly Wilde. She's hot. I'd bang her," the guy sitting on the other side of shaggy-haired dude—or Ansel, or whatever his name was—said, and Viper shot a glare in his direction.

"No thanks." I poured myself another round of vodka and tossed a lemon slice in the glass. Viper was practically boring a hole into my head with the force of his stare, but I didn't look at him again. I was still confused about what the hell had happened earlier. This morning he'd seemed fine, but as the day wore on, Viper's mood had deteriorated, and though he hadn't outright said it, I couldn't help but feel like it was somehow my fault. I replayed our short conversation, trying to put my finger on the issue, but Viper hadn't given any indication that he was upset at the time, so...maybe it wasn't me? Maybe something had happened after I'd gone down to the studio?

But if that was true, then why was he calling me Halo now? Since the time I met him, I'd always been "Angel," and for some reason, the name change bothered me more than his foul mood.

"So you're from New York too?" the girl beside me—Vanessa— said. She'd been perfectly nice, trying to engage me in small talk, since the others all knew each other and had inside jokes I knew nothing about. Not that I cared. I was too busy trying not to notice what was happening across from me.

I swallowed down some vodka before answering. "Yep."

She waited for me to add on to that, but when I didn't, she said, "Pretty different from Miami, huh?"

Viper had gone back to ignoring me, his head inclined toward

Ansel as the guy continued whispering in his ear, and when a sexy curve tilted Viper's lips, my stomach lurched.

"Mhmm." I kept drinking as I watched the scene in front of me unfolding. Would that guy end up in Viper's guesthouse tonight? I already knew the answer to that.

"Ansel's been talking about nothing but Viper since he heard you guys were in town," Vanessa said, her gaze following mine.

My jaw ticked as the alcohol buzzed in my veins. "Is that right?"

"Oh yeah. He said they hooked up last time the band was in Miami, and I didn't believe him, but I guess he was telling the truth, huh?"

"Looks like it," I muttered. *You knew what would happen. You know who Viper is.*

Yeah, I did, but it'd been less than twenty-four hours since I'd been the one in his bed underneath him, and already he had a replacement. It stung. Of course it fucking did. It didn't matter how prepared I thought I'd been for the reality of what would happen after spending a night with Viper—the actual aftermath was a harder pill to swallow.

It would help if he'd been shit in bed. But to have the most intense sexual experience of my life and then pretend tonight that it never happened? While Viper sat there looking so gorgeous and more edible than the damn steak on my plate? *Ugh.*

I ran a hand over my hair before remembering I'd tied it back this morning, and then sighed. How long did I have to sit here and watch Ansel pawing at Viper before I could leave? Would this be the way things were now? Me sitting on the periphery, watching Viper and his endless conquests?

You have to be okay with it. This is what you signed up for.

But foolish me for thinking I'd be satisfied with one night with Viper. We'd never discussed it, but I'd stupidly assumed whatever this attraction was between us would lead to more than just a one-night stand. Nothing as deep as a relationship—I wasn't delusional, after all—but a casual hookup every now and then.

Yeah, that's not happening, I thought, as I imagined throwing daggers into the side of Ansel's head. *Focus on something else. Anything else.*

I threw back the rest of the vodka and then laid my hand over the back of Vanessa's chair, angling my body to face her. She was definitely attractive, with heart-shaped lips and long, glossy black hair your hands could get lost in. As she smiled at me, I thought about how easy it would be to turn on the charm and end up with her slim body underneath me, writhing until the early morning hours.

But the thought didn't make my cock jerk in my pants. No, that honor belonged to the man across the table, the one with the hard, well-defined body and the sinful mouth that could wreck you with one kiss.

I brought my hand up to stroke the dimple in Vanessa's cheek. "I like these."

"You do?" Her smile widened. It was a beautiful smile, her pink lips full and wanting. Still, my dick refused to take notice. "Are you, um...busy tomorrow night?"

"You askin' me out?"

Her cheeks flushed. "Well, there's a bonfire at the beach, and it's always a good time..."

"You'll be there?"

She nodded.

But before I could answer, a low growl reverberated across the table, and Viper shoved his chair back, the legs scraping against the floor. He downed the rest of his drink and slammed it on the table as he got to his feet.

"Goin' out," he said, before he stalked off toward the back door that led to his guesthouse. I stared after him, belatedly noticing that he'd left alone. Ansel was half standing, his face almost comical as it fell and he began to sputter. For a moment, it looked like he'd follow Viper, but the guy next to him put his hand on Ansel's arm and said something in his ear, and Ansel sat back down, not looking happy at all about the turn of events.

I almost smirked until I realized Viper hadn't exactly left with me either.

As I dropped my arm from the back of Vanessa's chair, Killian tossed a balled-up piece of his roll in my direction.

"Yo, Halo," he said, his elbows on the table and the index fingers of his interlocked hands pointing toward where Viper had disappeared. "Why don't you go make sure he's cool."

I opened my mouth to protest, to comment that he'd been a dick all day, and I was pretty sure I'd only make things worse. But then Killian cocked his head ever so slightly, a knowing look on his face, and fuck. He knew. Somehow, he knew about Viper and me.

Pushing my chair back, I tossed my napkin onto my plate, and when I got to my feet, I was aware of everyone's eyes on me yet again. But fuck it. I didn't know any of these people, and they didn't know me, so I threw out an "Excuse me," and retraced Viper's steps.

Out of view of the dinner party, my hand paused on the door that led outside. I didn't know if Viper would even want to talk to me, but somehow I needed to squash this tension that had infiltrated today. He and I needed to clear the air, and it needed to be now.

With a deep inhale, I opened the door.

FIVE

Viper

FUCK THIS DAY.

That was the thought playing on a loop in my mind, as I slammed out the patio doors of the mansion and made my way across the back lawn toward the guesthouse. The night had chased the sun away, and as I stormed toward my sleeping quarters, I tried to shove aside the image of Halo and that Vanessa chick getting all nice and cozy at dinner.

When Ansel and his crew had first shown up, I'd thought it would be the perfect distraction for my shitty mood. Ansel was the kind of guy who was down for a good time with no strings attached. He was the ideal partner for someone like me. Someone who wasn't interested in forming attachments to the men he took to his bed, and while I'd known he'd been *up* for exactly that— since he'd guided my hand over the blatant invitation that could be taken no other way—my interests had stayed firmly fixated on the one seated across from me. The one who'd snuck out of my bed earlier that morning. The one who, for all intents and purposes, had dismissed me as though he was done...with me.

"Shit," I muttered as I shoved my fingers through my hair. This was so unlike me. I wasn't the kind of guy who cared whether someone *liked* me. I wasn't some starry-eyed virgin expecting proclamations of love, or dinner dates, or walks on the fucking beach. But when Halo had turned his body toward Vanessa and brushed his fingers over her cheek, making her blush like a damn schoolgirl, all I could think about was the way *he'd* blushed when I traced my finger along his—and I saw red.

Yeah, I thought, as I kicked a stone off the path I was walking along. *Fuck this night too.*

I had just about made it to the guesthouse when the sound of gravel crunching underfoot behind me caught my attention.

Jesus, don't let that be Ansel, I thought, because while I'd been ready to let him distract me at the beginning of dinner, by the end of it, I hadn't wanted anyone's attention but Halo's. And since that was out, I was thinking that locking myself in the guesthouse and getting off to the idea of the way he'd looked on his hands and knees last night would just have to do.

Not bothering to stop and acknowledge whoever it was behind me, I kept going, determined to get the hell away from anyone I might offend more than I already had tonight. I wasn't exactly in the socializing kind of mood. I was more in a fuck-the-angel-out-of-my-head kind of mood, even if it *was* only me and my fist doing the trick.

As I reached the door to the guesthouse, I pulled out a key and unlocked it, but it wasn't until I turned the knob and shoved open the door that I heard, "Viper."

There, standing in the exact same spot he'd stood the night before, was Halo. But unlike last night, the expression on his face wasn't one full of amped-up lust and arousal. No, currently stamped across the angel's face was confusion tinged with an underlying hint of...irritation.

Yeah, well, join the fuckin' club. I'd been irritated since I woke up at three in the morning and found him *gone*. I shoved my hands into my pockets and took a step toward him, and as I drew near, Halo glanced over his shoulder, no doubt to check we were alone. We were.

"There a problem?" I asked, which was a fucking laugh, because of course there was a problem. He was standing right in front of me, right within touching distance, and for the first time in my life, I had no idea if I was allowed to touch—or if he wanted me to.

This was why I didn't do relationships. Why I didn't play games. I sucked at trying to work out what another person was thinking. When it was just a fuck, it was clear, obvious—he got his, I got mine, everyone felt fucking amazing. There were no uncomfortable moments, no feelings to navigate. But this second-guessing shit? I failed every single time.

Halo's eyes flashed at my glib question; clearly he was coming to the limit of his tolerance when it came to my bullshit, but I wasn't in the mood to censor myself tonight.

"I was just about to ask you the same thing," Halo said, taking a step toward me, and I had to give the angel points for bravery. He was very brave to come closer with the way I was feeling right now.

He stopped when there were only a couple of inches separating us, close enough that I could smell the fresh scent of his soap on the night breeze. The same scent that was still clinging to my sheets.

I clenched my fists inside my pockets. "No problem. It's just like I said, I'm goin' out."

Halo eyed me for a beat, his gaze roving over me in a way that seemed to see straight through me, to the outright lie I'd just told. "Where are you going?"

"Why do you care?"

Halo shook his head. "Jesus. You can be a real dick."

My lip curled, the annoyance and frustration from the day bubbling up inside me and finally coming out in the argument I'd been spoiling for. "Well if anyone would know, it would be *you*. Right, Halo? If I remember correctly, you like that about me, a whole fucking lot."

I wasn't sure if it was what I said or the fact I called him Halo again that pissed him off more. But before I knew it, Halo was taking a step toward me.

"What the hell is your problem?" he said, his eyes glittering with a warning I was too far gone to heed. "You've been an asshole from the moment you set foot in the studio this morning. Did something happen? And if it did, do you want to, oh, I don't know, talk about it instead of biting everyone's head off?"

I took in the red tinge staining his cheeks, and then I leaned a fraction closer and said, "That offer's a really nice one. Really, it is, but I would've preferred it at around three o'clock this morning. Now, not so much."

When I flashed him a biting grin to accompany my final fuck you and good night, I turned on my heel, ready to get away from him before I did something *really* stupid. I was almost home free, until Halo grabbed hold of my arm and tugged me back around to face him.

"Is that what this is all about? Me leaving last night?" he demanded, and when I didn't answer, Halo shoved me in the arm and said, "Is it?"

And something inside me just...exploded.

"Yes," I shouted, and the volume had Halo's eyes widening and his mouth falling open. While he was caught off guard, I grabbed hold of his wrist and yanked him in until there was barely a millimeter separating us.

Halo blinked, those gorgeous eyes of his conveying his surprise but also his...arousal, and I lowered my head so my lips ghosted over his and said, "I wasn't done with you yet."

Halo sucked in a breath as a shudder racked his body, and when he flicked his tongue over his lower lip, that was it. A rough groan left my throat as I took his lips with mine in a brutal mating of the mouths. It wasn't gentle, it wasn't sweet, but when Halo opened for me and I drove my tongue inside to find his, it was exactly the way it should be.

Raw, hot, and sexy as all hell.

I let go of Halo's wrist and cupped the back of his neck, fusing our mouths together in a savage kiss that went from a wicked-hot flame to a blazing inferno in the space of seconds.

Halo grabbed hold of my shirt, balling the material in his fists as I walked him inside the guesthouse and kicked the door shut behind me. Fuck holding back. Fuck second-guessing myself. If he wasn't as into this as I was, then he would've put a halt to it by now. But as I leaned back against the door, Halo stepped between my legs and thrust his hips up against mine, a low moan rumbling from his throat.

"Fuckin' hell, Angel," I said, and tore my mouth free, and when my eyes found his, they were creased at the corners. He smiled at me as he rocked his hips forward again.

"So I'm Angel again, huh?"

"What?"

Halo chuckled. "You're calling me Angel again. So...this mood of yours, it's 'cause I left this morning?"

My breathing was coming faster now, harder as Halo ran his hands down the front of my shirt and slipped them up under it. His lips were teasing across mine as his fingers played up and down my rigid abdomen.

"Viper?"

I grunted in response—it was about all my brain could come up with—and Halo's lips curved in a grin that was all power, all sex, and just about had my knees buckling.

"If I'd known you were going to be in such a foul mood from me leaving your bed, I would've stayed," Halo said. "Last night was the hottest"—he nipped at my jaw line—"sexiest"—he sucked on my earlobe—"night I've ever had. I just assumed you'd want me gone the next morning."

I put my hands in his hair and pulled the elastic there free. As those golden curls fell down around his face, I grabbed hold of his ass, shoved forward from the door, and walked him across the room until his legs hit the back of the mattress. Then I raised my head to look down into his sex-hazed eyes.

"How about you stop making assumptions. Hmm? If I want you out of my bed, I'll tell you."

Halo's eyes flared, and his fingers dug into my waist, and then I was urging him back on the mattress. Back on the sheets that smelled like him. Back to the place where I'd lost myself inside him, and I'd been left feeling forever changed.

SIX

Halo

MY HEAD SPUN as my ass hit Viper's bed. I'd followed after him, expecting an argument, considering the mood he'd been in all day. Instead, I found myself in the same place I'd been last night, watching and anticipating as Viper removed his shirt and threw it on the floor.

My heart beat wildly as I took in the savage look on his face, the one that told me that he wasn't letting me get away so easily this time.

"This is where you belong," Viper said in a voice that stroked my cock as effectively as I knew his hand could.

I nodded as I kicked my shoes off and scooted back on the bed, and as Viper placed his hands on the edge of the mattress, he said, "Where you should've been when I woke up..."

As the words lingered between us, I lay back, my eyes not leaving his, as Viper prowled up the bed on his hands and knees. My breathing was coming faster now, my anticipation levels at an all-time high as he got closer, because fuck, I wanted this.

I'd spent the entire day remembering Viper like this. Intense, focused, and hunting me down with the primal look in his eyes that he had now. That look, that incendiary stare that had my temperature rising, screamed one thing—*you're mine, and you don't get to leave until I've had my fill.* And judging by the hard cock in Viper's jeans, that wouldn't be anytime soon.

As Viper made his way up my body, his eyes fell to the bulge between my legs, and when he stopped and lowered his head, I gasped. I could feel his hot breath through the material covering me, and my hips pushed up of their own accord, trying to get closer to that talented mouth.

"So glad we're finally back on the same page, Angel," Viper said as he brought a hand up and flicked open the button of my shorts.

"I never left this page," I told him.

"Just my bed..." As Viper drew my zipper down and parted my shorts, he raised those devilish eyes to mine, and the possessive light that shone out of them had me swallowing. Damn, he was potent. "You aren't going to do that again. Are you, Angel?"

Right then I would have agreed to never leave his side if that was what he wanted. But when I didn't immediately respond, Viper flicked the tip of his tongue over the head of my cock and said, "Angel?"

"Right..." I said on a rush of air, and the smirk that tugged up the corner of Viper's sexy mouth was so hot that I was close to overheating.

With his eyes still on mine, Viper bent his head and hummed against the underside of my shaft. "Hmm, good."

Shit. This was too much. *He* was too much. If Viper's intention was to drive me out of my mind, he was doing a damn good job, and as he slipped his fingers into the edge of my shorts to drag them off my hips, I arched up, ready to help. I was more than ready to be naked and under him again, as soon as fucking possible.

As Viper threw my shorts off the side of the bed, I peeled my shirt off and sent it flying too, and not a second later, he was back. His large hands were planted on either side of my hips, his powerful body hovering over me, as he dragged his tongue from the root of my cock to the tip. Of their own accord, my hands went to his hair, needing something to anchor myself to reality, and as I twisted my fingers through the dark strands, Viper glanced up my body.

"Whatcha want, Angel?"

I knew exactly what I wanted. But since words were a little difficult to think of right now, I tugged on the hair in my hands instead, and a grin that rivaled the devil's crossed Viper's lips.

With the stealth and grace of a true predator, Viper moved up the bed over me, and when he lowered his body, I automatically parted my legs.

Oh Jesus. That feels unreal. The rough feel of denim against my aching erection, and Viper's naked chest against mine? It was all too much, and had a needy moan slipping free of my throat. Viper rested his forearms on the pillow by my head, and as he rocked his hips in a slow, methodical rhythm, he brushed his lips over the top of mine.

"Fuck," I said, wrapping my arms around his neck, and Viper kissed the corner of my mouth, down along my jaw, and then he was licking a path up my neck. "*Viper...*"

"Gonna drive you crazy," he whispered by my ear, and my entire body shuddered at his words. They could've been a threat or a promise...hell, maybe both with the way he'd been acting today. But when Viper brought his mouth back to mine and sucked my lower lip between his, I didn't care.

I planted my feet on the mattress and curved my body up into his, rubbing my throbbing cock against him, and as I trailed a hand down the side of Viper's face, I marveled at the rough feel of his stubble under my fingertips.

It was so different from all of my past sexual partners that it probably should've alarmed me in some way or another. But when a throaty growl of pleasure hit my ears, all I could think about was how insanely hot I found it.

"Kiss me," I said, trying to capture Viper's teasing lips. But instead of taking my mouth with his, Viper put his hands on the pillow and raised himself off me until he was straddled on his knees over my waist.

"Oh, I plan to kiss you, Angel. I'm gonna kiss every single inch of you."

Fuck. Me.

I couldn't remember anyone ever looking at me the way Viper was looking at me right then. It was as though I was the sole focus of his entire world, and when I scraped my teeth over my lip and his eyes darkened, that look intensified.

Viper was looking at me as though I was his every sexual fantasy laid out for him to do whatever he wanted with, and he wasn't wrong. I was so far gone that I was ready to do anything he asked of me.

Once he'd looked his fill, Viper shifted back down to the bed, pressing a kiss to my Adam's apple and then making his way to the hollow at the base of my throat. As he flicked his tongue over the spot, a groan left me, and I reached for his hair.

A low sound of pleasure left the lips on my skin, as Viper then kissed his way down to one nipple, where he bit, sucked, and played with the sensitive nub, and I had to slam my eyes shut. He was destroying me, one kiss at a time, and the scary part about it was...I wanted him to keep going.

As if he knew what I was thinking, Viper continued with his sensual assault. His lips grazed down over my ribs, a warm caress that had me writhing underneath him, and as Viper moved farther down the bed until his body was between my legs and his tongue was following the V of my pelvis, I forced my eyes open. I didn't want to miss whatever was about to come next.

Viper turned his head and nipped at the inside of my thigh, and when I pushed my hips up against him, he ran a hand along the outside of the same leg and hooked his fingers under my knee, raising my leg to drape it over his shoulder.

I sucked in a sharp breath, my mind whirling at the possibilities. Viper then aimed those black eyes my way and touched my other leg, and I didn't need any further instructions. I shifted so I could hook my leg over his shoulder, and when I looked down my body and saw how open and vulnerable that made me in the face of Viper, a tremble racked my body.

"This," Viper said, his lips mere inches from my most sensitive skin. "This is what I was thinking about all through dinner, all through our studio session today. It's what I've been thinking about since I woke up this morning, and now? Now I'm going to have it."

"Oh God." I groaned, and considering Viper hadn't moved, had barely even touched me yet, I had a feeling this wasn't going to take long.

I could feel every pulse in my cock as Viper teased me with his words, his eyes, and his mouth, which was hovering precariously close to my balls, and it was taking every ounce of control I had not to come. Then Viper lowered his head and dragged his tongue over the hot skin there. A tortured groan ripped from my throat and my hips jacked up, and before I could form any words, Viper was sucking one of my balls between his lips.

Shit shit shit. How did he expect me to last through this? I had no idea. But as I shoved my hips closer to his mouth, Viper let out the sexiest fucking sound I'd ever heard in my life, grabbed a hold of each of my ass cheeks, and pulled my body even closer to his tormenting mouth. He dragged his tongue up, down, and all around my dick, and when he finally seemed to clue in that I was going out of my mind, Viper tongued the slit, licking up the pre-cum that had coated the head of my cock.

"Fuckin' delicious," he said, more to himself than me, and before I could respond, Viper parted his lips and swallowed me to the back of his throat. My entire body arched up, my shoulders and head the only thing remaining on the mattress, as the intense pleasure of being in the hot, tight heat of Viper's mouth flooded my senses. Then add in the sounds...and there was no way this wasn't about to come to an explosive end.

"Viper," I shouted, my hands finding and fisting his hair as Viper began moving his lips up and down my shaft. As my orgasm barreled down my spine, I crossed my ankles over Viper's back and shoved in deep, and the muffled groan and vibration of it around my dick was all I needed to send me over the edge.

Viper's fingers dug into my ass cheeks as he held me tight against him and swallowed every drop I gave, and when my body stopped shuddering and my cock was too sensitive to touch, Viper drew his lips free and let his gaze wander up my spent body.

When his eyes found mine, Viper brought a thumb to his mouth and brushed it across his swollen lip. As he sucked it inside, tasting the evidence of my lust that I'd left behind, I swallowed.

I'd never been so aware of my own body in my life, or another's, for that matter. But as I lay there barely able to move, all I could think about was how the first thing I wanted, when I could again, was to touch him.

Viper reached down to undo and remove his jeans. But when all he did was move up alongside me, I felt a wave of disappointment wash over me. As he stretched out on his back, I turned my head on the pillow to see him looking at me.

"Go to sleep, Angel."

"But—"

"But nothing," Viper said. "What I want, I can't have right now. That sexy ass of yours needs to recover after last night."

Oh, shit. I licked my lips, and he groaned.

"But I swear, if you sneak out of here before I wake up, don't think I won't come up there and drag your ass back down here to my bed."

I wasn't sure what it said about me, but that threat, that fierce look of determination in his eyes, sparked something rebellious in me, and as he turned away to look back at the ceiling, I felt a grin hit my lips. Because that threat almost made me want to leave, just to have him come and claim me again.

SEVEN

Halo

IT WAS STILL dark when my eyes flickered open in a room that wasn't mine, and it wasn't until I heard the quiet breathing of the man lying next to me that I remembered where I was.

I rolled my head to the side to look at Viper, where he lay sprawled out on his stomach, his arms shoved up under his pillow, hugging it beneath his head. In sleep, and without the acerbic comments that usually came out of his mouth, Viper looked like a sleeping panther—beautiful and peaceful, but deadly. Tendrils of dark hair fell onto his cheek, stopping short of his full lips. Those same lips that had ravaged my body for the second night in a row, the stubble along his jaw leaving their mark along my inner thighs.

I quietly moved onto my side, curling my arm beneath my head as I looked at him. With the sheets down around his waist, I looked over the smooth olive skin of Viper's back, his powerful body on display for me. I'd expected to feel changed in an irrevocable way by sleeping with—and now waking up next to—a man, but I hadn't felt any different yesterday, and the lack of morning-after regret was still missing now. Though I'd been ready for him, though I'd wanted Viper to the point of practically begging, a small part of me had still wondered if once the adrenaline rush subsided, I'd feel like I'd made a mistake.

But looking at him now? There was no way I'd ever consider what was happening between us a mistake. The only regret I had was leaving his bed yesterday, and Viper had rectified that fast.

I glanced back up at his face, his breathing still even, still dead to the world. My cock stirred with his nearness and with the way the sheet stopped just above the top of his ass, taunting me with what I couldn't see. Slowly, so he wouldn't wake—and because I was a creeper—I peeled back the sheet, pushing it down so that his smooth, rounded ass came into view.

Damn. How was it that I was mesmerized by just the look of him? I wanted to run my fingers over the curve of his body and explore all the hidden places, the ones he'd made me so curious about that I'd had to have him. I'd had to taste him, touch him, let him inside me in the way no one had ever been. I'd always been the one to dominate during sex, but letting Viper take control? Fuck, it was hot. Even hotter? That he'd confessed his foul mood yesterday had been because of me. *Me.* All because I thought I'd been doing him a favor by leaving.

But I'm not leaving now...

"You're thinking so hard it woke me up," came Viper's slow, gravelly voice, thick with sleep, and my eyes shot back up to his face.

A smile crossed my lips. "Maybe I wasn't thinking anything. Maybe I was just lookin' at you."

"Mmm." Viper adjusted the pillow beneath him so both eyes were on me. "Still like what you see?"

I pushed the sheet down farther, exposing more of his body. I was already busted—may as well own up to it. "I think you know I do."

"I think you like more than looking."

"Mhmm. That too."

"Glad I don't have to fuckin' drag your ass back here." As his eyes fell shut again, he reached for me, running his hand along my hip before trailing it down to the curls nestled around my dick. He moved leisurely, like he was still half-asleep, not gearing up for another round, and I relaxed back into the pillow, content to let him explore.

Hard to believe this was the same guy who'd lashed out yesterday, and all because he'd been...jealous? Disappointed? Feeling possessive? All of the above? That didn't go along with who he was at all, but he made it clear last night that he wanted me. Damn if that didn't send a thrill humming through my veins.

"There something you want, Angel?" Viper said, his eyes still closed.

Yeah, there was. No point in beating around the bush; Viper was a give-it-to-you-straight kind of guy, but I wasn't sure I wanted the answer yet, so I answered his question with one of my own. "And if there was? Would you give it to me?"

Viper lifted his head and pinned me with a scorching look. "With that face, does anyone ever say no?"

I grinned. "There's a first time for everything."

"And it is a week for firsts," Viper said, settling on his elbow, his head in his hand. "Any other firsts you'd like to try before the sun comes up?"

"Is that the deadline, then? You turn into a pumpkin?"

"Nothing that sweet," he said, the hand he had running circles along my pelvic bone coming up to brush over my lips. "I can see those wheels turning. Ask me, Angel."

I opened my mouth to say, *Ask you what?* but Viper was a smart guy, and he could probably guess what was on my mind.

"Okay," I said, bracing myself for whatever would come out of his mouth next. "What are we doing?"

"Well, *I'm* getting an eyeful of your delicious dick."

I looked down to where I'd inadvertently put my body on display when I pushed the sheets off. I wasn't shy about the way I looked, so I didn't bother reaching for the covers. I'd rather Viper get his *eyeful*.

"I mean...what is this?" I asked, gesturing between us.

"A mutual fucking attraction, emphasis on the fucking."

Snorting out a laugh, I shook my head. "Such a way with

words."

"Half of my charm."

"I know. I've been introduced to the other half," I said, looking pointedly at his cock. "Is that it, though?"

Viper's hand went over his heart like he'd been shot. "Geez, Angel, I think you just hurt my feelings."

"You know what I'm asking."

"Do I?"

Okay, so he wanted to hear me say it. "I need to know where we stand, since it's not like we're never gonna see each other again. And after what happened yesterday, we can't let whatever this is affect the band."

"Whatever this is..." Viper repeated, testing those words on his tongue.

I thought back to the pissy way he'd dealt with everyone and the way he called me Halo. To know that I was the cause of his turbulent reaction was an eye-opener, and I wasn't sure what that meant exactly.

"You were really upset that I left, weren't you?"

Viper adjusted the pillow under his head again. "You can do whatever you want to do, Angel."

"Except sneak out in the middle of the night."

"Hell, you can even do that if you want to. Doesn't mean I have to fuckin' like it."

"Huh. So is the problem that you didn't tell me I could go or that you didn't want me to leave?"

Viper opened his mouth to respond, and then snapped it shut.

"Viper?"

He sighed, rolling over to his back, and then he threw an arm over his eyes. "I don't know. Maybe it's both."

"I knew it," I said, grinning. "You're a secret cuddler, aren't you?"

He lifted his arm from his face for a second to shoot me a glare. "I don't fucking cuddle."

"Oh, yeah, you're right. That's absolutely not why you'd want me to stay all night with you. It wouldn't have anything to do with the fact that you'd want to touch me or maybe lie on top of me."

"Touching and fuckin' spooning aren't the same thing."

I had to fight back a laugh, because damn, he protested too much.

"You know who I am, Angel," Viper said.

"I do. But maybe this is more than that."

"Maybe you want it to be more than that because you're a romantic."

"So what if I do? What then?"

"Time for the truth, huh? Okay." Viper rubbed a hand over his forehead and then ran his fingers through his hair, pushing the wayward strands off his face. "I'm not a relationship guy. You already know that, but as far as what I want from you? That's up to you."

"Up to me?"

"I told you. You're a romantic. You'll want all the things I can't give you, so it's up to you to decide if you're okay with this being just this. Nothing more, nothing less."

So Viper didn't want just a one-night stand, but he didn't want a relationship either. Fair enough, and somehow more than I expected. Could I do it, though? Keep it to just fucking? With the way the band kept me busy most of my waking hours, I wouldn't have time for anything more anyway, so having a fuck buddy of sorts to get in a release? Yeah, I could do that. With one stipulation.

"What about others?"

"Fuck, Angel. Kinky," Viper said, his lips curving up.

"Not to join, asshole," I said, giving him a shove, but Viper grabbed my arm and rolled us so that I was on my back and his face was only inches from mine.

"Tell you what." He leaned in to nip at my lip. "I won't fuck anyone else while I'm fucking you."

That sounded an awful lot like something exclusive to me, but I wasn't about to call Viper out on it.

EIGHT

Viper

I'M SUCH A fucking idiot, I thought, as I stared down into the most stunning face I'd ever seen. Those were the words that were going to be written across my headstone when my time finally came, because this...*this* was a bad idea. And how did I know that? Because my reaction from yesterday was so far removed from the norm for me that this could only lead to trouble.

Such a fucking idiot.

"Viper?"

"Huh?"

Halo was looking at me as though he were waiting for an answer to something he'd just said, and when it was clear I had no idea what that was, he chuckled.

"I said okay. I'll do the same. No one else, while this is happening."

And that was really where the stupid part came in, right? Because if I wasn't fucking anyone else, then I was in a—

"I have another question."

Of course he did. The problem was that with every new question Halo asked, answers I didn't know I was going to give came flying out of my mouth. Maybe it would be smarter to just kiss him or fill his mouth with something so he couldn't talk.

Instead, I found myself fingering one of his golden curls and saying, "Ask away, Angel."

Halo shifted under me, and when he widened his legs a fraction, my body aligned itself nice and snug with his. The change wasn't lost on him at all, judging by his swift inhale, but he wasn't about to be deterred.

"So, does this need to be a secret?" Halo asked.

I stilled my fingers as I stared down into his guileless eyes, but before I answered, I wanted him to be a little more specific. "A secret from who, exactly?"

"Well," Halo said as his eyes roved over my face. "The guys, for one. I think Killian already knows. But what about Brian? The public? I don't know. I've never fucked a—"

Halo bit off his words, and I lowered my head and said against his lips, "Guy?"

Halo smoothed his palms over my hips so he could grab a handful of each of my ass cheeks and pull me tighter to him. "I was going to say rock star. But then I thought it might give you a swollen head."

My *head* definitely swelled, but not the one on my shoulders, and *not* because of what he'd said. No, my stiffening cock had everything to do with the fact the angel's fingers were digging into the crack of my ass. My hair fell down, curtaining our faces and making the moment even more private than it already was, and then I said, "I don't care if the guys find out, and they wouldn't say shit anyway."

As Halo nodded, I raised my head and brought my hands up to either side of his face, tracing a thumb over his lip. "As for Brian and the public..." *Tell him. Just fucking tell him and be done with this conversation so you can get back to the easy shit.* "That can't happen."

Just as I'd suspected, a frown furrowed Halo's brow. "Can't happen?"

"Right. It's just better if it stays here in this room, in the mansion. Trust me."

Halo's hands stilled, and when I went to lower my head to try and distract him, he brought a palm up to my chest to stop me.

"Um, you want to maybe elaborate on that?"

Knowing by now how determined Halo could be when he set his mind to something, I shook my head and rolled off him to the other side of the bed, where I stared at the ceiling.

"Viper?" Halo shifted onto his side, and I had a sudden desire to go and hunt down a drink from the bar.

"Look," I said, turning my head on the pillow. It was time to lay this all out for him. Let him know the way things were. The way they had to be. And why. "Things are about to change for you in ways you could never imagine. One of those things is your privacy —or lack of, I should say. And you, especially, have to be careful."

"Me?" Halo said, his face now a mask of confusion.

"Yeah, you. You're the frontman of the band, Angel. That means people are going to care where you stick your dick."

When Halo's gaze traveled down my body, I groaned, because it was more than obvious where he was thinking of sticking it right now—and *that* was the problem.

"You see, that look on your face right now," I said. "If you look at me like that in public and someone takes a photo? Your whole world is gonna blow the fuck up in two minutes flat."

Halo swiped his tongue over his lip and asked, "How am I looking at you?"

"Like you want to fuck." When Halo's eyes widened, I shrugged. "You asked."

"Okay." Halo chuckled. "But surely people don't expect me to be a monk? I'm in a rock band, for fuck's sake. Whatever happened to sex, drugs, and rock 'n' roll?"

"Social media." When Halo eyed me, as though trying to gauge my seriousness, I said, "No one cares who me or the rest of the guys are fucking. It could be a guy, a girl, hell, it could be two guys and a girl—no one would give a shit. But you? They're gonna care about you."

Halo sat up, pulling the sheet with him as he scooted up the bed until his back was against the headboard, and I moved up to sit beside him.

"When you think of iconic bands, the legendary ones, who do you think of?" When Halo said nothing, I reached over and turned his face so he was looking me in the eye. "I'll tell you who—the lead singer, the frontman. The one whose name and face is instantly recognizable, and starting now, that's going to be you. MGA is going to want to sell this perfect fuckin' face to the world, Angel, and the last thing they're going to want is you attached...to anyone." Wanting my words to really sink in so I never had to have this fucking conversation again, I added, "Just ask Trent."

"Trent? What do you mean?" Halo said, just as I knew he would, because if anything was going to bring it home for Halo, it would be this.

"You were a big TBD fan, right?"

When Halo's eyes narrowed, I could see him trying to guess where I was going with this, but he never would, no one would have, and that was the point.

"Right."

I nodded and dropped my hand away from his face. "Then did you know that Trent is bisexual?"

Halo scoffed. "Yeah, okay, that's why he only ever dated the latest lingerie model to hit the magazines."

"That's exactly why."

Halo's mouth fell open. "You're serious? You're not just saying that 'cause you hate his guts? Actually, why do you hate him so much?"

"It's hard not to resent the guy who destroyed your fuckin' band. How would you feel if you spent almost every damn day with someone and they walked out on you? When that level of trust is broken, you'd be fine telling that person to go to hell, trust me."

"But why did he walk out?"

"Dunno. Which makes it even more fuckin' frustrating. He didn't bother to talk to us like a normal human being. Just walked out of the studio one day and never came back."

"That's weird that he just left like that."

I rubbed my hand over my face and shrugged. "I should've seen it coming. Kill and I had noticed he'd been restless for a while. We'd all been fighting a lot, disagreeing over the direction of the band, and—" I snapped my mouth shut when I realized what had been about to come out. *Shit*, that was the last thing I wanted to talk about.

"And?" Halo prompted.

"And then he left."

Halo's eyes narrowed. "You're lying."

"I'm not fuckin' lying."

"Then you're not telling the whole story."

Perceptive angel. "That's because there's nothing to tell. Things were going to shit, we all got drunk one night..."

"And you slept together?"

My eyebrows shot up as he hit the nail on the head. "I wouldn't say slept together. I'd say had a drunken night of sex that didn't mean anything, and a week later he fucked off."

"Wow. Okay... I didn't know that," Halo said, as he digested that bit of info.

"No one knows that but Kill. Because it was a mistake and we both knew it. It'd be like me fucking Killian. It's just all wrong."

"So you and Killian have never...?"

"Fuck no." Done with the conversation, I straddled his lap and cupped Halo's face. "Can we please stop talking about this now?"

"Yeah, fine. But I just want you to know I get what you're saying about being careful. And no offense to Trent—"

"Offend him all you like. I don't care."

Halo snorted and wrapped his fingers around my wrists. "I'm not going to pretend to be someone I'm not, Viper. That's not who I am. I can't fake-date someone. I won't. But since we aren't dating, it doesn't really matter anyway, does it?"

No, I supposed it didn't...

Like I said—I was such a fucking idiot.

NINE

Halo

"CANNONBAAALL!" CAME THE cry as Slade ran toward the pool and jumped into the air, tucking his body into a ball. His aim was perfect—a massive splash of water drenched Jagger and his "lady friend," and as she shrieked, Jagger let out a string of curses in Slade's direction.

"Don't you pull that shit over here unless you wanna fuckin' starve," Killian said, where he was flipping burgers on the grill, the lifeguard he'd been hanging out with by his side. It'd been a long couple of days in the studio working with our producers and finally getting somewhere now that Viper's mood had taken a more...positive direction, and today was a much-needed day off to relax and rejuvenate.

"Halo, feel free to drown him while you're in there," Jagger said, as he toweled himself off and shot Slade a glare, to which Slade only gave him a big, cheeky smile.

I hitched my arms over the edge of the pool to catch my breath. I'd been taking full advantage of the Olympic-sized body of water in the backyard, swimming laps in the mornings after I slipped out of Viper's guesthouse—a luxury that was impossible to come by in New York.

"Viper," Killian called out toward the house, where Viper had gone to get the packages of hot dogs. "Bring another case of beer with you."

Viper emerged from the house, his sunglasses still on and black swim trunks low on his hips, the rest of him gloriously naked. I tried not to stare, since I didn't have shades on to hide behind, but it was damn near impossible.

"Already on it," Viper said, and when he reached the barbecue, he handed off the hot dogs to Killian and bent down to fill the cooler with more cans of beer. When he finished, he took a couple of cans from the bottom that had been chilling and sauntered over to the deep end, where I was still draped over the side of the pool. He placed a beer in front of me and then sat down, cracking open his drink as he swung his legs into the pool.

Nonchalant. That was the way we'd decided to play this thing around the guys, not giving them a clue what was happening behind closed doors. Or, more specifically, what Viper was introducing me to behind his closed door *nightly*.

"Thanks," I said, flipping open the tab and taking a long swallow, keeping my eyes directly ahead instead of where they wanted to be. But I could feel the heat of his body beside me, and that was enough.

"It's a shame you're wearing these." Viper's foot moved between my thighs, rubbing along my dick through my swim shorts as he kept his eyes on where the others were.

Jesus, the man was shameless, messing with me in full view of the rest of the band. But did I move away? No. Did I tell him to stop? Fuck no. Instead, I pushed my lower body forward, seeking out more of him, and as I did, the barest hint of amusement crossed Viper's lips.

"You're trouble," he said, and then took another swallow of his beer.

"*I'm* trouble?" Beneath the surface, I squeezed my thighs shut, trapping his leg between mine. Viper chuckled, but then quickly drew his foot away as Slade and a couple of the girls he'd invited over headed in our direction, most likely to teach them how to cannonball. I sipped my beer, watching as Slade reached for the girls' hands and they got a running start, aiming again for Jagger, who had enough sense this time to move before he got wet.

"See?" I said. "You keep starting things you can't finish."

Viper lowered his sunglasses to look at me, and the scorching heat I saw there told me I was playing with fire. "Don't think I won't make a scene in front of every damn one of them."

"You wouldn't," I said.

"No?" Viper set his beer down and lowered himself into the water beside me. He hooked his foot behind my leg and jerked my body forward, bringing me way too close to him. "It's not me I'm showing restraint for, Angel."

Shit, I knew he had a point, or at least the logical side of my brain did, but with the way he connected our bodies, and with the look he was giving me, all I wanted to do was grab him right there and kiss that taunting mouth senseless. But that wouldn't be smart, which meant the rational side of myself would win out, leaving only one thing I could do with Viper so close.

In one quick move, I pushed up off the side of the pool, shoved my hands down on his shoulders, and dunked him completely underwater. Before he could resurface, I was diving away from him, because once Viper came up for air, I had no doubt retaliation would be swift.

"Oh shit," Jagger said, as Viper broke through the water, sunglasses pushed halfway up his face. "You better run, Halo."

But dumbass that I was, I'd forgotten that I couldn't exactly get out of the pool yet, not with the hard-on Viper had stroked to almost full mast. So there I was, stuck on the opposite side from where I'd left Viper with no way to escape unless I wanted to give us away.

"Oh, Angel," Viper said, calmly removing his sunglasses and setting them off to the side before pinning me with a wicked stare. "That was a big mistake." Then he dove under the water, kicking off the wall and reaching me faster than I could get away.

Viper's hand clamped down on my foot, jerking me back, and I heard one of the guys yell, "Fuck, he's got him now," before my head went under. As soon as I resurfaced, Viper was there again, pushing me back under, and I had just enough time to grab a breath before he did. His attack on me was relentless, but I gave it back to him just as good, while the other guys cheered me on to "take his ass out." I did my best, channeling all that sexual frustration he ignited in me into a physical tug-of-war it didn't look like either of us would win.

"Hey, assholes," Killian said, pointing his spatula our way. "Maybe you could stop trying to drown each other and come eat."

I rose to my feet in the shallow end, wiping the water out of my eyes and taking a deep breath. Behind me, I thought I heard Viper do the same, but then his strong arms wrapped around my chest from behind, hauling me off my feet, and then I went crashing back into the water. When I emerged, laughs rang out, and Viper glanced over his shoulder as he climbed the stairs, smirking my way.

Fucker. He may have bested me this time, but I'd get a rematch of my own...later tonight.

But damn, why'd he have to look so good soaking wet? He ran his fingers through his dark hair, rivulets of water running down his broad shoulders and back, and then, as he turned toward me, I couldn't help but noticed the way they trailed down his chest as well. It made me want to lick them up, and in the back of my mind, I made a note to get Viper in the shower one of these nights.

"About time," Viper said to Killian as he grabbed a paper plate off the makeshift picnic table we'd set up earlier. "I'm suddenly hungry for a big, thick wiener in my mouth."

I sputtered out a laugh that came out more like a cough, and Viper looked my way. "Water in your lungs? Sorry about that," he said, looking not at all sorry about anything. Proud of himself, actually. *The fucker,* I thought again.

We all loaded up our plates and headed for the table, Viper taking the seat on the end beside me. It wasn't until we were all gathered around that it occurred to me that Viper and I were the only ones without dates.

"Got a call from Marshall," Killian said, between bites of his hamburger. I hadn't met the head of MGA yet, but Marshall Gellar had been a big enough presence in our studio sessions from the way the producers talked about him. "He's diggin' the new tracks."

"What the fuck ever." Viper broke off a piece of my hot dog and popped it in his mouth as Killian narrowed his eyes.

"Anyway," Killian said. "They got the numbers back for 'Invitation''s first week of release, and holy shit. It was streamed over eighty-five million times."

"What?" I said, my eyes wide, my plastic fork dropping onto my plate.

Killian grinned. "Yep. Eighty-five fuckin' million. And that's only the first week."

"But... We never even hit that high with 'More Than Enough,'" Slade said, the expression on his face—and all of the guys' faces, really—one of utter astonishment.

"Damn." Jagger let out a low whistle and then looked my way. "Hope you've got your passport, Halo."

Under the table, Viper squeezed my leg, the only acknowledgment he made of the news, and then he took a chip from my plate and popped it into his mouth. I could only sit there, dazed, as the guys continued to talk numbers I didn't understand, but there'd be plenty of time to ask them about it later. For now, I wanted to soak in the fact that "Invitation," a song that started as a riff in my head, was already a bigger first-week success than anything TBD had done. And damn—it felt good.

TEN

Viper

EIGHTY-FIVE MILLION STREAMS? Fuck me, that was impressive. Not that I was surprised. The first time I'd heard Halo playing that riff in Savannah, I knew it could be something extraordinary. But when that many people agreed with you, it was more than that. We'd had massive hits before with TBD, but for this single, from an "unknown" band, to blow those numbers out of the water and into the musical stratosphere, MGA had to realize that this was something genius—that *Halo* was a goddamn genius.

"We're so gonna get the green light for a stadium tour," Slade said, reaching for the ketchup.

Killian took a bite out his hamburger and nodded. "They're gonna want to see how some of the other singles hit, but they're super fucking impressed with the stuff we've sent them."

No shit. It was some of the best music we'd ever made, and all because of the man sitting to my left. Halo had lit a fire under our asses, made us think outside the familiar TBD box, and challenge ourselves, and hell if that didn't make him even more appealing than I already found him.

I looked over at the angel, who was staring at the rest of the guys in silence as though he were merely an onlooker to the conversation, instead of an integral part of it.

"You okay there, Angel?" I said, bumping his shoulder with mine, and when Halo turned my way, he shook his head.

"He's in shock." Jagger slung an arm around his lady's shoulder and tugged her in close to his side. "Not every day someone finds out his song has had eighty-five million streams in a week."

"Someone get him a paper bag to breathe into," Slade joked.

"Or just bend over and put your head between your knees," Killian suggested.

Or between mine.

"I heard it on the radio this morning," the woman plastered against Jagger's side chimed in as she aimed a flirty smile Halo's way. "I just love your voice."

Yeah, I was sure his voice was *all* she loved.

"Thanks, guys," Halo said, grabbing another handful of chips for his plate, since I'd eaten most of his. "I'm fine, it's just a little... wow, is all."

"You think this is wow?" Slade said, sitting back in his chair. "Wait till we get to start thinking about a tour. The sets. The lights. The pyrotechnics. It's gonna be off the chain."

Halo reached for one of the chips on his plate. "I can't even imagine."

"You better," I said, then drained my beer and looked to the cooler to find it empty. "You're gonna be center stage in a big way, Angel. We have to think up something epic for your virgin flight."

When Halo's eyes widened as though he hadn't thought that far ahead, I chuckled. Maybe it was time to bring out something a little stronger if the guys were going to start talking about stage setups and world tours. Poor guy looked like he was still coming to grips with the fact his music was being listened to...and loved.

Getting to my feet, I looked around the table and said, "How about we crack open something a little stronger than beer, yeah?"

When the rest of the guys nodded, I glanced down to Halo, who said, "Vodka?"

I reached across him for another chip from his plate and popped it in my mouth, and Halo's lips tugged up at the corners. "Maybe another bag of chips, too," he suggested.

"Anything you want, Angel," I said, and winked before I stepped around him and headed inside.

As I rummaged through the walk-in pantry, trying to find a flavor of potato chip I liked, the sound of one of the terrace doors opening and closing had me sticking my head out to see Killian walking across to the kitchen.

I went back to the task at hand, and when I spotted a package of salt and vinegar chips on the top shelf, I reached for them.

"Couldn't keep your hands off him, huh?"

Chips now in hand, I turned to see Killian standing in the pantry's doorway with his arms crossed over his chest and his shoulder up against the doorjamb, and I knew I could play this one of two ways.

One, I could pretend I had no idea who he was talking about, or two, I could just own that shit—and with the way I'd had Halo groaning under me last night, there was no doubt in my mind *who* I owned.

I opened up the bag of chips and stuffed my hand inside, and as I brought one up to my mouth, I stopped and looked Killian in the eye. "I told you I wouldn't be able to." Then I crunched down into it.

"Fuckin' hell." Killian laughed, shaking his head as he shoved off the door and walked inside the pantry. "I should've known better. If anyone could get a straight guy to fuck him, it'd be you."

I shrugged. "Who said I was the one getting fucked?"

Killian's feet came to a stop, his mouth falling open, as I shoved my hand back into the bag of chips.

"You're kidding."

I shook my head, enjoying this a little more than I probably should've. "I'm not."

Killian looked as though I'd smacked him over the back of the head with a two-by-four, and when he finally regained use of his motor skills, he managed, "Jesus."

Not shocked or bothered by Killian's response, I shoved the bag of chips against his chest and then looked around the pantry again. "Here, hold these, I'm trying to find the barbecue ones."

"Uh, don't try and change the subject, V."

"I'm not. I'm just trying to find the fuckin' chips."

"So that's the reason you were in a shit mood the other day. What'd Halo do, tell you no?" Killian reached behind my right shoulder and pulled a package of barbecue off the shelf, and then held them out to me.

As I snatched them out of his hand, I shot him the finger. "How about none of your fucking business."

"Okay, okay." Killian glanced over his shoulder out the pantry door. "So, you and Halo, huh? That's a severe case of opposites attract."

"It's a severe case of sexual fucking chemistry is what it is. And really, it's your own fault. You put him in front of me."

"Uh huh. Well, I'm glad the two of you worked your shit out, because I was about to kick your ass the other day."

"Whatever. You know I can take you any day of the week."

"And you know I won't let anything fuck with this band. *You* included."

I rolled my eyes, but knew Killian wasn't bullshitting. If he thought for a minute this thing with me and Halo could fuck shit up, he'd call us out in a hot second.

"Right," Killian said. "Well, you gonna come back outside and eat with the rest of us? Or do you need Halo to come in here and feed you?"

"You know, you almost sound jealous, Kill. That's sweet."

Killian flipped me off as I brushed by him and headed back out to the kitchen area to track down drinks. As I began looking through the cupboards, first the top and then the bottom, Killian came up to lean against the counter beside me.

"Jealous? Uh, no, I stopped thinking you were hot back in

middle school when you hung my underwear up the flagpole. But you do know that the two of you aren't foolin' anyone, right?"

I glanced up at him from where I was crouched down by his feet. "Um, news flash, we weren't trying to."

"No?"

I shook my head. "Nope. We just weren't telling you."

"That's the same thing, moron."

After locating a bottle of Ketel One, I got to my feet. "Not really. I could've lied right now."

"Yeah, and like I would've believed you. You've been feeling him up every chance you've had in the fucking pool. Not to mention disappearing at the same times, eating off his plate, getting his refills. What's next, V? You gonna take him on a date?" Killian scoffed, but then shoved me in the arm. "Wait—you already took him on a date. The Nothing..."

I screwed my face up at the thought. Killian had lost his damn mind. I didn't *do* dates. "That wasn't a date. We're fucking, not dating," I told him, as I also grabbed a bottle of whiskey. "You're an idiot."

Killian let out a loud bark of laughter. "No, you are, V. Oh my God. You are so fucking stupid, my friend."

Killian snatched up the chips and walked by me toward the glass doors, and with the alcohol in hand, I followed, calling out to the smug bastard, "Whaddya mean I'm stupid?"

ELEVEN

Halo

"THE RULES ARE simple," Killian said, standing in front of the movie screen in the mansion's decked-out home theater. Each of us had a drink of our choice with a refill jug beside us, and that alone told me this was no ordinary movie night. "This is an Ace Locke classic, so you have to take a drink every time one of the following happens: whenever Ace takes his shirt off, whenever he saves a woman, makes out with her, or has sex with her, and whenever he says, 'The name's Sinclair. Beckett Sinclair.'"

From memory, Ace was shirtless through most of the movie, so that meant we'd all be stumbling out of here in a couple of hours.

"We are gonna be so fucked," Slade said. He and Jagger had taken up recliners a couple of rows in front of me, and as Killian joined them, I looked toward the door, waiting for Viper. After the pool day and barbecue, we'd all ventured off to our separate corners of the house—me for a nap after a day in the sun, and the others to spend some one-on-one time with their guests. By the time nightfall came, it was just the five of us, and when someone suggested a movie night, I resigned myself to having to wait another couple of hours before heading to Viper's guesthouse.

"If you don't take a drink when you're supposed to and you get called out for it, you have to chug," Killian continued. "Everyone understand?"

As we all nodded, Viper came back with an armful of snacks. "Catch," he said, before tossing the packages out to each of us. I ripped open the bag of pretzels and inhaled a few, since it seemed like I'd be drinking my weight in Long Islands tonight.

Killian ran through the rules again for Viper's benefit, and then Viper grabbed his drink of choice and looked over the rows of chairs. When he looked at me and I raised my brows in an "aren't you sitting here with me?" way, his lips curved.

"Where to sit..." Viper said, and when I sent another pointed look at the recliner beside me, Jagger called out, "You know where you wanna sit, man."

"Yeah, Halo even saved you a seat," Slade said through a mouthful of popcorn.

Killian smirked at Viper. "Told you."

There was a snort from one of the guys, and then Jagger turned in his chair. "You thought we didn't know?" He threw back his head and laughed. "Please. You're not that stealth."

"Yeah, I busted Halo sneaking out of his room a couple of nights ago," Slade said. "Don't think he was going to the bathroom."

My skin warmed, and I resisted the urge to duck down in my seat. They all knew? I'd had a feeling Killian did because of the looks he'd given me before, but I thought my late-night trips and early-morning comings had been under the radar. Shit, what else did they know?

"Hey, I ain't complaining," Jagger said. "Ladies like that pretty boy look you got, know what I'm sayin'? This just means more for me."

Viper rolled his eyes and took the recliner beside mine, setting his drink in the cupholder. He didn't seem upset at the turn of events, only annoyed at the ribbing. "Start the damn movie," he said.

"Hey, Halo, you got somethin' in common with the actor in this one," Slade said, as Killian hit play on the remote.

"And what's that? More game than you could ever have?" Viper snapped, and the guys laughed.

Jagger recovered first and winked at me. "Ace was the ultimate ladies' man. A smooth fucking operator who bagged all the hottest actresses, lucky bastard. But then out of nowhere he's with the new Calvin Klein male model, and everyone loses their shit."

"It's always the hot ones who turn," Killian said, nodding.

Viper leaned back in his chair, throwing up the foot rest, and then he grinned. "And isn't that a fuckin' bonus." His eyes glinted at me in the dark, and I could only shake my head. I didn't know whether I should feel relieved that the guys knew or whether this opened up a whole new can of worms. After all, I was the new guy, but now I was the new guy messing around with Viper.

"Oh shit, he's already half-naked in the damn opening credits?" Jagger said, groaning. That was our cue to take the first drink, and as the liquor made its way down my throat, I kicked myself for not grabbing a bucket of lemons to chase the taste away. Killian had made this one strong.

I felt like I should say something to the guys, address the situation somehow, but I didn't know what to say. They didn't seem to care one way or another that Viper and I were hooking up, and that was when it hit me—this was the first time I'd "come out," in a sense, even though I wasn't sure that was the right term for it. Did my attraction to Viper mean I was gay? Or bisexual? I'd still never looked at another man the way I did Viper, so what the hell did that mean? Maybe I didn't have to put a label on it. After all, we weren't dating, we weren't together, and outside the people in this room, no one else would know. Granted, I told my sister everything, but there was no point in shocking the shit out of her over a casual thing.

"Let the chugging commence for the angel in the back who completely spaced during the make-out scene," Jagger said, and when I realized he meant me, I cursed.

After sucking down every bit of the Long Island, Viper leaned over and whispered, "Looks like I'm gonna get to see a drunk angel after all." The back of his hand brushed against the back of mine, sending an electric shock up my arm before he settled back in his seat. How was it that he could affect me like that by barely touching me?

I looked back at the screen just in time for Ace to introduce himself as Beckett Sinclair, and I barely had time to refill my drink before I was taking another sip. Already my head buzzed, and I had the thought that I'd been wrong earlier—I wouldn't be stumbling out of here. I'd be lucky if I could crawl.

The words were out of my mouth before I realized I was going to say them: "You guys really don't care?"

Killian popped his head up over his chair, and the other two followed suit.

"About what? This?" Jagger pointed between Viper and me and shook his head.

"I thought you would've had better taste, but..." Slade shrugged, and Viper threw a handful of popcorn his way. "What? You're a temperamental fuckhead on a good day."

"Fuck you too," Viper growled, and Slade grinned, looking back my way.

"He means that in a loving way, honest." When Slade faced the screen again, he cursed. "How many times does he lose his damn shirt?"

"Why do you think I chose this one?" Killian said. "Ace Locke naked for the majority of the movie? Duh. A fuckin' no-brainer."

Slade cocked his head to the side. "He is pretty hot for a guy, I guess."

"Swear to God we're gonna catch you in a gay bar one of these days. You download Grindr yet?" Viper said.

Slade's brow furrowed. "What's that?"

"Why don't you download it and find out?" Viper smirked, and then Jagger yelled out, "Drink!"

Once we'd all taken another sip, Jagger pointed at Slade. "You're my wingman. Don't you dare download that shit."

Slade shrugged and dug back into his popcorn, and a few seconds later, with all attention back on the movie, Viper's hand made its way to my thigh.

I raised my eyebrow, and when he looked my way, he moved his hand higher, inches away from my cock. I grabbed his wrist to stop him from going any farther and shot him a look. It was one thing for the guys to know about us; it was another thing for them to turn around and see it.

But Viper didn't move his hand, keeping it right where he wanted it, squeezing me there every so often to remind me he was there—as if I could ever forget.

The movie played on, and the more I drank and the more the liquor hummed through my veins, the more my inhibitions began to fall away, and soon it wasn't Viper who inched his fingers up my thigh. I slid my hand down to cover his, and then, feeling brave and really fucking horny, I dragged our hands up to cover my coming-to-attention dick.

His large palm cupped me, pressing down and stroking the length, and it was all I could do not to moan at how damn good it felt. The last thing I wanted was to draw attention back to us, though, so I bit down on my lip and reclined my seat a little so that Viper could have more access.

Our gazes were locked, a sly grin on Viper's lips, and then he mouthed, "Fuckin' trouble." But instead of pulling away, he quietly resituated himself in his seat, closer to me, and the pressure of his hand increased.

When he returned his attention to the movie, I forced myself to do the same, rocking ever so slightly into his palm.

Thank God for loud action scenes.

TWELVE

Viper

NEVER HAD A two-hour movie taken so long to be over, and that by no means was a dig at Ace Locke, whom I usually enjoyed staring at for a hundred and twenty minutes. But with the alcohol buzzing through me, and Halo's hard cock filling my palm, I wasn't in the mood to sit still and watch a movie I'd seen countless times before. I was in the mood to strip the angel beside me and—

"Drink up, suckers," Jagger shouted. "Okay, how many times does he need to tell people who he is? I mean, isn't he a badass detective? How come no one's ever heard of him?"

"It's for emphasis, moron," Slade said, then took a gulp of his drink. "Dramatic effect and all that."

As Jagger and Slade bitched back and forth, I raised my cup and swallowed the fiery mix I was getting to the end of, and as it warmed a path down my throat, I was aware that that wasn't the only thing making me hot.

Around twenty minutes until the end of the movie, Halo had gone from watching what was on the screen to flat-out watching me, and the heat from his intense focus was making it close to impossible not to lean over and attack those delicious lips of his. I could feel his cock throbbing beneath my palm, and every now and then he'd thrust up against my hand, wanting more attention.

"Viper...?" At the whisper by my ear, I turned and allowed my eyes to once again find his, and *Jesus*. It was going to be an exercise in restraint to last until the end of this movie before taking this any further.

"Yeah, Angel?" I said, making sure to keep my voice low, not wanting to draw anyone's attention our way. I could tell the angel had had a moment of reflection earlier when the guys were ribbing us about being together, and while I didn't give a fuck, this was new for him, and I wasn't about to scare him off by expecting some heavy-duty PDA. That didn't mean I was stupid, though, and if he wanted to take this further, then I wasn't about to stop him.

Halo's light eyes were a little glazed as they stared back at me, and I had to wonder if it was from the alcohol or—

"Undo my jeans."

—his arousal.

I lowered my eyes down to where my hand was massaging the bulge between Halo's legs, then he spread them slightly and my eyes flew back to his. When Halo flashed me a lazy, sex-drunk grin, I leaned across the arm of the chair until my lips were brushing over his and said, "And then what?"

As I flicked open the button of his jeans and drew the zipper down, Halo's lips parted, and he arched his back off the recliner. I slipped my hand inside the denim, and when I wrapped my fingers around him, Halo mouthed, "*Fuck...*" and I smirked.

"Oh, Angel. If I thought for a second you could keep quiet, I'd have your jeans down and you in my lap—"

One of Halo's hands came down on top of mine, his eyes flashing, and then I shoved a finger to his lips and chuckled. "But you can't. Shh..."

Halo's jaw bunched as my fingers tightened, and Christ, I was reminded of just how gorgeous he was. His hair was a tangle of curls around his face as he looked at me, his head resting back on the recliner, and in the dark of the home theater, the reflection from the massive screen gave off enough light to highlight all the angles of his stunning profile.

I could write songs about that face, I thought, as Halo's eyes fluttered shut and he pushed his hips up, sliding his cock through my fist. I could write albums, symphonies, all dedicated to how damn beautiful he was, and before I could stop myself, I was leaning over the arm of the chair and taking Halo's mouth with mine.

As soon as our lips connected, Halo let go of my hand to take hold of my face, and when my tongue slid in between his lips, he angled his body toward me, bucking his hips up off the chair. I'd totally forgotten about the movie, but luckily it was somewhere near the end, where all the explosions were going off all over the place, because Halo couldn't keep quiet to save himself.

He moaned and threaded his fingers into my hair as he craned up off the recliner to kiss me harder, his hips pumping as he chased after an explosion of his own, but I'd be fucked if that happened in the dark.

Tearing my lips from his, I clamped my fist around the root of his cock and put my other hand over his mouth. Halo's eyes flared with irritation, his frustration just as strong in that moment as the lust clawing at him. His breathing was coming in fast pants as his hips slowed until they stilled, and when I glanced over my shoulder to the credits that were starting to roll up the screen, he followed my gaze.

"Zip up, Angel." I reluctantly pulled my hand free and swallowed as I tried to readjust myself, but it was no use. There was no getting comfortable with how hard my dick was. There was no hiding it, either.

The lights flicked on barely a second later, bright enough to blind a normal person. But to those who'd drunk as much as we had, it did a fine job of making everything even hazier than the alcohol.

"Motherfucker," Slade said, wincing as he covered his eyes, and Killian started laughing by the door.

"Pussy. Since when has Jagger been able to out-drink you?"

Slade looked to Jagger, who seemed as put together as when

he'd walked in two hours earlier. "He can't. Were you following the rules?"

"You calling me a cheater?" Jagger said as he got to his feet. "I was sitting right next to you. I was throwing back as much alcohol as you when Ace was banging his way through the last half hour of the film."

Slade gestured to his cup. "Prove it."

As Jagger told him to fuck off, I turned to see if Halo had managed to get himself back in order, and what I saw had all of my patience and restraint taking a major detour right out the fucking door.

Halo had zipped up, yes. But he'd left the top button of his jeans open, and his long, thick cock was still clearly visible beneath the tight denim. When my eyes roamed up to his swollen lips, fuck-me eyes, and messy hair, I shook my head and got to my feet.

"Hey, assholes," I called out. When they all turned around to look at me, they took in my tight lips and strained expression. "This has been real great and all. But could you all please get the fuck out now?"

As their eyes fell to Halo, who was still reclined in his seat and silent, Killian smirked, Slade snorted, and Jagger's mouth fell open. Nothing else needed to be said after that. I was done spending quality time as a group. It was time for a little one-on-one.

THIRTEEN

Halo

MY COCK STRAINED to the point of torture as Viper made it clear to the guys that movie night was over, and thank fuck for that. If I had to wait any longer to get Viper's hands back on me, I would've reached down and finished off the job myself, audience be damned.

As the door shut behind Slade, I let out a groan, pushing back against the recliner and palming my covered erection. Viper had wound me up to the point of practically coming before he'd pulled away abruptly, and the irritation from his mouth leaving mine lingered.

He checked to see that we were alone, and then his gaze fell on me, to where I was busy stroking myself.

"I don't fucking think so," Viper said, starting toward me. When he hovered above me, he grabbed hold of the hand I had over my dick and pushed my arm up over my head. Then he leaned in so close that I could practically taste the alcohol on his breath. "No one touches what's mine except for me."

What's mine... A thrill shot through my body, and I arched up, trying to get closer to his mouth, but he pulled his head away just as our lips brushed together.

A frustrated sound ripped through me. "Don't be a fucking

tease, Viper."

"Or what?" He chuckled as he boxed me in, his hands on the arms of the recliner, keeping his distance.

I didn't know if it was all the alcohol I'd consumed that had me feeling bolder than usual, or if I could blame what happened next on the frustration Viper built in me, but I gripped his shirt and jerked him forward at the same time I wrapped my legs around his, holding him exactly where I wanted him.

In his surprise, he lost his balance, and I took advantage by slamming my lips against his. If I'd thought Viper would resist, I was wrong, because his lips immediately parted, and as he regained his footing, his tongue dove inside my mouth. But I wasn't content to let him take control this time. Oh no. I was burning up, horny as hell, and I knew exactly what I wanted to happen next.

As Viper's hand trailed down my body to land on my erection, I tore my lips away from his. "I want you to fuck me."

I could feel his mouth curve against mine. "That's the plan, Angel."

"Not like this," I said, as the pressure of his hand increased, and I halted his movements by grabbing his wrist. "Over there." I nodded toward the wall to my left, and Viper raised a brow.

"I know my dick's a fuckin' beast, but it won't reach you from all the way over there."

Smartass. I dropped my hold on him completely except for one hand tangled in his shirt, and as I tugged his face toward mine, I said, "You're gonna fuck me against the wall the way we were at The Nothing show."

"Mmm, an angel who knows what he wants." Viper sucked my lower lip into his mouth, eliciting a moan. "So this is what you're like when you're drunk. I approve." Then he straightened, a grin on his face as he walked over to where I'd indicated.

Under the glare of the lights, I got a killer view of his backside —those broad shoulders that tapered down into a strong back and an ass that made my dick harder than I'd ever thought possible. One day I'd like to get between those rounded cheeks, to see what

Viper would feel like inside, but that was a conversation for another day.

Right now, I wanted Viper pushing me up against that wall and taking me the way I'd fantasized about. In the days since we'd first had sex, Viper had surprised the hell out of me by refusing to get inside me again, telling me it was too much too soon, and I needed to go slow.

Viper? Go slow? That was even possible? And more than that, he cared enough to make sure this was a good experience for me? Utterly mind-blowing. So though I didn't understand why he was willing to restrain himself from going after what he so obviously wanted, I more than enjoyed the way he took pleasure in my body in other ways. If I'd thought his mouth and fingers were talented before I'd been introduced to his bed, now I thought they were nothing short of damn brilliant.

As I came up behind him, I ran my hand over his ass and then planted my back against the wall. Then he stepped forward, caging me in with his arms on either side of me.

My pulse raced to match the throbbing in my cock as his hips pushed up against mine, the friction of his rock-hard length making me tremble. It wasn't enough, though, and I gripped his waist, holding him tight to me as I rocked against him.

"Feeling needy, Angel?" Viper's voice, deep and low, stroked down my front like it was his hand, and as my head fell back and I thrust my hips forward, a throaty chuckle escaped him. "I'll take that as a yes."

Before I knew what was happening, Viper spun me around so that my front pressed up against the wall, and then slid his hand around my waist to pull down the zipper of my jeans. My jeans and boxer briefs were jerked down to just under my ass, and then Viper crowded in behind me, his hand going back down to wrap around my cock.

I muttered something unintelligible as his fingers circled the head, getting them nice and wet with my pre-cum before wrapping around my erection. Shiiit, it was just like the way he'd taken hold of me from behind backstage at The Nothing show, and it was just as hot now as it had been then. The only problem?

"Take your damn pants off." I panted as Viper continued to stroke me, and when he didn't immediately comply, I reached behind me for the button of his jeans and flipped the fucker open. Unzipping was a little trickier in my position, but with Viper refusing to take his hands off me—no complaints here—I did what I had to.

"Impatient," Viper murmured in my ear, squeezing around me, making me gasp. "I think I could get used to this side of you, Angel."

Then his hold on me disappeared as he shoved his pants down his hips, freeing his cock, and then, as he removed his shirt, I lifted my own up and over my head. I wanted to feel his skin on mine. Feel all those hard muscles tensing as he slid inside me, inch by delicious inch.

I sighed in relief when he touched me again, but as one hand worked me up and down, he brought the other up to my lips.

"Suck," he said.

I didn't hesitate or question why as two of his fingers slid past my lips. I treated them as I would a mouth-watering dessert—or his cock. Sucking and licking, I tasted every inch of him as Viper hummed behind me.

"That's it. Get 'em nice and wet, Angel. All the better to fuck you with."

A groan of protest left me, because I wanted more than just his fingers tonight, and Viper chuckled.

"Just a warm-up. Don't worry; I plan to fuck you until you can't stand."

Thank fucking God, because all this foreplay and lead-up over the past couple of days had made me desperate for what he'd been withholding, and though he'd said it was to let my body heal, I had a feeling that the real reason was to make me out of my mind with lust, leading up to this moment.

What was it about Viper that I couldn't get enough of?

FOURTEEN

Viper

THE ANGEL WAS on fire tonight. Fuck yes, he was. From the second the other guys had left us, until this moment, Halo had been demanding, impatient, and so damn needy that it'd been all I could do not to bypass the necessary build I knew he'd need before I slid my dick back inside the place it so desperately wanted to be.

As it was, I was finding it difficult to slow the pace enough to get him stretched and ready to take on the fucking he so clearly wanted. But there was no way I was going to cave and rush this. I'd been putting Halo off for a couple of days now, teasing and tormenting his body each night until I drove us both crazy, because I wanted him out of his mind for it this next go around. I wanted him begging me for it.

"So you want it just like that night at The Nothing do you, Angel?" When Halo nodded, I said by his ear, "Then your hands need to get up over your head...now."

Halo shuddered at the order, but not a second later, he stretched his arms up so he could press his palms flat against the wall. The move put the smooth skin of his back on delicious display, and when I shifted back a few inches to get a better look, Halo groaned and glanced over his shoulder at me.

With a smirk, I reached out and trailed the tip of my wet finger from his tailbone down in between his cheeks, and as I pushed it further down his hot channel, I licked my lips.

"This what you want?" I asked, rubbing my finger up and down, and moving back in so I could press my lips to his as I pressed the pad of my finger to his entrance.

"You know it is," Halo said against my mouth, and when I eased the tip inside him, he cursed.

"Gonna let me back in here a second time, huh?" As I slid my finger deeper, and then pulled it out to the tip, Halo's jaw clenched. "You're a brave angel. Or have you forgotten what I told you?"

When Halo's eyes narrowed, I nipped at his lower lip and said in a voice that was ragged with need, "I told you the next time I took you I was gonna drill you through the mattress. But since we don't have one here right now, I'm thinking this wall is just gonna have to do."

When I shoved my finger back inside him, Halo gasped, and I drove my tongue between his lips. He sucked on it as his body clamped down on my finger, and as I shoved him forward until his stiff, leaking cock was trapped against the wall, I pulled my finger free and pressed two against his tight little hole.

Halo bucked back, but I merely teased him by running my fingers up and down his crack.

"*Viper...*" he said as he tore his lips free.

I chuckled and probed at his eager entrance with both fingers now. "Right here, Angel."

Halo turned away and put his forehead to the wall, his fingers, which were still high above his head, pressing so hard against the surface his knuckles were turning white. Then he finally said, "I need more."

I lowered my head and pressed my lips to the top of his spine, and then I slowly eased both fingers back inside.

"Oh my God," Halo said as a moan of pure pleasure ripped from his throat, and he all but climbed up the wall to his toes as I flattened myself up against him.

"Fuck, you're tight," I growled by his ear. "Tight, hot, and so fucking sexy I could come all over you just from having you fuck my fingers."

"*No*," Halo protested, shaking his head.

"No?"

"No. I want you in me this time." Halo panted as I twisted my fingers and found his prostate, then he cursed and muttered, "I want you *all* the damn time."

Wasn't that the truth? Unlike my past sexual partners, Halo had somehow crawled beneath my skin. The angel with the bright eyes, and a face that I saw in my damn sleep, had gotten inside without even trying, and no matter how many times I told myself it would be the last time I kissed him, touched him, *wanted* him...it was never enough.

"Good, Angel. That's *real* good. 'Cause you're about to get me —*all* of me." I put my lips to his shoulder as I drew my fingers free, and then I shoved my hand into my pocket and pulled a condom and packet of lube out. Never had I been so fuckin' happy I carried that shit everywhere, because if I'd had to stop right then, I wasn't sure I would've.

I made quick work of the condom, and when I got the lube open, I slicked some over my dick before I sucked the skin on the side of Halo's neck and reached down to slide my slippery fingers back inside him.

"Fuckin' hell," I said against Halo's neck, as he shoved back from the wall, using his hands to propel himself harder onto my waiting fingers, and after several well-placed thrusts of my long digits, I had him all but whimpering. Then...

"Viper, now...*fuck*."

Pulling my fingers free, I reached down and spread his cheeks apart, allowing my cock the access it craved, and once I lined the head up with his hole, I wound my other arm around his waist and took hold of his dripping dick.

"You sure you're ready for me, Angel?"

Halo turned his head, and his eyes were the darkest I'd ever seen them. His lips were swollen from where he'd likely been biting them, and his face was tinged red.

"Please," he whispered, and I knew there'd be no denying that request. Hell, he could've asked me to rob a bank or commit a murder and I would've agreed right then. Halo had me under some kind of spell where all I wanted was to please him, and as I slowly entered his body, I crushed my lips down onto his. Halo moaned as I sank deeper and deeper, the heat of his body enveloping me until a groan rumbled up out of my chest and I was balls deep inside him.

"Hmm," I said against his lips as I stroked my fist up and down his stiff dick, and it wasn't lost on me that, this time around, Halo was as hard now, with me in him, as he had been before I'd entered him.

Whether that was the alcohol buzzing through him or the lust riding the angel, I wasn't sure. But there was no hesitation this time. No pulling away. This time he was rocking back, nestling his ass up against my pelvis as though he loved the way my dick was filling him up.

"Damn, you feel amazing," I said into the riot of curls in front of my face, and when that just wasn't enough, I nuzzled my nose into his hair and shut my eyes. When Halo craned his head back, his eyes shut as a blissful sound that was as sweet as it was sexy left him, and my body shook against his in response.

What the hell is he doing to me? I thought, as I dragged my tongue up his cheek to his lips, and when I got there, I said in a voice I barely recognized, "Kiss me, Angel."

Halo's eyes flashed open, and when they locked on mine, I knew he was as stunned as I was by the hoarse request. Since when did I ask for anything? But then he was kissing me, and I was moving behind him, no longer able to stay still.

As I slowly pulled out of him, I ran a hand up his length and squeezed the slick head, making him gasp, and when I grinned against that delicious mouth, he said, "Again."

I shoved back inside him, lowered my fist down his length, and told him, "Brace yourself."

Halo's eyes flared, and when he turned his head away from me and his arms tensed above his head, I released his cock and smoothed my hands down from under his arms. I trailed them along his ribs to his hips, and when my fingers dug into the naked flesh there, I pulled out of him, and this time when I thrust back inside, there was nothing slow or easy about it.

Hard, rough, and powerful. I tunneled inside the angel with all of the pent-up need and frustration I'd been feeling for him over the past few days, and the clawing possession I'd felt for him from the first moment I had him under me came hurtling back in full force.

Halo shouted out and reached down with one hand to jack himself as I hammered into him at an unrelenting pace, and as he slammed his other hand up against the wall, I bucked my hips harder, faster.

My breathing was coming in rapid bursts, and my heart was pounding a mile a minute, and suddenly I needed more of him. I wanted to feel Halo against me when he lost it, and I wanted him to feel me.

I slid my hands around his waist, and as I shoved back inside, I smoothed my palms up over his torso until my hands were flat on his chest. Then I pulled him off that wall so I was as deep inside him as I could get, and he was leaning back on me, fisting his cock as I gave him quick, hard thrusts in just the right spot.

Halo reached back with his free hand and grabbed the back of my head, and as he pulled me forward, he turned his face and captured my mouth with his, driving his tongue between my lips in a way that had my climax racing down my spine. But it wasn't until he said against my mouth, "I love the way you fuck me," that I lost it.

My entire body tensed behind his, and as I slammed our mouths together, I came deep inside him, capturing his shout of ecstasy as he came all over his hand, and Halo's body clamped around me in a way that had my toes curling.

As we stood there, both breathing hard, both shaking against one another, I was glad that Halo's back was to me, because I wasn't sure what he'd be able to see on my face, and I was positive it was nothing either of us were ready for.

FIFTEEN

Viper

"HEY, VIPER?" THE voice of Jared, one of our producers, cut through my headphones inside the recording booth, bringing me to a halt on the fifth go around for the background vocals of the track "Hard."

We'd been bouncing around ideas all afternoon, trying to get the chorus as edgy as I wanted it, but we hadn't quite hit the nail on the head, and when Jared had started waving his hands through the air midway through this cut, I knew we still weren't there yet.

Jared pressed the button that allowed me to hear him and said, "That was better, but I still think we're missing something. You're getting the frustration across like you want, but your voice is too smooth, my man. What do you do, drink hot tea and lemon every night?"

I snorted. "Nah. I get what you're saying, though. I want some gravel to it. Some grit. My voice just isn't cooperating."

Jagger got up from one of the couches in the mixing room where the rest of the band was seated and pressed down on the button. "Come on, V. We need you all growly. Can't you think of something that might make you feel like that? Bet I can..."

When Jagger glanced over his shoulder to the rest of the guys, my eyes automatically shifted to the other end of the couch, where

Halo was lounged back beside Killian. Dressed in navy shorts and a white polo that was tight enough it showed off his lean muscles, he could've been a Florida native. Add in the nice tan he'd gotten over the past couple of weeks, and he looked more like a sexy surfer than a rising superstar in the music industry.

"Hey, Halo?" Jagger said. "Vanessa, you remember her? Gorgeous, silky black hair, and legs for days? Yeah, she called up here this morning looking for you. Did Killian tell you?"

Fuckin' Jagger. He was having way too much fun with this. Ever since the three of them had found out about me and Halo, they'd been giving me nothing but shit. They'd been a little more restrained—if you could call it that—around Halo. But when he wasn't around, the fuckers never let up.

Not that I really expected them to. Finding out that I was fucking the new frontman, and *only* the frontman, had apparently been more than their little brains could handle. Hell, it probably would've been less shocking if Slade had told us all he was into cock. But since that hadn't happened yet, it seemed that I was their current entertainment.

Halo's lips curved into a smirk that made my cock twitch, Jagger's little ploy not lost on him at all, and I said into my mic, "Hey, asshole?" When Jagger turned back to face me, I shot him the finger.

Jagger chuckled. "Just tryin' to inspire you."

Killian grinned, as Slade busted up laughing, and after I'd done my best to glare them all to death, Jared came back to the mic.

"I've got an idea. What if we try this part in the morning?"

In the... "Huh?"

"In the morning," Jared said. "That's when your voice is the most gravelly, the deepest, right?" And before he took his finger off the mic, I heard Slade say, "What do you think, Halo? Is that when Viper's voice is the deepest?"

Even if I hadn't been able to hear what Slade had just said, I would've been able to tell by the way Halo's cheeks turned red that it had been something inappropriate. But when Halo's eyes found mine, he licked his lips and said something I couldn't hear but read crystal clear on his lips: *No way. It's deepest after he comes.*

That had the guys whooping and hollering so loud in the booth that I heard the vibration of it through the soundproof glass. But I didn't take my eyes off the angel, who was watching me with a look so hot that I was surprised the inside of the music booth hadn't caught on fire. Jesus. He was one surprise after another, and damn that was a turn-on.

"Right," Jared said, looking over his shoulder at Halo before turning back to me. "Since I'm positive I don't want to be around for that"—which only got more booming laughter—"how about we do this: tomorrow morning, I want you up at four a.m. and down here. I don't want you to talk to anyone—"

"Or come on anyone!" Jagger interjected.

"That too," Jared agreed. "Be here at four a.m. and I bet we can get it."

My mouth fell open. "Four a.m.? Have you lost your mind?"

"Nope," Jared said. "And I'm done with you, so get the fuck out so Halo can get in there."

Grumbling, I took my headphones off and hung them by the others on the wall before making my way to the door. When I pulled it open, I found Halo standing there with a grin on his face that made me want to kiss it the fuck off him.

"Proud of yourself?" I said, as he went to brush by me, and when he turned his head and ran his eyes over my face, that grin of his got wider.

"For...?"

Standing as we were between the booth and the mixing room, the wall separating the two may or may not have been blocking us from the others. But with him this close, and his words still rolling around in my head, I took a step forward until Halo's back was against the doorjamb.

His eyes were full of devilry—he knew exactly what he'd done to me with his not-so-innocent response—and I leaned forward to say in his ear, "For making me so fuckin' hard I'm about two seconds away from telling them we need a ten-minute break."

"Ten minutes?" Halo said, his lips but an inch from mine. "That wouldn't be long enough, and you know it."

I took in a deep inhale, because hell if he wasn't wrong, and when Halo's hands went to my waist and his fingers tightened in my shirt, the promise in his eyes made something other than my dick pound.

Lowering my head, I nipped at his lower lip, and the angel groaned in a way that made my entire body respond.

"Go on," I said, vowing that the second this was over I was going to make him groan again for me much louder. "Get in there and sing a song about how you make me hard."

Halo chuckled, and the sound was...arrogant, as he looked down my body. "Shouldn't be too difficult to channel."

I pushed away from him, and as I palmed my aching dick, Halo walked backward into the booth, his eyes on me until I shut the door, severing the connection.

As I walked around the corner and into the mixing room, Jared was already talking to Halo, but Slade, Jagger, and Killian were all eyeing me like they'd never seen me before.

"What the fuck are you three lookin' at?" I said as I moved to take the seat Halo had vacated.

"Hell if we know," Jagger said, running his eyes over me. "But we think it's a new species of...viper."

I narrowed my eyes. "Keep it up, Jagger."

"Pretty sure Halo's busy doing that," Killian interjected.

"Really, Kill?" I cocked my head in his direction. "I expected better from you."

"No, you didn't. Plus, even you gotta admit, you've been acting a little different lately."

"Hey, ladies?" Jared said as he let go of the button and looked over his shoulder at us. "Hate to break up this little gossip sesh, but you want to take a listen to your man in there—"

"You mean Viper's man," Slade said, to which I rolled my eyes, but Jared kept right on.

"Just see what you think, yeah?"

Jared turned back to Halo, and we all did the same. With the headphones on, his hair had been pushed back from his face, and the sharp angles of his cheek and jaw line—the same ones I'd kissed, licked, and bit—were all on full display.

When the music started up, I shifted forward on the couch, rested my forearms on my thighs, and clasped my hands together. Halo nodded along with the music we'd recorded earlier in the week, and as he stepped forward and angled his face up so his mouth was close to the mic, my eyes roamed up over his Adam's apple to his lips—lips that were now singing some of the filthiest fuckin' lyrics I'd ever written, all courtesy of him.

"Damn, Viper," Slade said, and I dragged my eyes away from Halo to look in his direction. "That's some love song you wrote for him to sing."

I ran a hand through my hair and was just about to tell Slade to bite me, when Halo belted out the lyrics:

I'VE THOUGHT *about how to fix it,*
   What might do the trick
   And fucking you for hours
   Just might get it licked

"DOES that sound like a love song to you?" I said, and Jagger chuckled.

"From you? Yeah."

Shaking my head, I went back to listening to Halo. Back to watching him, too. "You're all delusional."

"And *you* are all about the angel," Jagger said. "Admit it."

Choosing to ignore him, I kept my eyes forward.

"Come on, guys," Killian said, and I thought, *Finally, the voice of reason.* I should've known better. "Give it a rest. If V isn't ready to admit that he wants to go on long walks on the beach at sunset with Halo, who are we to push him?"

Slade snorted, as Jagger laughed, and I glared at Killian over my shoulder. He was grinning at me like a fucking idiot.

"I hate you."

Killian shoved me in the shoulder. "No, you don't. But come on. You like him...a lot. Just admit it."

"Why do you fuckers even care?"

Jagger's mouth fell open. "Umm, because you have *never*—in all the years the band has been together—dated, repeated, or sat moon-eyed over anyone. This is...it's..."

"Unprecedented." Slade shot a look at me.

"Do you even know what that means?" I asked.

Killian pushed his leg against mine. "Don't try and change the subject."

"Fine, you bunch of nosy fuckers." I shook my head and turned back to where Halo was singing. "I like him," then I added, "A lot," because I knew they wouldn't quit until they got some kind of confession. But that was all they were going to get, because I didn't even know what the fuck I was thinking or feeling yet.

"Now can you all please shut the fuck up so we can listen to him?" I said. "I don't think I heard any of that over all your damn yammering."

"Neither did I," Jared said without looking back at us, and I gave a pointed look to the three who were smiling smugly at me, and thought, yet again, that they were a bunch of gossipy fuckers before I turned back to hear Jared say, "Halo, can you take it from the top again, please?"

SIXTEEN

Halo

"HALO, WE SAVED you a seat," Jagger said a couple of hours later, when we'd taken a break for a late lunch. We still had a few hours' worth of work to do on "Hard," but it was coming together and would be done by the end of the day—well, apart from Viper's four a.m. session.

Speaking of Viper...

With a plate in hand and sitting on the end of the couch, Jagger reached over and patted Viper's knee, where he sat in the recliner beside him. "Right here good for you, man?" he said to me, shooting a wink my way while Viper swatted Jagger's hand away.

"If you don't fuck off with that shit..." Viper said.

Jagger laughed and moved down the couch, giving his spot up to me. I set my drink on the coffee table and sat down, and as soon as I did, Viper reached over and swiped my pickle.

"Hey," I protested, but Viper grinned before he pushed the pickle slowly between his lips, a move that looked almost indecent as he stared at me.

"Oh, for fuck's sake," Killian said, just as Jagger yelled, "Don't nobody wanna see that."

"Well, considering V was voted hottest guitarist alive in *Rolling*

Stone, I think a lot of people wanna see it," Slade said, then casually scooped leftover potato salad into his mouth.

Jagger shot him a look. "Dude."

"What?"

Jagger stared at him for a long moment and then shook his head. As Slade shrugged and went back to eating, I lifted my sandwich and stabbed the second pickle I'd grabbed with my fork. Bringing it to my lips, I bit off the tip, as Viper's lips curled.

Once I swallowed, I lowered my voice so only Viper could hear and said, "You're not the only one who likes a thick prick in his mouth."

His eyebrows shot up, and he coughed around the bite he'd been chewing. "Damn, Angel," he said, then grabbed my drink off the table and took a long swallow. "The shit that's comin' outta your mouth today..."

"Better than what's been going in it?" I asked, but this time Jagger heard it, and he jumped to his feet.

"Nah, nah, man. I don't wanna hear none of that," he said, moving across the room to sit, but there wasn't another open spot, so he sat on the arm of Killian's chair. "Tell them to take it to another room, Kill."

"Can't do that. We've gotta talk album names." Killian wiped his mouth with his napkin and then set his empty plate on the table beside him.

"Why don't we self-title it? There, done," Jagger said.

"We could, but don't you wanna come out with a bang?"

Jagger grinned. "I think Halo does."

When raucous laughter broke out, I could only shake my head. Yeah, the guys had been teasing nonstop since finding out about Viper and me, but I found that I didn't mind, because the alternative would've been much worse. Besides, it was kinda fun running Jagger off by freaking him out. Having the guys not give two shits one way or another had taken a weight off, and the result was me feeling more relaxed, more a part of the band than I ever had before. It helped that we were coming together so well musically, and our new producers, Jared in particular, had been great about giving us the space to work our songs ourselves while making sure we were still headed in the right direction.

"What about TBD?" Slade said. A few seconds later, he ducked, the pillow Killian had thrown at him barely missing his head. "Yo, it was a joke!"

"Speaking of TBD, what about *Destruction*? Like tearing down the past?" I said.

Killian nodded slowly. "Not bad. But do we want to focus on the past or make a statement about our future?"

Good point. As the others rattled off a few suggestions, I wolfed down my lunch. I hadn't realized I was so hungry, but performing always took a lot out of me, and trying to nail perfect vocals for hours was the hardest part.

Viper leaned in toward me, and I assumed he'd grab something off my plate, but instead he lowered his voice and said, "Now that's one way I'd like to see you eat my cock. Like you're fuckin' starving."

I dropped the sandwich, and Viper chuckled, taking the rest of my pickle from my plate as he sat back.

"Did you have something to add, V?" Killian said.

With his gaze still on me, Viper tilted his head to the side, those wheels turning, and when his mouth slowly curved... Well, shit. I knew that look.

"I think I do, actually," Viper said, tearing his eyes away to look at Killian. "We're Fallen Angel, and it just so happens we've got a fallen angel right here in this room."

Good God, here we go. Another contribution based on our sex life. Great.

"When Halo came to us, he was so...innocent, wouldn't you say?" Viper smirked at me. "But I think you'll agree after hearing some of the things that've come out of his mouth today, that he's been a bit corrupted by his association with us."

"With *you*," Jagger said with a snort.

Viper gave him a wolfish smile, like he was proud of his contribution to my demoralization.

"So what's the suggestion, then?" Killian said.

"*Corruption*," Viper said. "That's the album's name, because that's what fallen angels do. They corrupt others to fall. To join them in their sinful, wicked ways." He focused that wolf stare on me, and I felt the full weight of his words. Viper had been, and still was, the ultimate temptation, one I'd given myself over to after warring over "which way I'd fall," as Viper had said.

Guess that answer was pretty clear now.

"*Corruption*," Killian said, stroking his jaw. "I fucking love it." Then he turned to the others. "What do you guys think?"

"Sounds cool," Slade said.

Jagger stood up and crossed the room, holding his fist out to Viper. When Viper returned the bump, Jagger said, "Damn, man. First the band name and now the album title? You on fire."

Out of the corner of my eye, I saw Viper look at me again, and as my eyes met his, I saw the flames that lit that dark gaze. The heat in them warmed me from head to toe and sent my pulse racing.

"Nah," Viper said, still watching me. "Just been inspired."

The world faded away, the others disappearing until there was only me and Viper and his words. I'd inspired him. Hell, I was the inspiration behind the band name, and all because he had been as tempted by me as I had been by him. I leaned toward him, licking my lips, my eyes dropping to his mouth, and as I drew closer—

"That was the cheesiest fucking thing I've ever heard you say." Killian was shaking his head in mock disgust. "You two gonna make out right here? Maybe go get a room."

"Yeah, I'm with Kill. Get a damn room," Jagger said.

Realizing how close I was to Viper, I jerked away, but Viper was as quick as his namesake and grabbed my wrist.

"You know what? That's a great fuckin' idea," he said, rising to his feet, pulling me up with him. He took the plate out of my hand

and set it on the coffee table before towing me alongside him out of the room. "Later, assholes."

"We have to be back in the studio in twenty minutes, V," Killian called out.

"Noted." Viper stopped in the doorway and stuck his head back in the room. "And let Jared know I'll be ready for my vocals when I get back."

SEVENTEEN

Halo

————————

KICKING OFF THE pool wall, I cut through the water like a knife before rising to the surface, where I took in a quick breath and began to swim. It was a warm morning in Miami already, and as usual, I started the day off swimming a few laps, trying to get my blood flowing for a long day in the studio. We'd been working on tracks for over a month now, and I knew it wouldn't be too much longer before the album was finished and we were sent back to New York. And as much as I loved New York, I'd definitely enjoyed the slower pace of Florida, as well as the stunning scenery —and this pool.

"Hey, Angel. I got somethin' for ya."

I lifted my head, and when I saw Viper walking toward the pool, freshly showered and in nothing but a pair of shorts, it was enough to stop me.

I wiped the water from my eyes, and when I saw him slapping an envelope against his palm, I swam over to the side of the pool, crossing my arms up over the lip.

"What's that?" I said, as Viper crouched down to my level. His hair was still wet, and I had the brief urge to tug him forward into the pool, but curiosity over what he held in his hand won out.

Viper reached behind him to grab the towel I'd laid out, and once I'd lifted myself up out of the pool, I dried myself off and then Viper handed me the envelope.

"What's this?" I said, flipping it over, but the back was as blank as the front. I peeled it open to see a check, and I raised an eyebrow at Viper. "A check? That's nice, but I would've done you for free."

It was rare that I shocked him; he always seemed to have the upper hand, but when Viper's lips parted in surprise, I had to laugh.

"And I would've paid more," he said, as I took out the check to see MGA's address fixed to the upper left side. "This is your first official payment for Fallen Angel."

I blinked at the number on the check. There were more zeros than I'd made in the five years I'd been playing dive bars and scraping by. "How? I mean, I wasn't expecting anything yet. The album won't be out for a while."

"Angel, you wrote the most streamed song of the year so far. Trust me, you deserve every penny of what's on there and more. And there will be *a lot* more when we start touring."

My hands shook as I stared down at what one song had done. I couldn't have imagined this a few months ago, and even now, it was hard to believe. "This is unreal," I said. "Thank you."

"Don't thank me. Thank that head of yours."

I grinned. "Which one?" Before he could answer, I leaned over and kissed him. He moaned, bringing his hand up to hold the back of my head and deepening the kiss. Less than an hour had passed since I'd left his bed, but already I was hungry for him again.

With a groan, Viper pulled away. "Too fuckin' tempting, you know that?"

"You might've mentioned it a time or two."

"Because it's true," he said, and then nodded at the pool. "You done here?"

"Unless you wanna join me. Although if you do that, we'll be late to the studio."

"Mmm, about that..." Viper grabbed my chin and brought me

forward to suck my lower lip into his mouth, but before he let things go further, he said, "Jared's out sick today."

"Which means...?"

Viper snatched the check out of my hand and grinned. "We're gonna go celebrate."

"Seriously?"

"A check this big means you've gotta spend it."

I thought about my run-down apartment back home and frowned. "I should probably save it."

"There's more than enough here to do both. You deserve something you've had your eye on. You work harder than the rest of us assholes, so don't give me any of this 'I'm saving it' bullshit. We're goin' out."

Viper got to his feet, and I squinted up at him, bringing my hand up to block the sun. "Just you and me?"

"Well, I'm not inviting any of those fuckers. Are you?"

I grinned and stood up, toweling off. "Sounds like a date." When Viper didn't respond, just held my check out to me once I was done drying off, I thought about calling him out on it. We'd gone out a few times here and there, usually with the others, but occasionally on our own, and never once had he acknowledged it was anything more than "hanging out." I knew better, though. Viper may not want to admit it, but you didn't spend week after week with someone and not call it dating. But hey, if he wanted to live in denial, who was I to stop him?

"I guess we'll have to behave ourselves," I said, reaching for his hand. He didn't resist my touch—he never did—and I tugged him toward me, moving my free hand around to grab hold of his ass. "So none of this while we're in public, huh?"

Viper slid his fingers under the waistband of my shorts. "No."

"Or this?" I tilted my head up and pressed my lips against his.

"Nope," Viper murmured against my mouth. "It's just easier this way..."

With his hips flush against mine, I could feel his erection stirring behind his shorts, and I moved the hand I had on his ass to his growing cock. "I don't know. It feels pretty hard to me."

Viper groaned and brought his hands up to my face to take my lips in a vicious kiss before he jerked away and took a couple of steps back. "Fuckin' behave," he said, though his body was saying anything but. I found it ironic that the tables had turned and now it was Viper showing restraint, but as much as I didn't want to admit it, he was right. With the new album on the horizon, the last thing we needed to do was take our casual *whatever* public.

His eyes trailed down my body, taking in every soaked inch, and then he backed away, rubbing his face. "Get dressed or we won't be going anywhere."

"That a threat or a promise?" I called out after him, but the only reaction I got from him as he walked away was his middle finger.

"HOW DID YOU KNOW?" I circled the Manson MB-1 guitar slowly, my eyes roaming over the instrument and my hands itching to play.

"How'd I know you'd fuckin' orgasm over this baby? Please, Angel. It's like you think I don't know you at all." Viper smirked at my hesitation to come closer. "You can touch it. Play it. Lick it."

I stepped closer, my fingers running down the length of the body, and then with careful hands, I lifted the guitar out of its stand. The weight felt good in my arms, the long, lean body a gorgeous glossy red glitter. I looked around us, waiting for someone to run over and tell me to put it down, but when no one seemed to be paying attention, I quietly strummed.

"You can't pussyfoot with a guitar like that," Viper said, crossing his arms. "Play it like you fuckin' mean it."

I snorted, but the man had a point. Closing my eyes, I let loose, playing with no direction whatsoever, but relishing the unique sound of the guitar. This one came with a Korg Kaoss Pad too, which would make any noise my heart desired. I'd been dying to get my hands on this bad boy for years now, and it played even better than I'd dreamed.

"Fuck, that's hot," Viper said, and whether he was talking about the guitar or me, I didn't know, but I selfishly hoped it was the latter.

"Nice, isn't it?" came an unfamiliar male voice, and as I stopped playing, my eyes shot open. A man with a nametag that proclaimed him Paul, the store manager, watched me with a polite smile, but when he got a good look at my face, his mouth parted. "Are you...?" Then he looked at Viper, and even with a hat pulled low and sunglasses covering his face, a fan would recognize him in a heartbeat.

Paul stumbled back a bit, his hand coming up to cover his mouth, but then he seemed to shake himself, clearly trying to rein in his surprise. He swallowed, and when he spoke again, it was professional, though he was still obviously taken aback. When he held his hand out to Viper, I noticed the way it shook, and it made me think back to the first day I'd met the intimidating force that was Viper. Hell, I'd been shaking too.

"I'm Paul, the store manager here, and can I just say I'm honored you stopped by. I'm a huge fan." He shook Viper's hand, and then he turned to me, his arm outstretched. "And...Halo, isn't it? The new song is fucking killer—I mean, uh, just killer, sorry—"

"You can say fuckin' killer," Viper said. "He likes it."

Paul's face reddened, and then he managed a smile. I looked down to where he was still shaking my hand, and when he followed my gaze, he pulled free.

"Oh, sorry about that," he said, still looking between us as if we'd disappear at any moment. "Is there something I can help you with? Would you like more information about the MB-1?"

It was the first time I'd been recognized while Viper and I had ventured out, though he'd been stopped many times before. It felt a little strange for someone I'd never met to know who I was, but I guessed that was something I needed to get used to, huh?

"I think he's got a good handle on it," Viper said, inclining his head toward me. In response, I began to play again, as Paul stood quietly by, watching with wide eyes. It was easy to get lost in the guitar; it had so many functions I couldn't wait to try out—

Wait, was I actually considering buying it?

I stopped playing, much to Paul's apparent dismay, and as I put the guitar back in its stand, Viper said, "What are you doing?"

"I can't buy this." I shook my head, wondering if I'd lost my mind even coming here. I had two perfectly fine guitars already. I didn't need this one.

"Why?" Viper asked. "You don't like it?"

"It's more than several months of rent. I can't afford that."

"Oh, Angel." There was a smug look on Viper's face as he walked over to me and put his hands on my shoulders. "There's a few zeroes in your bank account now that say you can."

"But I don't *need* it. I just want it." Ugh, I wanted it so much. I could just imagine all the new sounds I could incorporate into the songs we were working on, and—

"Fine." Viper shrugged, dropping his hands and pulling out his wallet from his back pocket. "I'll buy it."

My mouth fell open. "What? No. I mean, unless you're buying it for yourself—"

When Viper handed a credit card to Paul, I snatched it out of his hands and shoved it against Viper's chest. "You're not buying me a guitar."

"Eh. It's a tax write-off."

"No," I said. "Absolutely not."

Viper looked past me at Paul. "We'll take it. Did you want the red or black, Angel?"

Fuck. He was really gonna buy me this damn guitar, wasn't he?

"Fine, I'll buy it," I said, taking out my own wallet and handing over my card. It didn't feel real that I had enough on there to cover the cost of the guitar, but I'd seen the check with my own eyes and knew just how many of these guitars I could buy with all that. I really did want it anyway, so having Viper's permission of sorts? Yeah, okay. Why not.

"Wonderful choice." Paul nodded as he took my card, and behind me, I heard Viper chuckle. "Which style would you prefer, and I'll get it ready for you?"

My eyes ventured over to where Viper stood in full black from his hat to his shirt to his shoes. "I'll take the matte black." As the store manager walked off, I moved in closer to Viper, who had a victorious grin on his face.

"You're welcome," he said. "What are you gonna name her?"

"Him," I said, my lips curving mischievously. "And I think I'll name him Viper." I leaned in close to whisper in his ear, "That way I can touch, play, or lick him whenever I want."

EIGHTEEN

Viper

THE RUSTY PELICAN was one of the hottest restaurants in Miami. It catered to all kinds of clientele, including celebrities, locals, and tourists. With its waterfront views overlooking the Miami skyline, the guys and I had discovered the hotspot the first time we'd been sent down here to record and made it a point to visit whenever we were in town.

That was exactly what I was doing now, I told myself as Halo walked beside me, down toward the entrance—just, you know, minus the other guys. Nothin' unusual about that. We'd gone out, spent some of Halo's hard-earned cash on something he more than deserved, and now we were gonna throw back some drinks, eat some food, and have a good time, which all would've seemed completely normal if I hadn't started it by—

"Here, I got it," I said, reaching for the door when we got to the entrance.

As soon as I had it pulled open, I realized the move for what it was, and so did Halo, judging by the way he stood there staring at me like I'd grown two heads. There was no way in hell I would've opened a door for Killian, Jagger, or Slade, and up until a second ago I would've added Halo to that list, but that second had obviously passed.

Halo's lips twitched. "Thanks."

"Yeah, no problem," I said like a total lame-ass, and then rolled my eyes as Halo walked off in front of me. As I followed after him, I gave myself a mental uppercut. *This is just a fucking meal.* But as my eyes swept around the blue lights that illuminated the shadowed interior, it suddenly felt like a whole lot more. Not that I would know.

"Good evening," the hostess said with a brilliant smile as she looked to Halo. "Do you have a reservation?"

"Uh," Halo said, and then looked back at me, a questioning look in his eyes.

"No, sorry. We don't," I said, moving up beside Halo, and when the woman's eyes shifted to me, I flashed a grin that had her mouth falling open. "But Sabrina told me to stop by anytime I'm in town. Is she around?"

"Oh..." She laughed. "Um, I mean, no. Sorry. She's off tonight. But of course we have a table for you, Viper," she said, reaching up to push some of her chestnut curls behind her ear.

As she looked down at the list and map in front of her, my eyes found Halo, who was smirking at me. I arched an eyebrow, daring him to voice the mocking taunt I could see in his eyes, but he remained silent as he turned back to the woman.

"Would you like to sit inside or outside?" she asked.

I was about to answer, but then found myself saying, "Angel? You got a preference?"

Then her eyes lit up on Halo, and she grabbed a pad of paper from her stand and rushed around to us. "Oh my God, you're the new guy. The new singer for Fallen Angel."

It took everything I had not to correct her. Halo was the *only* singer Fallen Angel had had. But Halo was already nodding and taking the pad of paper she was all but shoving at him.

"Will you sign this for me? We get everyone who's famous to sign a Rusty Pelican menu, napkin, whatever. We have all the other guys up there," she said, indicating the wall behind us, and sure enough, there was my signature along with the rest of TBD's, including that fucker Trent's name. We needed a new group signature up there sooner rather than later.

As Halo handed the pad back to her, she tucked it into the front of her black apron and then grinned at us again. "Sorry, did you say inside or outside?"

Halo looked at me and shrugged. "Outside okay for you?"

Outside was perfect, and where I would've chosen anyway, and when I agreed, we followed the hostess to the doors that led outside to the tables lining the patio. She led us past the busiest section to a table on the far side of a sleek fire pit, and as we took our seats, she placed our menus down and said, "Kyle will be out to take your orders soon."

As she disappeared back inside, Halo looked out at the spectacular view of Miami at night, and me? I looked at Halo. With the string lights hanging between the palm trees that dotted the edge of the patio, Halo's curls shimmered and his eyes all but gleamed, and wanting that face aimed my way, I said, "Do you approve?"

Just as I'd wanted, Halo turned his head in my direction, his lips curving. He cocked his head to the side, and his astute stare had me doing something I'd never done in my life—I shifted nervously in my seat. *What the fuck?*

"Do I approve of the restaurant?" Halo asked, and I had a feeling he was fucking with me.

"Yeah..."

Halo pursed his lips and looked back at the multimillion-dollar view before returning his attention to me. "That sounds an awful lot like something a *date* would worry about."

When I narrowed my eyes, Halo added, "Would you care what Killian thought?"

"Hell no, but I'm not fucking him."

Halo licked his lips, drawing my eyes again. Damn, I really wanted to be the one tracing my tongue over them, then he said something that had me just about falling off my chair.

"Good. I'd be jealous." Halo then leaned a little closer over the table and said, "That's also something a date would say, just so you know."

Smartass. "You havin' fun?"

Halo chuckled and then leaned back in his chair, eyeing me with a smirk that made my cock jerk behind my jeans.

"Just pointing out some facts."

"About dating?"

"Mhmm. It's the least I can do, since you've never been on one before."

"Keep it up, Angel, and I'm gonna—"

"Good evening, guys. Welcome to The Rusty Pelican." Kyle, presumably, came to stop by our table just in time to save Halo's fine ass. "Have you decided what you'd like to eat tonight? To drink?"

Luckily for us, it seemed Kyle had been informed in advance as to who we were and we didn't have to go through the whole *oh wow, you're so-and-so* moment, because right then all I wanted was to be alone with Halo. Shit, maybe I did want to be on a date with the angel—a really fucking private one.

I hadn't even looked at the menu, but I liked anything seafood, and before I could say a word, Halo was talking.

"We'd like to share the three-tiered seafood tower, thanks."

"Got it," Kyle said. "And to drink?"

Finally locating my tongue, I said, "The best whiskey you have on hand for me."

"Vodka for me, thanks," Halo added, then Kyle vanished, and I heard myself say, "Is it also customary for one party of the date to order for the other?"

"Are you finally admitting that's what this is?"

"You're pushing awfully hard tonight, Angel, for someone who told me he was cool with things being as is." I watched him closely, not quite sure what it was I expected to see. Denial, indifference, humor? But what I got was an intensity I didn't have a clue what to do with.

I'd been looked at many ways in my life, with awe, lust, hunger, and power. And as Halo's eyes ran over my face, I saw all those things, but when they finally settled and locked on mine, there was also a fierce interest in getting to know the person sitting opposite him—and *that* was a first.

"And you're avoiding the question," Halo said. "Look, I know what I said, and if that's still all you want, then I guess that's cool—"

"You guess?" I chuckled.

Halo rolled his eyes. "Well, yeah. It's not like anyone could *make* you do anything."

I rubbed my hand over my jaw. "Oh I don't know, Angel. I find myself doing all kinds of things for you. Things I never thought I'd do."

Halo's cheeks colored, and fuck, something in my stomach flipped from knowing I'd caused that reaction. The same way it had from the very beginning.

"Like opening restaurant doors?" Halo asked.

And finally I gave in and nodded. "Like opening restaurant doors."

"So it *is* a date?"

"Jesus." I laughed and ran a hand over my face. "It's a fucking date. Happy?"

"Delirious."

As Halo crossed his arms, I muttered, "Smug fucker."

"Hey, don't even try to take this away from me. How many firsts have you given me over the past month?"

I touched the tip of my tongue to my top lip, thinking about each and every one of them. "A lot. I've enjoyed every damn one of them, too."

"Mhmm. And this is me giving you a first. Your first date. Aww, welcome to being an adult, Viper. How's it feel?"

"Right now? Pretty fucking painful."

A booming laugh that made me want to grab him left his lips.

"Seriously."

"Seriously," I said, sitting forward in my chair. "It feels...right. *You* feel right."

Halo's grinning lips clamped shut, but before he could respond, Kyle showed up with a tray and the most delicious-looking tower of seafood I'd ever seen. A second waiter put our drinks down in front of us, then, without any further lingering, they disappeared back inside.

"So this is what you thought we should eat tonight, huh? What if I don't like seafood?"

Halo arched a brow at me. "Yeah, okay. You brought me to a seafood restaurant. And even if you don't, too bad. Live a little. You always eat off my plate anyway."

I'd like to eat off you right this second, I thought, and as though Halo knew exactly what I was thinking, his lips kicked up at the sides.

"I also saw a dessert on the menu that I thought we could order to go. It had three sauces, ice creams, and things you dip in it before you suck it off. I'll share that with you too. *If* you're nice to me."

I reached for some lobster and shrimp, as Halo took some sushi.

"Not sure I know how to be nice, Angel," I said, finding that I actually meant it. What if we did this thing, dated, and I fucked it up because I was an asshole? The probability of that was pretty damn high, and—

What the hell? Since when have I been so goddamn insecure?

Halo dipped his sushi in a bit of soy sauce before eating the whole thing in one bite. Once he'd swallowed, he licked a drop of sauce off his finger and said, "Yeah, but by nice I mean bad. Come on, Viper. You said earlier that you know who I am, so how about you give me a bit of credit here, huh? I'm not exactly naive when it comes to you."

No, I didn't suppose he was. And yet here he was, wanting to... date me. A guy. Someone he'd never even considered until I made him. And that had me thinking.

"What was her name?"

Halo's hand froze midway to his mouth. "Who?"

I could tell he knew what I was asking even though he hadn't answered. But if he thought I was going to back down then he was in for a shock. The angel had said he wanted a date, and wasn't this what people did on dates? Asked about exes?

"The girl you sang about in your audition video. The one who broke your heart. What was her name?"

Halo's mouth fell open, and I could see the question *why* in his eyes. But before he could ask, I said, "She still in the picture at all?"

When he seemed to get past his shock, Halo popped the rest of the tuna sashimi into his mouth, and once he was done, he picked up his drink, took a long sip, and then wiped off his mouth.

"You jealous?" he asked.

I snorted but didn't answer.

"Viper? Are you jealous?"

Was I? I thought back to the hundred and one times I'd watched that audition video of Halo before we agreed to permanently hire him, and remembered thinking what a dumbass someone would've been to let him go.

Was I jealous? *Yeah, I'm fuckin' jealous. Of some nameless girl I don't even know.*

"And if I am?"

Halo grinned as though the idea pleased him immensely, but instead of giving me shit, he put his napkin down and said, "Phoebe. Her name was Phoebe. And to save you the agony of asking a question I know you're dying to ask but probably won't, we dated for three years."

"Three years?" Fuck me, that was, like...twenty-one in dog years. I couldn't imagine waking up with the same person for—

"You freaking out over there?"

"No."

"Liar," Halo said, and when he smiled, I tried to imagine *not* waking up and seeing his face. "Anyway, she wanted different things to me. Or should I say *for* me. She thought I was wasting my time in the dive bars when I could've had a career more like my mom's. With the symphony."

I was listening to everything Halo was saying, but instead of having anything remotely intelligent to say, I blurted out, "She was wrong. You don't belong in an orchestra. You belong center stage, Angel. Under a fucking spotlight."

A pleased sigh left him. "Do you remember that night at Li's when you said people would look at me, at us, and wonder who I was to you?"

I nodded. I'd purposely been fucking with him, and it had worked. He'd looked totally freaked out that the other customers might think we were together. But when Halo leaned over toward me tonight, there was no concern in his eyes, not even a hint.

"Tonight, I wish I could tell everyfuckingone," he said.

NINETEEN

Halo

WHEN I WOKE the next morning, the soft strumming of a guitar filled my ears. It was a beautiful sound, one of my favorite sounds in the world, though the song itself was unfamiliar.

Keeping my eyes closed so Viper would continue playing, I let the music lull me, my thoughts drifting back to last night, when he'd finally admitted we were on a date.

Yep, the perennial bad-boy bachelor of the group had gone on an official date, and somehow, even with all the choices available to him, it'd been with me. That filled my stomach with a million damn butterflies, because though we'd gone out alone before, last night had been different. He'd opened the door for me, for God's sake, which I knew had surprised him as much as it had me.

Somehow, over the last few weeks since we'd been in Miami, I'd gotten over the shock of falling for a man—although that was largely due to the fact that no one in our inner circle had questioned what was happening with Viper. Sure, the guys gave us shit for it, but Viper had assured me they would've done that regardless of gender. But in the back of my mind, I considered what would happen when we got back to New York. Here, it was like being in the safety of a bubble, but what happened when we ventured outside of that? What would my family say? My friends?

And more importantly, would whatever this thing was with Viper continue once we were back to reality?

Not wanting to think any more about the what-ifs, I opened my eyes to see Viper sitting in a chair across the room, naked and with my new guitar across his lap. Dawn was just breaking, sunlight filtering in through the opening where the curtains met, giving me just enough light to see him.

Damn, he was beautiful. Not a word I ever thought I'd associate with a man, and not one Viper would ever want to be called, but it was the truth. Every inch of his smooth olive skin was on display, and it surprised me now, as it always did for some reason, that Viper wasn't covered in tattoos—or that he didn't at least have a few hidden ones. No, the only thing hidden on his body was the Prince Albert piercing at the head of his cock, and *that* had most definitely been a welcome surprise—especially because he knew just how to use it. The thought of him inside me made me shudder and lick my lips, and the small movement caught Viper's attention.

He looked up. Strands of dark hair covered his face, and when he saw that I was awake, he tucked them behind his ear. We didn't say anything for a long time, just stared at each other. I wondered what he was doing awake so early, but I hadn't recognized the song he'd been playing, so maybe inspiration had struck, as it sometimes did in the dead of sleep.

"*The* Viper is christening my new baby, I see." I gave him a lazy smile, content to lie there and listen to him all morning.

"Just playing with myself. Something I like to do often," he said, shooting me a wink.

"Mmm." I moved onto my back so I could get a better look at him. "Don't stop on my account."

Viper ran a hand through his hair, and as he bent down over my guitar again and began to play, I stretched out and kicked off the too-warm covers. Cool air glided over my naked body, and as I angled my head to watch Viper, his eyes shot up, immediately darkening.

"Angel..." It sounded like a warning, which only made me want to go further.

Under his perusal, my cock stirred, and as he continued to play, I decided I should join in and put my fingers to good use.

I brought my hand up to my neck and, keeping my eyes on Viper's face, let my fingers trail down over my throat and then down my chest, pausing only to encircle one of my nipples. As Viper licked his lips, he stopped his movements, and I stopped mine.

"You play, I play," I said, and he stared at me for a long moment before shaking his head.

"Someone woke up a fuckin' tease."

The music started up again, and I tweaked my nipple between my thumb and forefinger before flattening my palm and sliding it down over my abs. As the tips of my fingers reached the tight crop of curls below my hips, a low growl sounded from across the room, and I grinned in satisfaction.

Feeling every bit of Viper's heated gaze, I brought my hand up to my mouth, and when I sucked two fingers deep inside, the song stuttered before he was able to get it back on track. Once my fingers were good and wet, I wrapped them around my growing erection, and Viper cursed.

I groaned and arched up into the tight feel of my fist as I slid my hand up and down my length, but when the music stopped again, so did I.

"You're fuckin' serious about this 'you play, I play' shit, huh?" Viper shook his head, and as his fingers plucked at the strings again and I resumed jerking myself off, he stood up from the chair and walked over to the edge of the bed. I writhed under the shadow of him, loving the way he watched me so intently, and the way he bit down on his lip like he was struggling not to say "fuck it" and climb in the bed for a taste. I'd never be opposed to that, but shit, his gaze on me as I got myself off was so hot that my pre-cum more than coated the entire length of my dick.

I matched my movements to the music, a slow, seductive

melody that allowed me time to inch my way up from the base of my cock to the head in a delicious yet tormenting slide. Viper's eyes locked on my grip, and the longer he played, the faster the music became. I wasn't even sure Viper noticed the change as I began to pump my cock with more urgency than I had before, but as I steamed closer to release, I heard him say, "So goddamn sexy, Angel."

Spreading my legs farther apart, I continued to stroke myself with one hand while reaching down with the other to run my fingers along my perineum, and Viper's knee hit the mattress. He was so close, but had enough self-control somehow to merely watch, even though the angle he was at now showed me exactly how turned on he was behind the guitar.

It reminded me of the times I'd gotten off watching Viper on my laptop, and here he was now, in the flesh, close enough to touch, and devouring every move I made. He made me feel like the hottest motherfucker on the planet, and suddenly I was too far away.

Releasing my hold, I crawled to the edge of the bed and sat up on my knees. There were only inches between us as I gripped my cock again, and as a bead of sweat trailed down my neck, Viper leaned in, swiping it away with a long lick that sent a shiver through my body.

Fuck this no-touching shit. I wanted his mouth on me.

Before he could move away, I dove in for a kiss, but as my lips brushed his, he jerked away and smirked.

"Uh uh," he said, taking a step back. "That's against the rules."

"Fuck the rules."

He tsked. "How about you fuck yourself instead?" Then he moved back toward the bed, angling his head so that I could feel his breath on my neck. "Show me how you got off that first night we got here when I heard you come, Angel. Let me see you."

My head fell back as I grunted, my balls drawing up tight. Shit, how would I ever resist Viper and his damn mouth? I'd been fully in control of this show, but a command from him and I was ready to fall apart for him.

I'd been lying down that first night, but with my orgasm barreling down my spine, I didn't have time to move. I could only watch Viper watching me, and when the explosion finally hit, I moaned his name as the world went white.

TWENTY

Viper

———————

SOMETHING HAD CHANGED. Nothing that you could see or touch. But something between the angel and me had definitely shifted.

I wasn't sure when it happened exactly, but if I had to pinpoint it, I'd guess it was the moment I'd opened the door for Halo at The Rusty Pelican last night. That seemed to be the moment I opened a whole lotta other things, too. Things I wasn't familiar with. *Things* that had been bangin' around in my head so loudly last night that I hadn't been able to sleep.

What the fuck was I doing? That seemed to be the question at the top of the list, and no matter how many times I asked myself, I couldn't seem to come up with an answer. Not a good one, anyway. Not one that made any sense.

From the moment I set eyes on Halo, I'd wanted to get closer to him. I'd wanted to touch him, taste him, fuck him—things I'd now done, many times over—but where that would've usually been enough, the hunger and the need satisfied, I found myself wanting more. More time with him, more tastes of him, more everything. What the hell was that all about? It was that realization that had me knocking on the bathroom door and telling him, "Meet me in the kitchen," instead of joining him under the warm water. I needed a minute to myself, and a minute to get my head on straight.

The mansion was quiet as a church as I made my way down the hall, the guys still dead to the world, and I knew they'd be that way until at least noon. They'd still been out when Halo and I got home last night, so there was no way any of them would surface until lunch. So for now I was making breakfast for two, and when my stomach tightened with pleasure at the idea of having the angel to myself for a little longer, I rolled my eyes.

Halo had me so wound up that I wanted to steal him away so he only looked at me, talked to me, thought about me, and the idea of having even a couple hours more with him alone this morning made me happier than a kid at a damn candy store.

Jesus. Thank fuck the guys couldn't read my mind, or Halo, for that matter—they'd laugh me out the house. I knew if it were one of them I'd never let up, but I couldn't seem to help it. The second Halo walked into a room, I—

"Gonna cook me breakfast this morning?"

—wanted my hands on him. "I figured you might be hungry after that performance of yours."

Halo chuckled as he made his way to where I was grabbing a frying pan out of one of the lower cupboards. After his shower, he'd pulled on a pair of faded jeans that fit him in all the right places, with a shirt the same light green as his eyes. He'd left his feet bare and pulled his hair into a knot at the back of his neck, and he was so damn appealing I wanted to take his hand and tug him in close enough to kiss.

Fuuuck.

"You okay?" Halo said as he sidled up close to me, and I wondered what he'd say if I told him I was fine, I just wanted to hold his fucking hand.

Yeah, how about keep your mouth shut, Viper.

"Sure," I lied as I put the pan on the stovetop. "Why do you ask, Angel? Don't I look fine?"

Halo's eyes lowered to my jeans and up to the black The

Nothing shirt I wore, then he grinned. "You look sexy. You should've joined me in the shower."

As he reached for me, I took a step back, disguising the dodge by moving over to the fridge. But I needed some distance; he was messing with my head. Hell, my whole body.

I pulled the doors open and looked inside. "Eggs and bacon work for you?" I called over my shoulder.

"Sounds perfect. You want some coffee?" Halo asked as he moved to the Nespresso machine at the far end of the counter.

"What do you think?"

"Yes. You aren't human until you have your coffee."

As I grabbed some butter, the carton of eggs, and a package of bacon, I felt a hand on my lower back, and then the fresh scent of Halo's soap wafted around me as he moved into my personal space and peered over my shoulder into the fridge.

"Will you pass me the milk?" he said.

The question wasn't anything out of the ordinary, but with his warm breath on the back of my neck, every nerve ending in my body was on high alert, and when he ran his hand down to my ass and squeezed, I quickly turned and held my full hands up. "You'll have to grab it."

Halo chuckled as I sidestepped him to head back to the stove, and as I went, I shut my eyes and told myself to pull it together. Since when was I hyperaware of every single thing another person did? This was bordering on ridiculous.

"So should I be worried you're cooking for me?" Halo asked as he shut the fridge and made his way back to the coffee machine.

I flipped on the burner, and after I had the frying pan and butter heating, I glanced over to where Halo was busy getting out two cups and the coffee pods. "Nope. Mom made sure I knew how to cook. Told me if I was gonna survive being some poor musician traveling the country in an RV with a bunch of yahoos, I needed to know how."

Halo laughed, and when I looked at him, he was leaning up against the counter watching me. "So you all cook?"

"Fuck no." I scoffed. "Killian can grill, and I can cook, but everyone else? Forget it. And Trent, he was the fuckin' worst. Couldn't even boil an egg, that guy."

"Seriously?"

"Seriously. I'd be surprised if he even knew where they were in the grocery store." I chuckled as I thought about the time he'd "helped" with dessert at Killian's parents' house, only to pour a shit-ton of salt into the cake mix instead of sugar.

"You guys have been friends a long time, huh?" When I cut my eyes to him, Halo added, "I mean you were."

"Right," I agreed, then heard myself say, "He would've liked you."

When Halo's eyes widened, I tried to understand why I'd said that. I didn't give two shits what Trent Knox was doing these days. I didn't even care if he liked what we were doing here with Fallen Angel. But I figured Halo would like to think that the man he'd come in here to replace would approve of him.

"You think?"

I nodded, dragged my eyes away from his, and went back to stirring the eggs, shoving aside the emotion that was making my heart thump a little harder at the pleasure I saw in Halo's eyes. "I do. Okay, how many pieces of bacon?"

"Oh," Halo said as he took the cup from the machine and brought it over to me. When he put it down beside me, he aimed a smile at me that did jack shit to calm my thumping heart. "How about four?"

"You got it."

Halo's eyes narrowed, and when he cocked his head to the side, I thought he was going to call me out on being a fucking weirdo this morning. But instead he said, "What time did you say *Rolling Stone* was coming tomorrow?"

Oh thank fuck. "Um, I think Kill said nine?"

Halo nodded as he walked backward toward the coffee machine. "Got it."

"You nervous?"

"Yes and no."

I chuckled as I picked up the pan and divided the eggs onto two plates. "You haven't got anything to be nervous about—you know that, right?"

"Uh, no. They're going to be asking a bunch of questions and taking a million photos that are supposed to 'launch' Fallen Angel. That's only slightly terrifying."

"You're going to do great." As I laid the strips of bacon in the pan, I glanced down the counter to where Halo was looking over at me, seeking my approval, as he always did when he was unsure.

"You think?"

Was there really any doubt? I'd been mesmerized from the second Halo walked in the door, and I was starting to believe there was no damn cure for it.

"Angel, they're not gonna know what hit 'em."

TWENTY-ONE

Halo

THE *ROLLING STONE* feature was in full swing at the mansion the next morning. I stood beside Viper in the corner of the kitchen, both of us drinking our coffees as we watched crews of people pouring in: hair and makeup artists, costume designers, the lighting crew, the photographer and his assistants, a catering team, the journalist who'd be interviewing us, and a rep from MGA, since Brian was currently across the country dealing with one of his other artists. People everywhere, and a knot in my stomach the size of a damned grapefruit and still growing.

"Don't be nervous," Viper said, then took a sip of his coffee as he surveyed the chaos.

"I'm not."

He snorted and looked at me out of the corner of his eye. "Yeah, okay. Because I can't read you like a fuckin' book."

"You don't read books."

With a chuckle, Viper shook his head. "Someone woke up a smartass. Care to use that mouth on me while we wait?"

I jerked around to make sure no one was within earshot, and when I saw the coast was clear, I said, "You can't say that shit to me today. Not with all these people around."

"Relax, Angel. No one's paying us any attention...yet."

Yet was the operative word, because soon the spotlight would be directed our way, and who knew what kind of questions would be lobbed at me. The only saving grace was that Viper and the other guys would have my back, since we'd be doing the interview and photo shoot together.

"Can I get Fallen Angel to gather on the outside patio, please?" the director of today's shoot called out over the noise.

"You ready?" Viper flipped on the faucet and rinsed his cup out, and after I downed the rest of my coffee, I did the same.

"Do I have a choice? Can I sit this one out?"

"Gotta come out sometime, Angel." Viper shot me a wink to go along with the double entendre, and I rolled my eyes.

"Wasn't planning on it today." I followed him out onto the patio, where Killian, Slade, and Jagger had already gathered around a small woman with bright fuchsia hair that was shaved on one side and flipped over on the other in a punk-rock style. As we stopped beside her, she peered up at us, her eyes rimmed heavy with purple liner, and then she put her hand out.

"You must be Halo. I'm Imelda Wainwright. I'll be the one interviewing you guys today and making sure everything runs smoothly. If you need anything, anything at all, you come to me, got it?"

I nodded and forced a smile as I shook her hand, her grip surprisingly fierce in spite of her petite stature.

"Thanks, Imelda," I said, hoping I'd somehow charm the pants off this woman and the rest of America. Well, not *literally*.

As Viper shook Imelda's hand, he lifted his chin toward me. "Take it easy on this guy. It's his first time."

"A virgin, huh?" Imelda's eyes glittered as she looked back at me. "Can't say I'll take it easy. He looks angelic, but I bet he's a guy who doesn't mind it rough."

It was too damn early in the morning for the heat to hit my cheeks, but it did anyway, especially as I heard Viper cough out a laugh and Jagger say, "As someone who rooms a few doors down from Halo, I can confirm the headboard banging."

My eyes practically flew out of my head as I stared at my soon-to-be-dead bandmate, but Jagger only grinned.

"Breaking hearts already," Imelda said. "You guys are gonna be fun."

She told us to hang out and grab some food and drinks from the catering table while she checked on the setups happening inside, and after we'd piled our plates high, we sat beneath the open umbrella. The sun was already beating down, and combined with the humidity from an overnight shower, it was stifling at the early morning hour.

"Sorry, Halo," Jagger said, pulling apart a croissant. "You know I gotta give you shit."

"Long as you know payback's a bitch."

Jagger spread his hands. "Hey, I didn't say *who*."

"Good fuckin' thing," Viper said. "I'd hate to have to drown our best keyboardist."

"I'm your only damn keyboardist," Jagger protested.

Viper sent a pointed look in my direction. "Halo's pretty good on the keyboard. You can be replaced."

"Fine." Jagger held his hands up. "My mouth is zipped."

When Imelda came back out again, she took the open seat beside Killian, set her phone in the center of the table to record the conversation, and then settled back with a pen and a binder of notes.

"All right, guys, go around the table and say your name so when I play it back I know who's who," she said.

Slade started things off, and once we'd done our introductions, Imelda dove into the questions.

"Let's start at the beginning, shall we?" she said. "When Halo joined the band, you guys were still reeling from the departure of former frontman Trent Knox from TBD—"

Viper mumbled something rude as Jagger sighed and Slade

rolled his eyes. Only Killian kept a professional stance, but the reactions didn't slip by Imelda.

"I'm guessing that's a sore topic for you?" she said.

Viper crossed his arms and leaned back in his chair. "Just an *in the past* fuckin' topic."

"Well, I need to give the readers a bit of background, though I know many are familiar with your story." Imelda looked at Killian, the only one who didn't seem bothered by the line of questioning, and directed her focus his way. "Killian, had the plan to bring Halo in always been to replace Trent in TBD, or was the goal to form a new band?"

"To be honest, we needed a singer to finish out the album we'd spent months working on, and we needed to get back on tour," Killian replied. "It's not uncommon to hire a new singer, so yeah, Halo was brought in based on his ability to fit in with us as a band."

"An already formed and supremely popular band," Imelda added. "But within weeks, you guys did an about-face, dropping TBD altogether and starting over as Fallen Angel. What was the catalyst for the change?"

"Rude fuckin' assholes," Viper said.

Jagger laughed but shook his head. "Dude."

"What? Imelda wants honesty, right?" Viper looked at her for confirmation, and when she nodded, he shrugged. "Might as well tell it like it is."

"Maybe not that much honesty, V, yeah?" Killian said, and then he turned back to Imelda. "Once we began rehearsals, we quickly realized how talented Halo is. He plays every instrument, he writes his own music, he's a phenomenal singer, an all-around showman. It didn't seem right to have him try to fill someone else's shoes when he should be standing out on his own."

Damn. Nice workaround, Kill.

"So it had nothing to do with you guys getting booed offstage at the Savannah charity concert?"

Viper cursed, but Killian winked at Imelda. "Maybe that too," he said.

Imelda smiled at him and jotted something down, and then she was looking my way. I braced myself as she said, "Halo. You just got quite the endorsement from your fellow bandmate. At only twenty-three, how does it feel to be playing alongside legends in the rock world?"

"Surreal," I said, running a hand over my hair. "I grew up listening to these guys—"

Groans sounded from around the table, a balled-up napkin was thrown my way, and Slade mumbled, "We're not *that* damn old."

"Obviously *that's* their sore spot," I said, grinning at Imelda. "But to answer your question, it feels like..." Shit. Everything I wanted to say sounded so corny in my head, but...fuck it. It was true. "It feels like I'm exactly where I'm supposed to be."

"Aww," Jagger said, leaning over to throw his arm around my neck. "I mean, you hear that and then you look at this face. How will anyone resist him?"

I laughed and shoved him away. "Fuck off."

"I think many of our readers will agree with Jagger," Imelda said, rolling the end of her pen over her chin. "It's unbelievable what's happened since the release of your first song, 'Invitation.' How did your rehearsal video find its way onto the Warden's Instagram feed?"

"Your guess is as good as ours," Killian said. It didn't escape my notice that he didn't elaborate on that and throw our manager's name into the mix...probably because Brian was a dick who didn't deserve the shout-out.

"Well, however it happened, it's been a massive introduction to your new sound. Can you talk a little bit about the change in direction and what we can expect from the new album?"

Content to sit this one out, I grabbed the energy drink I'd snagged from the catering table and popped the tab as Killian launched into a long-winded answer. Out of the corner of my eye, I saw Viper's arm inch closer to mine and inwardly smirked.

Couldn't keep himself away, could he? All of his protesting about not dating and not being a relationship guy, and his actions told me the complete opposite. Here we were in an interview, and I knew he had to be sitting there forcing himself not to touch me.

And *that* was fucking hot.

TWENTY-TWO

Viper

___

IMELDA WAINWRIGHT WAS a seasoned music journalist who'd been around the scene about the same amount of time as we had. She'd been interviewing us for years, and when Brian had told Killian she was the one the magazine would be sending our way today, I'd known we were going to walk away from this spread golden.

Always the professional, Imelda was known for bringing the readers of the magazine exactly what they were after through edgy and interesting articles, coupled with provocative photos that would burn up the pages.

I knew that was what was worrying the angel this morning. I'd known even before we all filed out here to start with the sit-down portion of the day, and it was going to be a task to be anywhere around Halo and not look at him or touch him in a way that would scream *the two of us are fucking*. But I'd managed to keep my hands to myself as we sat out here by the pool...so far.

"Fallen Angel now seems to be a name that's rolling off everyone's tongue when you ask them what they're listening to. It's like we've been listening to you guys for years instead of a couple of months. Can you tell me how the name came about? What made you guys settle on Fallen Angel?"

Logically, I'd known this question would come up. Just as I'd known I would never forget the first time those words had left my tongue—the same tongue that had still tasted of Halo after I'd swallowed him down my throat in his apartment—but when Killian inclined his head in my direction, and Imelda turned her attention to me, I had a difficult time not jamming the heel of my palm against my twitching dick.

"Oh, was this your idea, Viper?" she asked, tapping the end of her pen against her lips, and out of the corner of my eye, I caught Halo shift in his seat beside me.

Don't look at him. Don't fuckin' look at him or your semi is gonna turn into a full-blown hard-on. Keep your eyes on Imelda.

"Yeah, I guess you could say that. I mean, it was kind of a no-brainer. Our new frontman's name is Halo and, well, look at him."

When Imelda did just that, I allowed my eyes to shift to the gorgeous fucker beside me. Halo was chuckling and shaking his head, and when he ran his fingers back through his hair, Imelda nodded.

"As you know, I'm not exactly known for writing *sweet* lyrics," I continued, and when Halo turned his head in my direction, his lips curled in a wicked smirk. "And that hasn't changed. While the band is going in a completely different music direction, and there are some songs that are more mellow, the lyrics will still be sexy. And trust me, once you see him on a stage singing them, you're gonna see his halo fall right off his head."

That delicious flush that heated Halo's neck and cheeks whenever he was excited or embarrassed appeared at exactly the same time Jagger smacked a hand to his thigh and gave a hearty laugh.

"Mhmm," Jagger said, flashing his charming smile at Imelda. "He's gonna set the ladies on fire and have all the men thanking him for getting them laid."

"Is that right?" Imelda's eyes swept over the group. "And what song would you say is the one that will be the most tantalizing for the fans? The most shocking for you to sing?" she said, her attention back on Halo.

But before he could reply, the rest of us all said, "'Hard.'"

Imelda let out an inelegant snort as Halo tried to glare us all to death. Poor guy was so tense and we were trying to get him to relax. This was just another day at the rodeo for us, but for Halo, it was a first. He was overthinking every little comment he made, not to mention every move, and the sooner he realized he was fucking amazing, the easier this would be.

"'Hard'?" Imelda said. "As in...?"

I snorted. "We're five guys, Imelda. What do you think?"

"Did you write that one?"

When I nodded, she looked to Halo and said, "I think you *must* be a rock star if you can sing one of his filthy songs and make him like it."

I was close to telling her *how* much I liked it, and that he'd inspired the whole thing. But at the last second, I remembered I wasn't allowed to announce that the first night Halo had really nailed this song we'd *both* been hard.

Then Halo said, "Yeah, I'm not too worried. I can handle Viper."

Jagger choked on his swig of soda, clearly as dumbstruck as I was at the smartass double entendre, and Killian thumped him on the back as he stepped in and saved the day—as always.

"What he means is, we all get along really well," Killian said, and aimed his lazy grin Imelda's way. Fuckin' charmer. "It's crazy how music can bring people together, and it's been unreal discovering our new sound and coming up with lyrics and songs we hope people are going to go crazy over."

"Yeah, Halo's breathed new life into us," I said, and when I looked at Halo, I realized for the first time that he had done the impossible. He'd made me fall even more in love with music than I already was. That was some fuckin' gift right there. Tearing my eyes away from his, I refocused on Imelda. "He's inspired us to be creative and pushed us to be more."

Okay, so maybe that's what he does to me, I thought, when no one else agreed.

But then Killian spoke up. "I agree. The way he commands anything he touches is...insane. Almost unbelievable, really." At those words, my eyes cut to Killian, who was focused on me.

Imelda whistled. "That's some seriously high praise, Halo. But I can understand. I'm as obsessed with 'Invitation' as everyone else is, and after meeting you, I just know you are going to have people eating out of your hand. So tell me a little more about you. Where are you from? Your family?"

As Halo began talking to Imelda, I saw Killian smiling in my direction like a damn moron, and I reached up to scratch my temple with my middle finger. So I liked Halo—a lot. Was that a fucking crime? No. Was it totally freaking me out? Yes. I had no idea how to deal with this...this...whatever this was. And I had a feeling that Killian, Jagger, and Slade all knew that, which was exactly why they were taking such delight in torturing me.

The timing couldn't be worse for me to develop an obsession with the angel. He was about to explode on the music scene in ways he didn't even know, and have so many opportunities thrown his way. Opportunities that could be greatly hindered if it got out he was sleeping in my bed each night, and I was sleeping in him.

As Halo continued to talk with Imelda, the thought that I should put an end to this thing between us now, before we left Miami, crossed my mind. But as I ran my eyes over his profile, down his neck, to the red T-shirt that hugged his biceps and showed off his tanned arms, I knew I wasn't going to be the one to call a halt to whatever this was between us. I was a selfish bastard, and I wanted Halo, and until he told me to get the fuck out of his bed, I planned to take that angel over and over again.

But until then, I had to pull my shit together and get my mind back in the game, because the *game* was about to get a whole lot more complicated.

"Right, guys," Imelda said, putting her pen down on her pad. "I think I have all that I need here for now. If you want to go with Drew over there, he's going to take you inside and get you ready for the photoshoot. You ready for your close-ups?"

TWENTY-THREE

Halo

_____

CLICK CLICK CLICK.

"Halo, could you lower your chin a bit? Yeah, right there." The photographer moved around in front of the five of us, snapping away at different angles. "All right now, Viper, bring your left foot forward a couple inches and turn in... Perfect."

I held the position, front and center, between Viper and Killian, with Slade and Jagger on the ends beside them. The rest of the band had been outfitted in a shit-ton of black—all except for me. I was the lone man in head-to-toe white, playing off our name. Like I didn't already stick out like a sore thumb, but as long as they didn't put an actual halo on my head, I was fine with whatever the magazine wanted.

"Eyes on me but don't move an inch. Set those jaws." The photographer climbed up on a ladder to shoot us from above, and as I looked up, the light was blinding. I tried not to squint, but Jesus, it was like "move, but don't move, look at me, but don't look _at_ me, keep your eyes open and try not to blink, look badass but not like an asshole," and shit, how did models do this for a living? It was exhausting. I would've rather been answering invasive questions than have to do this. Then again, it was _Rolling Stone_, as in a cover and feature story, so if I had to stand here all day and pretend to scowl at the camera, then I'd do it. It just went to show how unglamorous things felt behind the scenes, even if the end result was kickass.

"All right, I wanna try something. A various stages of undress photo," the photographer said.

"You want us to get naked, Jacques?" Jagger grinned, like he was totally down for it. Hell, he was already stripping his jacket off when the photographer—apparently named Jacques—held up his hand.

"Uh, not quite," he said, waving his assistant over to fuss over our clothes. Jackets were stripped off, my pants were unbuttoned and slightly unzipped, and beside me, Viper lost his shirt. Great, like he wasn't enough to look at fully clothed—now I had to stand here with Viper half-naked and positioned so all that warm skin brushed against me. They'd lifted my shirt up over my head but kept the sleeves on so that all of me was on display except for my arms. I had them crossed over my chest, which was a good damn thing, because it meant I couldn't reach out to touch Viper, but skin on skin in front of everyone? Fucking torture. How the hell was I supposed to focus now?

"Can't wait to get an eyeful of this when the magazine hits," Viper murmured in my ear as the assistant adjusted the lighting. Taking advantage of the brief break, I looked back at him, but quickly caught my own eyeful. Viper's hand was shoved down his pants. Down. His. Pants.

"What are you doing?" I said, not even bothering to mask my surprise.

Viper shrugged, but he had a smug grin on his face like he knew exactly what effect he was having on me. "Just doin' what I'm told." He trailed his eyes down my body to where my own pants were open and riding low on my hips and let out a low whistle. "Fuck me, Angel..."

"Later, if you're lucky."

"Really?" Viper's eyes darkened. "I just might take you up on that."

"Fuckin' hell," Jagger said from beside Viper, and then he leaned forward to seek out Slade on the other side. "Hey, man, you wanna switch?"

"Switch? Why?" Slade asked.

Jagger shot him a look, and when it was clear Slade wasn't following, he inclined his head toward me and Viper. But when he still didn't get it and the photographer turned around, Jagger said, "Uh, 'cause the right side's my better side."

"You look fine from both sides," Jacques said, waving him off, making it clear Jagger was stuck right where he was.

"Sorry," I whispered to him, and Viper snorted.

"Suck it the fuck up, asshole," he said. "You're just jealous."

Jagger shrugged. "Yeah, well, Halo *is* really pretty."

Viper turned around, and I could only imagine the glare he gave Jagger then, because Jagger put his hands up and mumbled something I couldn't hear, but it was enough to have Viper facing forward again.

We went through another series of shots for Jacques' "various stages of undress" theme, and by the time it was over, I'd never been so glad for a food break.

"Halo, don't go too far," Jacques called out after me as I pulled the shirt off my arms and took off for the catering table. "We've got solo shots, but I'll start with Killian. That goes for the rest of you too."

Solo shots? Screw the food; where was the damn alcohol?

"I don't think I've ever seen you look so miserable, Angel," Viper said, coming up beside me.

"I preferred the interview, which should say a lot."

Viper reached for one of the water pitchers lined up at the end of the table. He poured a couple of glasses and handed me one.

"No thanks. I need something stronger than water."

"That's not water."

I sniffed the glass and reared back. "Holy shit."

Viper chuckled and swallowed a mouthful. "They know how to keep their artists happy. Get 'em naked and liquored up." Viper's eyes heated as he took in the way my pants were still undone, and the fact that I'd gotten rid of my shirt. "Have to say, I fuckin' approve."

God, now was not the time to be looking at Viper the way I wanted to, not with all the people milling around. I needed to steer clear of him for the rest of the shoot unless I wanted to give us away.

"You need to go away." I sipped my vodka and turned my attention to where Killian had finished his solo shoot and they had moved on to Slade. Even he looked more comfortable in front of the camera than I'd been. Maybe the alcohol would help me loosen up a bit.

"You can't get rid of me that easily, Angel. Like I'm goin' anywhere when you look like you wanna jump me."

I snorted out a laugh. "That's exactly why you need to get the fuck away from me. What happened to keeping this shit on the down-low?"

Viper smirked and brought his drink to his lips. As he lifted his arm, he brushed it against mine, and that meant the bastard was too close. If he was making it his mission to taunt me, he was doing a damn good job.

"Halo, you're up," Jacques called, giving me the out I needed to get away from the tempting man beside me. I took a long swallow of my drink, tossed it in the trash, and walked away before Viper could say another word.

Keep it professional and try not to look like you're in pain this time, I told myself as I stopped in front of Jacques. He pursed his lips as he looked me up and down, and that was when I remembered I'd stripped out of the long-sleeved shirt after the group shoot.

"Sorry, it was hot and I didn't want to get anything on the shirt," I said, but Jacques held his hand up, still studying me, and then he snapped his fingers at his assistant.

"Molly, get the oil," he said, and as his assistant rushed off, my eyes bugged out.

"Did you say *oil*? What's that for?"

"You wish to be naked, I will accommodate," Jacques said. Molly came running back, the bottle uncapped and already pouring oil into her hand.

I backed up before she could reach me. "That's okay, I'm good with a shirt. Or a jacket. A shirt and a jacket, even."

They paid my protests no mind, Molly slathering a palmful of the oil across my abs as I inwardly cringed.

"Is this really necessary?" I asked, as she spread the oil over my chest, my shoulders, even my back, which probably wouldn't even be in the shot. A snicker sounded to my right, and I looked over to see Viper grinning and whispering something to the photographer. "Just wait till it's your turn," I told him.

He winked at me. "Don't forgot his biceps. He works so hard for those." Viper's eyes were full of devilry as Molly went to work on my arms, and I couldn't glare him down enough.

When my body was a complete oil slick, Jacques moved me into position, which just so happened to be in direct view of the sun, making me feel like I was an egg in a frying pan. I could practically hear my skin sizzling as he snapped away.

I told myself to relax, that this was the last thing I'd have to do today, and then I could take the longest shower known to man. *Almost done...almost done...*

"Halo, turn your face an inch to the right...a bit more... Why don't you try looking at where Viper's standing? Yes, that's it." Jacques' camera snapped away as I stared at the man I'd been trying to avoid looking at all day. Viper ran a hand through his black hair, and I couldn't help but notice the way his muscles stretched with the move. His olive skin had darkened during our time in Miami, and somehow that only accentuated the ridges of his body and made him look even more enticing.

"Hold that look," Jacques said, and I froze, not sure what it was he was seeing, but realizing if I'd been having thoughts about Viper, it was probably nothing good. A few more clicks of the camera and Jacques beamed at me. "Beautiful man. Thank you."

"I'm all done?" I asked.

Jacques nodded and gestured for Viper to take my spot, but before I went anywhere, there was one thing I needed.

I caught Molly's attention and gestured to what felt like an inch-thick layer of oil covering me. "Could I get a towel?"

"Of course." She had rushed off again before the words were fully out of her mouth, and as I waited, Viper sauntered to where I stood.

With his back to everyone, he let his gaze travel down my chest and abs. "You sure you want that towel, Angel? This could be a fun *slick* and slide..."

I licked my lips, the sexual promise in his words so damn tempting that when the assistant came back with what I'd asked for, I thought twice about wiping myself off.

"Halo, you stay right there," Jacques called out suddenly. "Molly, get rid of the towel."

"Huh?" I squinted and brought my hand up to shade my eyes as I frowned at Jacques. "I thought I was done?"

"You were, but this..." Jacques gestured between me and Viper. "*This* I can work with. Molly? Oil up Viper."

TWENTY-FOUR

Viper

IF I THOUGHT Halo had looked worried before, the expression on his face as Molly rubbed oil into one of my arms, and then the next, was close to horrified. His eyes were wide and his mouth had fallen open, and when he glanced at Jacques and said, "Work with us *how*, exactly?" I almost lost it.

Jacques wasn't known for elegant, proper photographs. He worked for some of the edgiest magazines in the world. So when he walked to where the two of us stood in our half-zipped jeans with our oiled-up torsos, to get a better look at Halo and myself, it didn't take a genius to see where his mind was wandering.

"I like the feel of you two together. This vibe," he said, as he wandered around behind Halo, whose head whipped to the left to peer at Jacques, who was now behind him.

"Uh, what vibe? Slick and uncomfortable?"

When Jacques stopped beside us, he grinned at Halo and shook his head. "No, no. Dark and light. Good angel," he said to Halo, before turning to me and saying, "Bad angel."

I snorted, because Jacques had just hit the nail on the head.

Jacques was nodding as he rubbed his fingers over his chin, his eyes roaming all over the front of me, much like Molly's slippery hands. "I'm right, no?"

"No," Halo said a little louder than I thought even *he* expected.

"No?" Jacques chuckled. "I can't imagine Viper is a *good* angel." When Jacques winked at me, I smirked, and his eyes lit up. "Yes! That right there. That's all I need in the shoot. That expression and a guitar."

"Huh?" I said, confused, then he gestured to my jeans.

"You can lose everything else," he said.

"As in...?"

"Strip." Jacques clapped his hands together. "Yes. Oh, I can see it all now."

Uh, pretty sure that everyone would be seeing it *all* if he was serious.

"You with your guitar, slung across your hips, and Halo, we'll have you next to him holding on to the neck of it. The curve of your hip mimicking the guitar and—"

"Wait, wait—*what?*" Halo said, his eyes close to bugging out of his head as they flicked between Jacques and myself. "I'm not getting naked."

"Oh dear. See, good angel," Jacques said as he moved between us, his hands coming up to frame Halo's face without touching him. "I promise no one will see anything they shouldn't. We'll keep your modesty intact."

The blush that hit Halo's cheeks then was so endearing that I couldn't help the chuckle that slipped free. At the sound, his eyes flew past Jacques' shoulder to find mine.

"No. I'm not doing a naked photoshoot," Halo said, shaking his head. "What about the rest of the guys?"

Jacques looked over at Killian, Jagger, and Slade, who were over by the catering table out of earshot, then turned back to Molly.

"Molly? While the men are stripping, can you go and get Viper's guitar for him and close off the area to everyone who isn't needed? Looks like we've got ourselves a shy one here."

Molly scurried off and Jacques faced Halo again.

"There. That's better, no?" Judging by the alarm pouring off

Halo in waves, I was thinking...no. But before Halo could find the right words, Jacques said, "Both of you strip down and we'll get the rest of you oiled up. Then we'll start. This is going to be incredible."

As Jacques left us to "strip down," Halo didn't move. In fact, I wasn't even sure he was breathing, as a dozen crew members began ushering people out of the backyard and erecting those collapsible poles that they then attached massive black privacy curtains to.

Out of the corner of my eye, I saw Killian look our way, but before any kind of explanation could be exchanged, his face disappeared as the curtain blocked him out.

"Are you out of your mind?" Halo stage-whispered as he took a step toward me, his eyes a little wild as he ran them all over my face, no doubt trying to see what screw had come loose in my head. "We can't do this."

"Can't do what? Get naked together?" I said, my lips curving at the sides. "Pretty sure we've already done that, Angel. Many times."

Halo moved in even closer to me and said between gritted teeth, "Would you be serious for once in your life?"

I lowered my eyes to his slicked-up chest and licked my lower lip. "I'm being very serious, and you are supposed to be stripping."

Halo shook his head. "I can't do that."

"No? Well, if you need me to help, I can..." As I raised a hand, Halo took a hasty step back from me.

"How about you keep your hands to yourself," Halo said, and when I reached for the zipper of my jeans, he groaned. "God. That's not any fucking better."

With my jeans hanging open, I glanced over my shoulder to where Jacques was fiddling with his camera and lighting, and then turned back to where Halo was looking like he might pass out. Knowing the only way Jacques was going to get the shot he wanted was if I managed to get Halo to chill the fuck out, I put my hands on his shoulders and said, "Breathe." Halo glared at me, clearly unamused, but when I cocked my head to the side and said, "Fucking breathe," he did.

In and out. In and out. He took several deep breaths, and when he finally looked as though he could stand without falling, I let him go.

"What's the main issue here for you? Me? The nakedness—"

"How about you and the nakedness?" Halo said, then he lowered his voice. "How am I supposed to stand next to you naked and not get...get..."

"Turned on?"

"*Yes.*"

Fucked if I know, I wanted to say, but I didn't really think he'd appreciate that much honesty. So instead I said, "The same way I'm going to stand next to you and try and do the same."

"Umm, that's *not* the same," Halo said. "Did you forget the fact that you get a prop?"

Oh, that's right. Well, shit. When I chuckled, Halo's jaw clenched. *Right, maybe don't laugh, Viper.*

"I wouldn't worry about it," I said. "Jacques is a professional and it's only going to be you, me, him, and Molly. He's not going to care if you get turned on. Hell, he'll probably like it more. He made it pretty fuckin' clear he thinks you're gorgeous...*beautiful man.*"

"That's your pep talk?"

Halo ran a hand over his face, and I leaned in to say by his ear, "No. This is my pep talk. You look hot as fuck naked, and I can't wait to frame this picture and hang it above my bed so I can get off to it each night you're not there. Now strip, Angel. Or I'm gonna rip those pants off you."

That did the trick. Halo took a less-than-steady step back, his eyes full of fire as he reached for his zipper, and it was me who had to turn my back on him then to finish getting undressed without attacking.

"Okay, you two," Jacques called out a couple of minutes later after all was clear and Molly had handed me my guitar. "Let's see if we can find a position we all like."

Halo made a noise that sounded like a tortured groan, and then, with his hands crossed in front of himself, ambled over to where Jacques was standing in front of me. I looped the guitar strap over my shoulder and slung the instrument across my lower body and hips, and when I aimed a grin in Halo's direction, he quickly tore his gaze away.

"So let's try this," Jacques said, as he eyed me. "Viper, I want you front on, facing me and the camera. The guitar looks perfect where it is, but let's get your right hand sitting loosely over the strings."

I did as instructed—my feet planted on the ground slightly parted, the fingers of my right hand resting low on the strings.

"Good, good." Jacques nodded. "And let's have the left hand down by your side."

By my side? That was interesting. But hey, I wasn't the photographer, and if that was what he wanted, I wasn't about to argue with him.

"Yes, just like that. Now, Halo," Jacques said, and when he looked to Halo, I did the same. The angel looked awkward and uncomfortable, and when Jacques crooked a finger at him and said, "Come closer," Halo's cheeks turned scarlet.

Halo took the couple of steps needed to bring him in close to my right side, and when Jacques looked down our bodies, Halo mumbled, "This is fucking crazy."

"Okay," Jacques said. "I want you to straddle his leg."

"What?" Halo said, and took an immediate step back. "I'm not straddling anyone. Viper? My parents are going to see this."

And if *anything* was going to kill a hard-on, that was it.

"Your parents—" Jacques pulled up short, and when what Halo had said registered *and* offended, he shook a finger at him. "I don't do porn, young man. I want you to put a foot on the front and back side of Viper's thigh and then angle your body to hide your..."

Jacques gestured to the lovely cock Halo had forgotten to cover in his minor freak-out. "For that very purpose."

How Halo managed to look chagrined and fuckable all at once, I had no idea. But when he gnawed on his lower lip and said, "Sorry," I wanted to grab his hand, take him somewhere private, and bite down on that lip myself.

"Right, well, if you're done questioning me," Jacques said, "could you please move into position?"

With color still high on his cheeks, Halo lowered his eyes and moved into my side, placing a foot at the front and back of my right thigh. He then angled the lower half of his body away from the camera so the shot would be of the curve of his hip, and that phenomenal ass.

"Yesss," Jacques said, his excitement at what he was seeing now shoving aside his irritation from the earlier interruption. "Now, Halo, I want you to reach across Viper's chest and grab the neck of his guitar with your right hand, and then look over your shoulder at me."

With Halo standing so close I could feel his cock brushing against my thigh, I had to admit that I was pretty damn happy for the prop I had across my hips, because nothing could've stopped the blood from rushing south.

"Oh my God," Jacques said as he walked backward, his hands coming up to frame us as he continued to his spot. "This is it. It's perfection. Hold it just like that. Let me get my camera."

As he rushed to grab his camera off Molly, I caught Halo's eyes and said, "I don't care what's scheduled for after this shoot. I'm scheduling you, me, and a fucking shower."

Halo swallowed, but I felt his hips inch in closer to my thigh, his dick now as hard as my own, but angled as he was there was no one to see what I could feel.

A mischievous light now replaced the anxiety from the beginning of the shoot, and he grinned. "A *fucking* shower, huh?"

I was about to tell him he'd be lucky if he made it to the shower, when Jacques called out, "Okay, you two. Let's give everyone in the country something to talk about. I want sex. I want fire."

Jacques got both in spades. He had the shot he wanted in less than five minutes, and I had Halo in a shower in less than ten. All in all, I'd say that was one helluva successful photoshoot, and I couldn't wait to frame the fucker over my bed.

TWENTY-FIVE

Halo

"I CAN'T BELIEVE you've been living at the beach for two months while I've been in snow up to my knees," Imogen grumbled as we FaceTimed a couple of weeks later. To rub it in my sister's face, I'd walked out to the private beach in front of the mansion and planted my ass in the sand, giving her a view of the house behind me and occasionally flipping the camera so she could look out at the sun setting over the ocean. I didn't think I'd ever get enough of this view, but I also knew our time here was coming to a close, since the album was almost finished.

"You can still come visit," I said.

"Ugh, I wish. I'm so pale I'm practically translucent, and you guys are gonna come back here all bronzed sun gods. Have I mentioned I hate you?"

I laughed. "Not in the last five minutes."

"Yeah, well, I do. And speaking of coming home, when are you? I miss your face."

"From hate to missing me in the span of two seconds. You're all over the place, Im." I brought my legs up so I could rest my elbows on my knees, my toes digging into the warm sand. "We don't have too much longer here. Jared, one of our producers, thinks we'll have things wrapped in the next two weeks."

"Thank God. You're not allowed to leave again."

"No? You gonna come on tour with us?"

Imogen's eyes widened. "You're talking tour already?"

"There's been some rumbling about it happening before the end of the year. They want the album out stat, so it makes sense a tour would follow pretty quick."

"It's just all happening so fast."

"You're telling me."

Imogen's lips thinned into a straight line. "And are you okay with all this? You've been thrown into something huge and overwhelming, so if you aren't okay, you'd tell me, right?"

The concern on her face made me wish I was there to give her a big, reassuring hug. She wasn't usually the type to worry—that was my job—so the fact that she cared enough to check in on me made me slightly homesick.

"I promise I'm good. It's been insane, I won't lie, but there's nothing else I'd rather be doing. Swear."

She let out her breath and nodded. "Okay, good. Because—"

"Angel, I know you might think it's romantic to fuck on the beach, but trust me, sand gets in all the wrong places. How about you get your hot ass back in my bed?"

I jerked around to see Viper sauntering down the beach toward me, and then realized Imogen would've heard him and looked back at the screen to see her eyes wide and staring past me.

"Is that—" she started, but I quickly cut in.

"That's code for the studio. Gotta go." Before she could say another word, I ended the call and turned my gaze up to where Viper grinned and sank down onto the sand beside me. I could only stare at him, mouth open, because shit. Had Imogen heard what he said? The look on her face told me she had, and... Shit.

I held my phone up. "I was on a call with my fucking sister."

"Something wrong?"

"Yeah, something's wrong. She heard what you said."

"So?"

"So? So I haven't exactly told her about...this."

Viper stretched his legs out and settled back on his hands, unperturbed. "She gonna have a problem with it?"

"I..." I scrubbed my hands over my face and sighed. Would she? How the hell would I know? She'd never guess in a million years that I'd even look at a guy, so it wasn't exactly something that had come up...ever. "I don't know. I tell her everything, but I haven't told her this, and I feel...I feel..."

"Guilty?"

I let out another sigh, staring out at the lapping waves tinged golden by the sun's dying light. "Yeah. I feel guilty."

"Because you never planned to tell her?"

I tore my eyes away to look at Viper but found I couldn't read his expression. "I'm not sure it would do any good to tell her something that could cause problems between us. Not when this is just..." I didn't voice the rest of those thoughts, because he knew as well as I did that whatever this was between us was fleeting. It wasn't anything serious...right?

"Uh huh." Something in Viper's tone sounded off.

"What? You think I should tell her?"

"I'd never tell you what to do, Angel."

"But you think I should? Wait... Do you think I'm ashamed or something?"

Viper shrugged, a casual move, but his jaw was set a little firmer than usual, and he didn't look my way. "Are you?"

"No. Of course not." I shifted, angling my body toward his. "But you have to understand that telling my sister or my parents or even my friends about this would upend my life."

"It would."

"Right. And since you've made it clear this is only fucking, why would I risk my relationships? It's not like I'm gonna date men exclusively after this ends."

Surprise lit Viper's features. "You're not?"

"Well, no. I mean, I haven't really thought about it. But I haven't had a reaction to anyone the way I've had to you, so..." I shrugged and looked away, feeling heat creeping into my cheeks, and I wasn't sure why.

We were silent for a long time, and though I wanted to ask what Viper was thinking, because it was obvious something was on his mind, I didn't want to open my mouth and insert my foot again. Had something I said upset him? It wasn't anything he wouldn't have said to me, so I doubted his feelings were hurt by my honesty. Maybe I was overthinking things.

I shoved my cell into my shorts pocket and dropped my legs, mimicking Viper's pose. With no one else around, we stared out at the water, listening to the sound of waves crashing. Had we ever just sat like this? Still and quiet, not saying a word?

The longer we sat there, the more the anxious thoughts about what Imogen had heard left me. My shoulders relaxed; I was content to have the stable force that was Viper sitting beside me.

"I was eight when I told my parents I was in love with one of the boys in my class." His words came from out of nowhere, but it was clear he'd been thinking over what to say.

I smiled slightly. "You? In love?"

"Believe it or not, my heart wasn't so black when I was a kid."

"Who was he?"

"Hiroji Onaga. His family had moved from Japan at the start of the school year, and I guess I found him fuckin' fascinating."

"Enough to come out to your parents, huh?"

Viper's lips twisted. "You wouldn't think it'd be such a surprise. I was a flashy kid. Into music. Never into girls."

"I would've liked to see a young, flashy Viper," I said. "How'd they handle it?"

"Mom knew. She always knew." A faraway look entered Viper's eyes as he stared ahead.

"And your dad?"

"You could say that was the catalyst in a long, messy divorce." When he saw the shock on my face, he lifted a shoulder. "He'd rather have no kid than a gay kid, and I'd rather have no dad than a homophobic asshole."

"Shit, Viper. I'm sorry."

"Don't be. I'm not. I helped Mom pack his shit."

"And you never had a relationship with him after that?"

"Never even heard from him again." He glanced at me and shook his head. "Don't look so sad, Angel. It happens. We're better off."

God, I couldn't even imagine what that would be like. To show who you are to someone you love and to have them reject you in that way. Viper had only been a kid, and he hadn't deserved a father who deserted him. No one deserved that.

"So I can understand why you wouldn't wanna say anything," Viper continued. "You said you're tight with your family. I get it."

I frowned, looking for what he was really saying. "But it bothers you? Tell me the truth."

As I studied Viper's profile, I found myself holding my breath. From the day I'd met him, I'd sought his approval, and I found myself wanting it now. If he was disappointed in me, would it change anything? And if he wasn't affected, would that bother me more?

God, when had things become so complicated?

TWENTY-SIX

Viper

"VIPER?" HALO'S VOICE found me over the waves that lapped upon the sand and chased each other into the shore as I sat beside him looking out at the fading sunlight. When I'd come down here looking for him, I had one goal in mind: find the angel and convince him to come and spend an hour in the guesthouse before heading up to the mansion for dinner.

But instead, I'd stumbled on him mid-conversation with his sister—a sister he'd hidden me from—and now I found myself sitting on the sand staring out at the water ahead of us, hoping that he didn't reach for me, because I wasn't sure I wouldn't jerk away.

Fuck. When had I let this get away from me? When had I started to...*care* this much?

"Hey," Halo said, and I didn't need to look his way to know he was staring at me. Probably wondering when I'd lost the ability to speak. "If I said something I shouldn't—"

"You didn't." I finally made myself talk, and turned to look his way. "I just don't have anything to really say about this. It's not my decision to make."

"Okaaay..." Halo said, the hurt at my blunt dismissal exactly what I'd been aiming for.

But when Halo bent his legs as if he was about to get up and leave me sitting there, which was exactly what I deserved, I reached out, put a hand on his leg, and said, "Shit. I shouldn't have said that."

"Then why did you?"

I shrugged. "Because I'm an asshole."

Halo said nothing as he searched my face—looking for what, I had no clue. But when he swallowed and raised his hand to put it over the top of mine where it rested on his thigh, I shook my head. "I'm not good at this, Angel. Fuck." I gave a self-deprecating laugh. "I think it's safe to say I'm horrible at it."

"What's that?"

"This," I said, gesturing between us. "Talking."

"I don't know. You seem to have a pretty good handle on the English language."

I rolled my eyes. "Smartass. You know what I mean. I'm not good at talking about my feelings. About opening up to others."

Halo stretched his legs out in front of him again, and once he was settled back in place, he said, "Would it help to know you make me nervous as hell?"

When he angled his head and his eyes found mine, I did something I couldn't remember ever doing. I tightened my fingers around his in a comforting move—but who I was trying to comfort was anyone's guess.

"I make you nervous? Angel, you scare the fucking daylights out of me." Halo's eyes widened, and I chuckled. "Do you think I'm the kind of guy who usually sits on a beach at sunset holding hands and talking about my feelings?"

"Well, no."

"Yet here I am," I said, raising our joined hands, and Halo spread his fingers to interlace them with mine.

"And...?"

As I lowered our hands, I shrugged. "And I like it. I like you, Angel, or I wouldn't be out here, trust me. But that doesn't mean I have any idea what the hell I'm doing. You asked me if it bothers me that you aren't going to tell your family about this...about us."

Halo nodded and lowered his eyes to our hands, a frown marring his forehead. "Right."

I knew I could take the easy way out here and lie, but instead I heard myself say, "It shouldn't."

Halo's head snapped up. "But it does?"

"It does." I didn't say more than that, but the shy smile that stretched across Halo's lips let me know this small admission from me was what he'd been looking for.

Halo looked back out to the waves, and then leaned in to bump his shoulder against mine. "See, this is what I mean. I don't understand why you pretend to be such a hard-ass. Why you don't date. There are millions of guys who'd die to be sitting where I'm sitting tonight if they had the chance."

I glanced at Halo's striking profile, and when the wind ruffled the hair around his face, I said, "I don't want a million guys. I want the one who's already here."

Halo turned to face me and leaned over until his lips were a whisper over the top of my own. "You're so much better at this than you think."

I highly doubted that. "Sure I am," I said, but didn't move. I didn't let go of his hand either, finding that I enjoyed the feel of it in mine.

"You are," Halo said, and brought his other hand up to hold my face as he traced his thumb over my lip. Then he lowered his hand and sat back, but kept our fingers locked.

"Teasin' me, Angel?"

"No," Halo said, shaking his head. "I just know if I kiss you now, I won't stop."

"And that's supposed to deter me?"

Halo grinned. "No. But before I give you that, I want to know something."

I was convinced Halo could've asked me for anything then as

long as it got his mouth back over the top of mine. "And what's that?"

"What ever happened to Hiroji?"

The question was so unexpected that a burst of laughter escaped me. "I have no idea. Why?"

Halo was laughing too, but then he sobered. "I don't know. I was just wondering if he's the only person you've ever loved."

I eyed Halo for a beat and then dropped my gaze to our interlaced fingers. I ran my thumb over the back of his hand, and when I raised my eyes again, I told him something I'd never told anyone other than Killian and Trent: "There was someone else. A long time ago."

When I paused, Halo shifted in closer to me but said nothing else, as if sensing what I was about to say needed to come from me willingly or it wouldn't come at all.

I shoved my free hand through my hair and looked out to the lights twinkling across the water, finding this conversation easier if I wasn't looking anyone in the eye. "His name was Owen, and we'd been dating on and off for a couple of years, until the last year, when things got serious."

"Serious?" Halo said softly.

I didn't turn toward him, knowing if did, I wouldn't finish the story. I would kiss him, make him forget what it was he'd asked in the first place. But for the first time in a long time, I realized I *wanted* to tell this story. I wanted this beautiful man beside me, this man who'd ignited the same euphoric feelings I'd had as a twentysomething-year-old aspiring musician, to know who I was, to see me...the real me.

"We lived together. Shared this crappy little run-down apartment where the only heat in the place was from the oven if we left it on. We were wildly in love. The kind of blind, stupid love that makes you think you can live off a packet of ramen noodles the rest of your life, as long as you're sharing it with that one person." I brought my legs up until I could rest my arm over it, and took in a breath before continuing. "But I was a struggling musician and he was a struggling artist. Shit wasn't easy, but it was something I didn't think about because I was—" When I bit off the word *happy*, I wondered if Halo would push. But he merely sat there, patiently waiting for the next piece of the fucked-up puzzle I was trying to piece together for him.

"Owen came to every show, followed TBD across the country. He knew every secret I had, knew everyfuckingthing about me. And then one day an agent from MGA came to one of our shows in New York. He watched us play at one of the local dive bars, and the day after we got a call to come in for a meeting. To MG fucking A. We were so excited, Jesus. I mean, you get it." I looked at him, and Halo nodded, but the smile on his lips was strained.

"I'd never been so fucking pumped about anything in my life. This was what Trent, Kill, and I had been waiting for. We'd been dreaming about this our whole damn life, and when we got in there and they started talking songs, albums, and tours, the shit you never think is going to happen to you, there was no hesitation from us. We signed those contracts in a fucking heartbeat. Our careers went from the bottom of the barrel to swimming with the big fish overnight. It was insane. But while my career took off, Owen continued to struggle."

Halo's expression softened, even as his eyes narrowed, and I made myself look away from him before I decided to just end things there.

"I don't really remember much about the days before the story broke, or if I maybe missed something with Owen. But I do remember waking up to Killian on the phone telling me that there were photographs of me and Owen on *Entertainment Daily.*" I paused and cocked my head, looking at Halo. "Do you remember those?"

I wondered what Halo would say to that. If he was a true TBD fan he would know about those photos—and he'd also know that was the day I told everyone I was gay, and if they didn't like it, they could go fuck themselves. But instead of turning the media off, it had ended up earning me my nickname. When he nodded, I smirked.

"Yeah, well, Owen had decided if I was going to make it big, then he would too. Who cares if it wasn't due to any talent but by selling private fucking moments between us to the highest bidder? As long as he got his cut too, then it was fair, right?"

I ran a hand over my face, and when Halo said, "That's so fucked up," I nodded.

"I won't ever let anyone have that kind of power over me again. Not ever. So now I make sure anyone I'm involved with knows the deal upfront. One of the hardest things about becoming the person you're about to become"—I raised Halo's hand to my mouth, pressed a kiss to the back of it, and closed my eyes—"is that you never know who is with you for the right reason and who you can trust. Millions of people out there are going to want you because of everything you can give them."

Halo cupped my cheek with his other hand, and when I was looking him in the eye, he said, "That might be true. But I don't want a million people. I just want the one who's already here."

As my words from earlier lingered between us, I opened my mouth to tell him I wasn't what he wanted or needed. That I was, in fact, the exact opposite. But before I could get a word out, Halo leaned in and pressed his mouth to mine, and just as he'd said earlier, the second he kissed me, he didn't stop—and the scary part about that was that I didn't want him to.

TWENTY-SEVEN

Viper

"THAT'S A WRAP." Jared's voice came through the headphones each of us had on in the sound booth, but when none of us reacted, the mic opened up again and he said, "Hey, guys? Did you hear me? That's a wrap." When he added two thumbs up, the five of us gathered around the mic and looked at each other as though someone had just pinched us all on the ass.

"Hell fuckin' yes," Killian said. "I can't believe we're done."

I flashed a smile in Halo's direction, who was standing between Killian and me with a megawatt grin on his face, and it was all I could do not to grab a handful of his shirt, haul him in, and kiss him.

It was Friday afternoon, and the only time we'd been able to find alone lately was at night after spending hours in the recording studio with the other guys, and while that would usually be enough to take the edge off for me, I found that with the angel, I always wanted more.

More time.

More attention.

More. More. More. *Fuck.*

Maybe getting back to New York would be a good thing. It would give a little space, bring me back to reality. We'd all busted our asses these past two weeks finishing up the background vocals for "Corruption," "Dark Angel," and "Invitation," and it seemed our hard work had paid off. We were done, and I should've been over the fucking moon. Sure, there might be minor changes needed once we got back home, but for now we were free, and all I could think about was the fact that once I got back to New York, Halo wasn't going to be in such close proximity to me.

Again...*fuck*. There was no reason I should be feeling this wave of disappointment that was washing over me, but there it was. We'd been in Miami for nearly two and a half months, and it had definitely lived up to the promise of paradise. There'd been sun, sex, booze, and music, and while I was pumped to be wrapping up an album that I knew was going to blow everyone's mind, I couldn't shake the *less* excited feelings too.

"Damn." Jagger let out a low whistle. "We came in before deadline, too. That has to be some record."

"No shit," Slade said.

I glanced at the two of them. "If that doesn't make Brian hard, I don't know what will."

"Uh, no offense, but the last thing I want to think about is Brian hard," Killian said as he hung his headphones on the hook along the back wall. "I want to think about the serious celebrating that's gonna happen tonight. We're still going with tradition, right?"

"MGA's yacht?" I said, thinking back to the other times we'd taken to the ocean after wrapping an album.

"Mhmm. What do you all say?" Killian asked, as the rest of the guys hung their headphones.

"As if anyone's gonna say no to that," Slade responded, and when we all turned to Halo, we found him still standing over by the mic, silent.

We all faced him and cocked our heads to the side.

"Aww, look, our little boy's all grown up," Jagger said. "Want us to take a photo of you by the mic to send to your mom?"

Halo blinked as though realizing Jagger was talking to him, then he chuckled and shot a finger in his direction.

"I was being serious."

"He was," Slade said. "Remember how long it took him to pick out a 'special jacket' for the photo he sent to his mom?"

"Forfuckingever," I said, rolling my eyes.

"And she now has it proudly on display in her foyer, I'll have you know." Jagger walked to the door of the booth and pulled it open. "Don't be hating on me because I take the time to look good, V."

As Jagger walked out of the booth with Slade and Killian following, I called out, "I don't need time. I roll outta bed looking this fucking amazing."

A chorus of whatthefuckevers could be heard as the door closed, blocking them out, and I turned to see Halo now hanging his headphones.

"So how's it feel, finishing your first album?" I asked as I leaned a shoulder up against the wall and crossed my arms and ankles—all the better to keep my hands to myself.

"It feels..." When Halo's eyes found mine, they were bright with excitement. Then he took a step closer to me and reached out to finger the hem of my shirt. "Unreal."

"Yeah?"

"Yeah. I can't believe this is my life. Writing music, recording it, living in mansions, celebrating on yachts? I keep waiting for someone to pinch me. To wake me up and say, 'Just kidding.'"

Unable to keep my hands off him, I reached down to his hand and brought it to my mouth, where I nipped at his fingers and said, "Wake up. This is now your life."

"How?" Halo said, and swayed closer, and there was that draw again. That need and urge for more, more, more. I wrapped my other arm around his waist and pulled him flush against me so I could brush my lips over the top of his.

Halo closed his eyes and moved up to his toes to get closer, and when he wound an arm around my neck, I said against his mouth,

"This is your life, because you are the most talented person I've ever met."

Halo's eyes drifted open like he was in as much of a daze as I was, and I wondered for a moment if he was experiencing that same pull as me. Was I weaving some kind of spell over him the same way he was me?

"You really mean that, don't you?" he said.

"I wouldn't say it unless I did."

Halo chuckled and leaned away from me to run his gaze over my face, making me wonder what it was he was searching for.

"That first day when I auditioned for the band." Halo flashed a grin that would soon win over hearts around the world, and my stomach tightened. "Killian asked you what you thought of me. Do you remember what you said?"

I did. My standard answer when I didn't want to show my hand was *not bad,* and that day I'd been battling a serious hard-on for the angel who'd wowed me as soon as he opened his mouth. I'd been so busy trying to decide if I could work alongside someone that I had such an intense attraction to. The answer to that was apparently yes, as long as I could be *in*side him too.

"You told me I wasn't bad."

I shrugged. "I lied."

"So you basically freaked me out for nothing?"

"No. I just didn't think telling you that you made me hard from singing my song was very professional."

Halo let out a laugh and shook his head. "You're probably right. But I have to say, hearing you say I'm the most talented person you've ever met..."

"Yeah?" I said, and when Halo punched his hips forward, I groaned.

"That makes *me* really hard."

I smoothed my hand down to grab at his ass and then scraped my teeth along his jaw. Halo tilted his head to the side and moaned as I kissed my way up to his ear.

"Viper...shit. How long until we head to the boat?"

"Not long enough for what I want," I said, and Halo reached up to grab my hair and tug my head back. Those light eyes of his had now darkened, and when he licked over his slick lips, I couldn't help the growl that slipped free of my throat.

"Does this boat have rooms?" Halo asked.

"Five staterooms, from memory."

Halo ran his palm down my front to my erection and aimed a shameless look my way. "Then how about we pick this up later in one of them? You, me, and the nice, slow rocking of the waves." Halo punctuated his words with a firm squeeze, and when he took a step back, he winked at me. Oh, how the angel had fallen.

That was when I knew it wouldn't matter if we were in Miami, New York, or the North fucking Pole. If Halo was there, then I was going to want to be there with him, and I had no idea what to do with that.

TWENTY-EIGHT

Halo

_____

IF THERE WAS one word to sum up my life over the last few months it would be *surreal*.

Joining an insanely popular rock band? Check.

Recording an entire album of songs I'd helped write alongside the most talented musicians I'd ever met? Check.

Living in a mansion in Miami to do all that? Check.

And now here I was, celebrating all of the amazing events by partying it up on a freakin' *yacht* with the band? How had this become my life? It was everything I'd ever wanted, and on top of it all, it'd come with an unexpected, sexy surprise.

Viper.

He'd barely moved from my side since we'd boarded the yacht hours ago, leaving only to grab us refills, and even then I usually went with him. It was strange how used to having him around I'd gotten, and I didn't know how I'd feel once we were back home. Without the ease of only walking distance between us, things would surely change. Maybe that was the reason he'd stuck to me like glue tonight: he knew our time was almost up.

Shit, way to turn things morose, I thought, drinking down the last of my Long Island iced tea.

"Tequiiilaaa!" Slade shouted over the music as the bartender poured another round.

There was a tug on the side belt loop of my jeans, and then Viper's breath was on my neck. "Good timing. You need a refill anyway." His teeth grazed the sensitive skin below my ear, and I shivered.

"You're just trying for drunk angel round two," I said, thinking back to the way he'd taken me against the wall after one of the movie nights. Damn, I wouldn't mind if *that* happened again, so bring on the drinks.

I could feel his lips curve against my neck. "I am. You turned into a wild fuckin' beast last time. My cock wouldn't mind trying to tame you into submission."

If Viper was dead set on teasing my dick tonight, he was doing a damn good job. Ordinarily, I wouldn't have minded. After all, he'd told me there were bedrooms on board, but fuck if the guys hadn't locked them and ruled there would be no hookups on the yacht, ensuring tonight was strictly a band celebration and not a way for me and Viper to sneak off for an hour or two.

Dammit.

A cold breeze brushed against my neck as Viper moved away, inclining his head toward the bar, and as we gathered around, the bartender handed out the shots, screw the salt and lemon.

"All right, assholes, I'd like to make a toast," Killian said, looking down the bar at each of us. "A few months ago, we were in a rut. A place of what-the-hell-do-we-do-now and nonstop auditions by some of the most painful singers we've ever heard. Am I right?"

"My ears are still bleeding," Viper muttered, as the others voiced their agreements.

Killian grinned and then lifted his shot glass toward me. "Then one day, this guy walks into the studio and blows everyone outta the goddamn water. This shit may be a whirlwind for you right now, Halo, but trust me when I say we never thought we'd end up here again."

"Too true, too true," Jagger said, nodding and lifting the glass to his lips, but Killian's arm shot out just in time to block it.

"I'm not done, fucker," he said, before straightening. "In this life, you're lucky if you can count your successes on one hand. Hell, one fucking finger. But here we are, all these albums under our belt and we've never been better. There's a reason for that, and he's standing beside that asshole Viper."

I laughed, joining in with the others as Viper flipped them off.

"Halo," Killian said, "thank you, man. For joining us. For sharing your talent. There was a review I read after we did the Carly Wilde show that said you 'breathed new life' into the group, and honest to God, that's the fuckin' truth. We wouldn't be standing here right now if it weren't for you, so before we all get so trashed we can't walk straight, I'd just like to take the opportunity to let you know how stoked we are to have you as the voice and face of Fallen Angel. We've got a hell of an album, and we've got you to thank for that."

I blushed under his praise as Viper's head turned toward me, and he lifted his shot glass. "To Angel."

"To Angel," the others chorused, and as they threw back their shots, I could only stare at my fellow band members. I was really a part of this thing, huh? Not just lurking on the outside, but a real part of it all. I wished I could say the thought didn't bring tears to my eyes, but the sting hit behind my lids and I quickly took my shot to avoid anyone's gaze.

"By the way, we're never letting you leave, so don't even think about it," Jagger added, and then looked at Killian. "That was in his contract, right?"

"In the fine print." Killian winked.

"Good." Jagger pushed his shot glass forward and waved his hand. "Another round."

As the bartender poured more tequila, the music changed, our song "Hard" blaring through the speakers.

"Oh shiiit," Slade called out, taking his shot glass to the center of the boat, where he began to dance, moving his hips back and forth like he had a partner, the alcohol obviously well in his system.

Jagger grabbed his shot too and joined Slade, singing along at the top of his lungs, and I had to laugh. Jagger was definitely not a singer, tequila or no tequila.

As the two of them began to do their dance moves, Killian laughed and took out his cell phone. I wasn't sure if he was snapping photos or taking a video to blackmail them with later, but before I could ask, Viper moved in behind me, his arm circling my waist so his hand covered my lower stomach to hold me right where he wanted me. And right where he wanted me was with my ass flush against his hips, his cock straining behind his shorts as he nestled it in between my cheeks.

He began to grind his hips against me, moving us to the music slowly, sensually. Viper's voice was low in my ear as he sang along to the song he'd written for me—*about* me. "I want to get inside you, and show you exactly what you do. Whenever your eyes invite me to fuck you like I want to..."

Shit. Did he have any idea the effect he had on me? The way my pulse sped up and my heart raced when he touched me? The way my cock throbbed at his words? We were polar opposites, but somehow we attracted each other the way magnets would, and once we fell together, it was hard to pry us apart.

Wanting my eyes on him, I circled Viper's wrist and pulled his arm away enough that I could turn to face him, and what I saw nearly had my knees giving out. Fire swirled in those obsidian eyes, drawing me closer, and as our mouths crashed together, he moved his leg in between mine so I straddled his thigh. Tongues tangling, he rocked our hips along to the beat again, a slow grind, my erection pressing hard against his leg.

He dove in, taking more of my mouth as the words he'd written and I sang filled my ears. I barely noticed the guys laughing and joking in the background, too zeroed in on the way he kissed me like it was the first time he'd ever gotten a taste. I moaned into his mouth and could feel the way his thick length grew harder against my hip.

"All right, all right, break that shit up," Jagger called out. "If I couldn't bring a date, then you two can't suck face all night."

Viper pulled his mouth away long enough to tell him to fuck off before he moved back in, but I laughed and put my hands on his chest, keeping those deadly lips away from mine. If I didn't, I knew where it would lead.

"And that is why we locked the bedrooms," Killian said, and when I looked over my shoulder, he waved us over to join them.

I had to adjust myself before I went anywhere, and Viper groaned at the move.

"Seriously, Angel? You're asking for me to bend you over this goddamn bar right here, right now."

I trembled at the promise in those words, because I had no doubt he'd make good on it if I let him. But tonight wasn't about us. It was about the band, and so with that in mind, I wrapped my hand around his wrist and tugged him along behind me toward the makeshift dance floor, Viper grumbling the whole way.

Killian grinned as we joined in the celebration. "Someone change the song to something less fuckable."

"Hard" stopped abruptly, and as "September" by Earth, Wind & Fire began to play, the bartender brought out a tray full of drinks. Considering my head was already buzzing pretty damn good, I had no doubt we'd all remember maybe only half the night later.

Before any of us could take a sip, Slade said, "Wait, I wanna make a toast too."

"Oh God, here we go," Jagger said under his breath, but Slade heard him and went to punch him in the arm. It would've hurt if Slade hadn't swayed on his feet and missed Jagger completely, stumbling into a nearby deck chair, half of his drink sloshing over his hand.

As he cursed and righted himself, the rest of us broke out into a peal of laughter until Viper brought his hand to his mouth and let out a loud whistle.

"How about I take this one, Slade," Viper said. Slade responded with a shrug, licking the spilled alcohol off his hand, and then Viper lifted his drink. "To us, motherfuckers!"

"To us," we all chanted. And as we guzzled down our drinks and the rest of the night turned fuzzy, a feeling of warmth spread through my chest at belonging to something bigger than myself. I'd known I was part of the band, but it hadn't been until tonight that I felt truly, one hundred percent accepted.

TWENTY-NINE

Halo

———————

ONCE WE'D GOTTEN back to New York, MGA didn't waste time calling us all together for a meeting. I still hadn't unpacked, though I'd been home for a couple of days, and I had to rummage through the back of my closet for something decent to wear. Apparently we'd be meeting with Marshall Gellar, the head of MGA, and the last thing I needed to do was show up in a pair of ripped jeans from high school.

I settled on a light grey Henley shirt, sleeves pushed up, and managed to find some dark jeans that would suffice, and then I grabbed the jar of styling cream from my bag and headed to the bathroom. I ran it through the curly mess in an attempt to tame it a bit, which was never an easy feat. While we'd been in Miami, I'd taken to wearing it up, away from my face since it was so hot and humid, but for today I needed to make a little effort. Not to mention Viper liked when I wore it down, or at least I assumed he did, because he could never keep his hands out of my hair.

Once I was satisfied it was as good as it was gonna get, I took a step back and looked myself over in the mirror. Imogen had already given me hell about the way my skin had bronzed under the Miami sun, and I had to admit, it looked a lot better than the pale white I was accustomed to in New York winters. But the city had thawed out since we'd been gone, the days growing longer and warmer, and I wasn't complaining.

As I wrapped my leather strap around my wrist, my cell buzzed on the counter, and I looked down to see Viper's text.

Viper: Get your sexy ass in the car, Angel.

Grinning, I shot back a quick message and grabbed my wallet from the nightstand. The worries I'd had over whether this thing with Viper would fizzle out once we got back to the city had been unfounded, though I hadn't seen him since we'd landed. He'd needed to check on his mom, I'd needed to visit with my family, and really, I'd seen him every day for over two months, so two days apart should've been a breeze.

Talk about fucking torture.

I missed him. Yeah, I *missed* Viper, and I practically ran out of my apartment and down the stairs to where he was waiting in the back seat of the car MGA had sent. But before I opened the door that led outside, I took in a deep breath. My stomach flipped at the thought of seeing the man I'd gone too long without. It almost felt like I had first-date jitters or something, which was crazy considering we wouldn't exactly be alone on the ride to the record company's offices.

My phone buzzed again.

Viper: You've got five seconds or I'm coming up.

Impatient fucker, I thought with a smile as I threw open the door and headed out toward the SUV idling by the curb. I jumped in the back seat, in the open spot beside Viper, and once my ass hit the leather, Killian said, "About time. I thought V was gonna go all Hulk and carry your ass down."

I raised a brow at Viper. "You driving everyone nuts?"

"No more than usual," he replied, giving me a smirk that told me exactly how much of a menace he'd actually been. As I gave him a long once-over, I noticed that despite his protests that MGA could kiss his ass, he'd dressed up for the meeting. Or as dressed up as Viper generally got—black boots, black jeans, and a black shirt he'd left half unbuttoned. It wouldn't matter what he wore;

the man would always be the most stunning person to walk into a room, and with the eyes of the other guys on us, I had to tear my own gaze away or risk the possibility of making a move.

As if he could sense my struggle, Viper placed his hand on my thigh, resting it there like it was the most normal thing in the world as the guys began to talk about what they'd been up to since we'd been back. I couldn't hear any of it, though. My mind and every part of my body was now solely focused on the hand on my thigh. It was a possessive move, not one a simple fuck buddy would do, and I wondered if Viper even realized he'd done it.

One way to find out.

I moved my hand to cover his and waited for him to pull away. He was mid-conversation with Slade and didn't flinch or even look my way, but lifted his fingers up, grabbing hold of mine and interlacing them.

Stunned, I swallowed, looking down at our hands. He'd only done this once before, back on the beach in Miami after I'd Face-Timed with Imogen and the conversation had turned a bit heavy. We were alone then, and we definitely weren't alone now.

Feeling someone's gaze on me, I looked up and met Killian's eyes. Unlike me, he didn't seem surprised by what he saw. In fact, his mouth tilted up slightly on one side, as if he were pleased by Viper's actions. He winked at me before turning his attention back to what the others were saying, while I sat quiet and unmoving so Viper wouldn't notice what he'd done and pull his hand away.

Twenty minutes passed in the blink of an eye, and once we arrived, we filed out of the SUV, and I missed the warmth of Viper's hand immediately. But now wasn't the time to think about that or him, because in a few minutes, I'd be coming face-to-face with Marshall Gellar. I craned my head back to look up at the Keystone Building, where MGA held their offices.

"I wonder which floor they're on," I murmured, mostly to myself.

"The top five," Viper said. "Gellar's office is the corner one right there." He pointed to the floor-to-ceiling glass windows on the highest floor, and then we all made our way inside to go through security before loading into the elevator.

It was odd, but I'd felt more nervous about seeing Viper again than I did about meeting the man responsible for putting out our album. Maybe because I knew the others could handle whatever was lobbed our way, since they'd been working with him for so long.

Once the elevator doors opened, we were ushered into Mr. Gellar's office, a massive room that overlooked the East River. His chair faced away from us, but from the sound of his voice, it seemed he was on a call, so we quietly took up spots in front of his desk and sat there taking in the gold and platinum albums adorning one wall. More than five of those belonged to TBD, and I let myself visualize our Fallen Angel album taking up residence beside them. It was gonna happen. I could feel it.

"Guys," Gellar said, spinning around in his chair and setting his phone in the cradle. Then he stood and came around the desk to shake Killian's hand. "Sorry to keep you waiting. You fellas need anything? Drinks?"

As he went down the line to greet each of us, we shook our heads, and when Gellar stopped in front of me, I mustered up some of the charm and confidence my parents and Imogen claimed I had.

The CEO of MGA was lean and tanned, with a headful of salt-and-pepper hair and the intimidating stare of someone who knew how to do business. His handshake conveyed that much as well— firm and unyielding.

"You must be Halo," he said, smiling at me, but it wasn't an overly friendly smile. It was more what I imagined a wolf looked like as he lorded over his prey.

"It's good to finally meet you, Mr. Gellar," I said, and a roar of laughter left him.

"Mr. Gellar? Call me Marshall." He gestured for us to sit as he walked back to his oversized chair—throne, more like—and then he wasted no time getting down to business. "Gentlemen, I have to tell you, I've listened to your album..."

Out of the corner of my eye I could see Killian holding his breath, and I found myself doing the same. Sure, we'd heard he liked some of the things we sent his way while we were in Miami, but shit, what if he'd changed his mind? The pressure in the room was intense.

Marshall shook his head, and my stomach dropped, but then a wide grin spread across his lips. "You boys have outdone yourselves."

A collective sigh went through the room as Marshall continued.

"If I'd known this is what you were capable of, I'd have kicked Trent to the curb for you a long time ago." Then he held his hands up. "Kidding, kidding. But *Corruption* is gold. You haven't made it easy to narrow down the singles."

Beside me, Killian reached over and gripped the back of my neck, giving me a shake as if to say, "Fuck yeah, Halo." Not that it had been all me doing the work by any means, but all of us together?

Magic.

THIRTY

Viper

I WASN'T SURE when Killian and I had appointed ourselves Halo's personal bodyguards, but as we walked into Gellar's office, the two of us had taken up position on either side of him like soldiers going into battle.

As longtime clients of MGA, we knew what it meant to be granted a meeting in this office—either something fucking momentous or something akin to battle—and with our most recent trips down here as a gauge, both Killian and I hadn't been sure what direction it would go. It appeared, however, today was going the route of really fucking momentous.

"So, Halo, Killian tells me you're responsible for the new sound and direction of the band. What do you say to that?" Gellar said, zeroing in on the angel. I glanced at Halo to see him gripping his thighs—in an effort not to fidget, would be my guess.

"Well, I," Halo started, and then stopped and regrouped. "*We* all came up with the new sound—"

"Aw, stop being so modest, Halo," Jagger said, and when he peered around Slade's broad frame to look in Halo's direction, he added, "It was totally you. Own that shit."

Halo's eyes widened a fraction, and when his cheeks reddened, I took pity on the guy and let my attention shift back to the man with the money. Marshall Gellar was watching Halo like he was an interesting new toy he'd just acquired and was still trying to figure out.

But there was no way in hell Halo was about to tell Gellar that he'd single-handedly saved all our asses. Halo also wouldn't tell him that he was a musical fucking genius—but I sure as shit had no problem saying so.

"Halo is definitely the one responsible for the direction Fallen Angel has taken. He has more talent in his little finger than all of your other artists combined." When I broke the silence, I felt Halo's stare bore into the side of my head, but I refused to look his way. I also refused to shut up, because Gellar needed to understand that he had someone special sitting in his office right now. Someone he better not fuck with.

"He not only sings and plays the piano like a fucking rock star, he can play any instrument you put in his hands. He writes, composes, and he looks like *that*." I gestured with a thumb toward Halo. "And is humble to his very core. He's going to make you millions, Gellar, and you know it."

Gellar's eyes found mine as he leaned back in his chair and steepled his fingers over his chest. "You certainly speak highly of him for someone who usually doesn't give a shit either way."

That was true. The last few times I'd seen Gellar, I'd been less than charming, to say the least. We'd gone at it many times over in the past about music, lyrics...Trent, and I wasn't about to let him bait me now. This was about the band, not my less-than-stellar personality.

"He's talented," I said. "And if you're looking for suggestions on which song to release next, then I'd go with 'Dark Angel.' It shows off Halo's grittier side but is less in your face than—"

"A case of blue balls?" Gellar said, and Halo coughed out a strangled laugh beside me. Killian, Jagger, and Slade were less discreet, laughing, cursing, and grinning like a bunch of morons.

Gellar smirked. "That one had your name all over it."

I shrugged, not in the least bit sorry. "Happy to see you know me and my dick so well."

Halo's head whipped my way, his mouth hanging open, as Gellar said, "You're such a fucking reprobate. But here's an idea: how about we talk about something *other* than Viper's cock?"

"*Please*," Killian said, and I shot a finger his way.

"Right," Gellar said, and then sat forward to place his clasped hands on top of his desk. "Let's get down to business. You five ready to go on tour when this bad boy hits?"

"Fuck yes, we are," Slade said, and Gellar nodded, his eyes running up and down the five of us who were all waiting with bated breath, as his attention finally landed on Killian. Gellar understood the hierarchy in the room.

"If 'Dark Angel' hits as well—"

"*When* it hits as well," I said, and Gellar's eyes flicked to me for a second. He nodded before turning back to Killian.

"Right. *When* it hits as well as 'Invitation,' we're going to go ahead and give you five lucky fuckers the green light for a stadium tour. What have you got to say about that?" As Gellar let his words sink in, he sat back in his chair and a smug smile curled his lips. Then he delivered the icing on the already fucking amazing cake: "And if *Corruption* hits the way 'Invitation''s numbers all seem to indicate it will, then we want this to be worldwide. It'll be the biggest, most spectacular production the rock world has seen in years."

Holy fucking shit.

When no one said anything, Gellar let out a booming laugh. "So this is all I need to say to get you guys to shut up?"

That set them all off. Jagger was on his feet shaking Gellar's hand, Slade was *hell yeah-ing* and fist-bumping the man behind the desk, and Killian was busy asking questions I couldn't hear, because I was too busy trying to wrap my head around the fact that four months ago MGA had been close to kicking us out on our asses, and now they were talking worldwide tours. I mean, we'd all been fantasizing about it down in Miami, and thought that we might get a shot at a nationwide tour—but worldwide stadiums?

Holy.

Fucking.

Shit.

I glanced at Halo, the only other person who hadn't moved, to see he was looking at me with shock stamped all across his face, but his eyes were lit with pure excitement.

I wanted to kiss him. I wanted to grab the back of his neck, haul him in, and kiss him. I wanted to share this perfect moment with him by sharing my own pent-up feelings of relief, excitement, and total respect I had for him for getting us to this spot today. But I couldn't do any of that, so instead I winked at him, and Halo grinned even wider as he got to his feet to shake Gellar's hand.

When I went to do the same and we were all standing gathered around Gellar's desk, he took my hand and said, "Remember, this is all contingent on whether this album, and Halo, are as good as you all think they are."

I tightened my fingers around his and leaned over a little and said, with no hesitation whatsoever, "He's even better, and you know it. Otherwise you'd never have signed off on this in the first place."

When I let go of Gellar's hand, he looked at all of us, and I added, "Drop 'Dark Angel' next. If that shit doesn't top 'Invitation''s numbers in the first week, I'll shave my fucking head."

"I'll hold you to that," Gellar said, and I shrugged.

Jagger's mouth fell open. "Shut the hell up," he said, as Slade muttered, "You crazy-ass motherfucker."

And when Killian said, "You wouldn't," I looked over at Halo, who was eyeing my hair as though he hated that idea, but I wasn't worried.

All of America was waiting for what this dark angel beside me was going to do next. My hair was going nowhere, but Fallen Angel? We were going on a worldwide tour, and I couldn't fucking wait.

THIRTY-ONE

Halo

IT'D BEEN A chaotic month. "Dark Angel" had dropped, edging out "Invitation"'s sales by a number that blew my mind, the stadium tour was officially greenlit, and, best of all, Viper had gotten to keep his hair. Thank God.

I turned my head on Viper's pillow to look out his floor-to-ceiling windows at the Manhattan skyline. It may have been after midnight, but lights twinkled across the city like stars, countless others as awake as I was. Beside me, Viper slept soundly on his stomach, his face angled toward mine and his arm draped over my waist. More often than not lately, I found myself staying over, not leaving until well after dawn, because if I was gone when Viper woke up, all hell broke loose. I'd already seen what happened when I snuck out in Miami after our first night together, and I wouldn't be repeating that mistake anytime soon.

Those were all good excuses, because it wasn't like I wanted to leave. Sure, his place was a helluva lot more comfortable than mine, but I'd feel the same even if our situations were reversed.

I looked down at the arm he had lying across me and covered it with mine, gently so I wouldn't wake him up. It was this small move Viper made in his sleep, as well as a hundred other little actions I don't think he even realized he did, that told me this thing between us had veered into complicated territory. When we'd been in Miami, I worried that we wouldn't be able to continue the casual hookups once we were back in New York, but now that we were here, I worried that neither of us would come out of this thing unscathed.

Viper stirred, his arm tightening around my waist before he stilled again, and as I looked at his face, my stomach flipped. Somehow along the way, and I couldn't even pinpoint when, my guard had dropped and I'd fallen for him. I couldn't even deny that truth to myself anymore, though I'd deny it to anyone else who asked—especially to Viper.

I rubbed my eyes with my free hand, wondering how the hell I was supposed to navigate this now. We'd both been on the same page, agreeing to the same terms about our non-relationship, and here I'd gone, doing something as stupid as falling for Viper. If he knew what I was thinking, I doubt he would've minded me running out on him at two a.m.

Dropping my hand, I let my eyes roam over his face. I wanted to reach out and trail my fingers along the stubble that lined his jaw, but if I did that, I'd keep going, down his neck, across his chest, over his abs, and farther down...

My stomach let out a growl of hunger, and I realized we hadn't actually managed to eat the dinner we'd ordered. Viper had shoved the pizza in the fridge before dragging me into his bed, and that was the start of a marathon fucking that had lasted until about an hour ago. It hadn't taken Viper long to fall asleep, but I'd stayed wide awake, my mind unable to shut the hell up.

When my stomach growled again, louder this time, I slowly moved out from beneath Viper's arm, sliding out of the bed without waking him up. I quietly stepped into a pair of jeans and slipped out the door, heading toward the kitchen.

I made my way across the hardwood floors, grabbed a glass from one of the overhead cabinets, and then opened the fridge. I reached inside for the pizza box and put it on the counter before turning back for the Parmesan cheese, and then I reached for the bottle of Coke on the side door. Once I had everything I needed, I turned around to hunt down some napkins but startled when I found Viper leaning up against his kitchen counter watching me. With his arms crossed and jeans hanging low on his hips, it was close to impossible not to say screw the food and just go to him. Viper was so effortlessly sexy—even standing in his kitchen having just climbed out of bed, he oozed more sex appeal than someone who'd spent a good hour trying to look hot.

"You scared the hell out of me," I said as Viper pushed away from the counter and walked toward me, his eyes taking a tour of all that I'd left bare. With the fridge still open behind me, it lit the kitchen area up enough that I could see the hunger in his dark eyes, but whether it was for me or the food we hadn't eaten earlier, I had no clue.

"Did I?"

I chuckled as he took the Coke and cheese out of my hands and put them on the counter, and when he turned back to me and walked forward, trapping me between himself and the open fridge, I had my answer.

That hunger, the craving I could see in his eyes? It was all for me.

"You gonna let me shut the fridge?" I asked as Viper held my chin in place, then he leaned in and flicked his tongue across the corner of my mouth.

"Not yet," he said as he nipped at my lower lip. "I like the way the light makes your skin look...like gold."

I groaned and reached for Viper's hips as he trailed his fingers down my throat, and then he slid his palm around under my hair to grip the back of my neck. As he kissed his way along my jaw and slid his fingers into my hair, I tugged on the loops of his jeans and ground my stiffening cock against him.

Viper growled and pressed his lips to the soft skin behind my ear, his warm breath in direct contrast to the cool air of the fridge behind me.

"Why can't I get enough of you?" he said by my ear, and I

wasn't sure if he wanted an answer or was voicing the question I kept asking myself. Why was I so drawn to him? How was it that I'd allowed myself to become so involved in what we were doing with each other that I wasn't sure I'd ever be able to be free?

Instead of answering, I turned my head and captured his mouth, knowing that that was the answer Viper would prefer over the crazy notions running through my head, and he was right there to tangle his tongue with mine.

"Viper..." I said as I ran one of my hands up his back and took a step toward him, molding my body to his as I walked him back to the counter. I didn't let go of him, or bother stopping to shut the fridge. I moved directly between his legs and took his face between my hands, as I dove in and took a long, deep taste of him.

Viper opened to me in an instant, moving his hands to my ass as he rocked forward, and I moaned in response, and it was times like this—when he was obliterating any common sense I possessed —that I felt a slight tinge of desperation creep in.

I had no idea how long I had to enjoy what was happening between us, and whenever I thought about it being over, I found myself wanting to hold on to him tighter, to kiss him harder, to mark him in some way as mine, so he'd be just as affected if he decided to walk away.

I sucked on his bottom lip, making that rumbling purr escape his throat, and when Viper's head fell back, I took full advantage, lowering my head and licking a path across his throat.

"Angel...*fuck*. You're killin' me here," Viper said as I ran my hands down to his open jeans.

"Hmm. Not my fault." I slipped my hand down into the denim and wrapped my fingers around his throbbing cock. "I was going to get something to eat, and then you came out here and interrupted me."

As I swiped my thumb over his Prince Albert, Viper cursed and shut his eyes. "I woke up and you were—"

"Not gone." I grinned against his lips, knowing exactly where he was going. "Just in a different room."

"Too fuckin' far away," he said, and those words made my heart skip much faster than they probably should've. *He means for sex,* I reminded myself. *Nothing else.* But when Viper opened his eyes and reached down to wrap a hand around my wrist, stilling me, the emotions swirling in those mysterious depths made my breath catch—and so did the next words that left his mouth. "Wake me next time."

I nodded, and Viper glanced over at the pizza box before turning his attention back to me.

"I suppose I should let you eat, huh?"

"I wouldn't object," I said, taking a step away from him and zipping my jeans to at least try and contain the erection that was dying to get free. Then I turned to shut the fridge and moved back over to the counter. "Sorry I woke you."

Viper shook his head, as he too readjusted and zipped up. "You didn't. I missed—"

My hand stopped midway to opening the box as Viper cut his words off, because there was no way he'd been about to say *I missed you*, was there?

THIRTY-TWO

Viper

_____

I MISSED YOU? I fucking missed you? Did I seriously almost say that out loud? But when Halo glanced over his shoulder at me with curiosity in his eyes, I knew that I had.

I shoved my hands into my pockets and shrugged, trying to blow off my major faux pas. "I just woke up, that's all."

The side of Halo's mouth crooked up before he turned back to the pizza, and I rolled my eyes at myself. *Jesus, think before you talk, Viper.* Maybe then I wouldn't word-vomit every thought that ran through my head. Even if it was true.

Over the past month I'd gotten used to waking up and finding the angel sprawled out in bed next to me. With his tangle of curls and warm, smooth skin, Halo was a welcome addition to my bedroom each night, and when I woke up to find him missing, I'd had a flashback to that first time in Florida.

"Are you hungry?" Halo asked, giving me the out I so desperately wanted from the previous conversation.

I shamelessly took it, not wanting to look closer at all the reasons I might feel anxious over the thought of this man leaving my bed, even to go and get something to eat from my damn kitchen.

"Yeah, I could eat," I said, and then I busied myself by grabbing a couple of plates and a roll of paper towels from the cupboard under the sink. "But not here." I balanced the Parmesan on the plates with the towels then grabbed the glasses. "You bring the food and drink."

As I made my way to the bedroom, the lights from the surrounding buildings spilled inside, illuminating the way, and as we entered, I passed the unmade bed and headed for the couch set up in the corner.

Halo put the Coke down and slid the pizza box onto the small table, then put a couple slices on each plate and took up a seat next to me on the couch, directly facing the magnificent view.

We wolfed down our first slices, both obviously hungry from missing dinner and our extracurricular activities, and once the initial hunger was satiated, I reached for my drink and washed it down with a gulp of the soda.

When Halo chuckled, I arched an eyebrow in his direction, and he gestured to the glass with a tilt of his chin.

"I'm shocked you didn't bring in a bottle of whiskey to add to that."

I smirked as I slid the glass back on the table. "I was tempted."

"Why am I not surprised?"

"You tryin' to say I drink too much?"

Halo took a bite of his second slice and shook his head. "No."

I eyed him for a beat, trying to see if there was more to that answer under the surface. But one thing I'd begun to realize about the angel was that what he said, he meant. There wasn't any kind of underlying message to decipher with him. No bullshit lurking around a corner to bite you in the ass later, and that was something I could appreciate.

"Well, if you were saying that you'd probably be right. Smoking, drinking, fucking around, all nasty habits I picked up from years of touring." As soon as the words left my mouth, I frowned and added, "Habits you should steer clear of."

Halo let out a loud laugh and lowered his half-eaten slice to the box before turning to me. "Is that right?"

"Yep." I took a bite out of my second slice. "I mean, the fucking you can do—with me. But you really shouldn't drink as much as we do, or smoke for that matter."

"Right." Halo's lips twitched. "Because you're the poster boy for abstaining."

"Eh, I'm too old change my ways now."

"Old?" Halo fell back on the couch and laughed. "You're thirty-three, not seventy-three. And I don't know, it sure hasn't hurt Mick Jagger and he's what?"

"Seventy-five."

"See," Halo said with a grin. "Maybe I *should* start smoking."

I wasn't sure why I cared, but the idea of Halo picking up a habit that just might kill him made my stomach revolt. "Don't you fucking dare."

Halo pursed his lips. "Well, since you asked so nicely..."

"I'm not fucking joking. That shit will kill you."

Halo sat up and leaned over to brush his lips over mine. "I know. So why do you still do it?"

As his eyes locked with mine, I wondered if he was about to ask me to quit, and as he continued with the silent stalemate, I couldn't help but wonder what my response would be if he did.

It was an answer I never had to give, though, because Halo grinned and shifted away to reach for his half-eaten slice. "No need to worry. I don't plan to take up heavy drinking or smoking. I plan to enjoy this kickass life that seems to be happening right now."

"Uh, what's this 'right now' business?" I said, stretching my legs out and crossing the ankles.

Halo shrugged. "Well, you never know in the music industry, right? Highs, lows, and all that? I'm just trying to keep my expectations in check."

And that was another thing I really liked about Halo—how damn humble he was. It was rare that someone with as much talent and charisma could remain so modest. But something told me that nothing—money, fame, success—would ever change Halo's temperament. And that was so damn attractive after spending the past decade surrounded by overconfident assholes who all believed you should get on your knees and thank them for just looking your way. Hell, I'd made it my mission to become one just to fit in. But Halo was in a league all on his own. One I planned to make sure no one fucked with, or they'd have me to answer to.

"Angel," I said, and Halo glanced over his shoulder at me. "With your talent, there are only going to be highs from here on, I can tell you that right now."

The shy way Halo smiled made me sit up and cradle his cheek so I could kiss him. *God*, I'd tried to push aside what I'd said out there in the kitchen. But as Halo melted under my touch, there was no shoving aside the question that I couldn't get out of my mind. Why couldn't I get enough of him? And as Halo opened to me, I made myself let him go so he could finish his dinner, because I knew if I didn't get my hands off him, it would all be over.

"Eat, Angel. You're hungry," I said, and shifted back to my spot.

Halo licked his lip, getting another taste of me before he went back to his meal, and I pressed a palm to my frustrated cock.

"So the pre-release party. Are you excited?" I asked, trying to get us back on track.

"Yeah. A bit nervous, but more pumped, you know? The pressure is off a bit since I already know Marshall loves it and 'Dark Angel' did so well. So I'm going to try and just breathe and enjoy it."

"Oh yeah? And how do you think that'll go?"

Halo scoffed. "I have no clue. Ask me Friday."

"Will do," I said, and shut my eyes as Halo finished eating his food.

A few minutes later, I felt myself dozing off when Halo settled back on the couch beside me. As his arm brushed up against mine, I shifted "accidently" to brush his hand with the back of mine. Halo then traced his fingers over the top of mine, and I tried not to think of all the reasons I might've just done that, or why I loved the way he interlaced our fingers.

"You asleep?" Halo said into the shadow-filled room as he

shifted down the couch a little further, and his hair tickled my shoulder.

"Nope," I said, my voice thick with the sleep that was coming back to claim me.

"What are you doing tomorrow night? I was thinking that maybe we could pick out some movies and stuff our faces with popcorn and—"

"That sounds great, Angel, but it's Monday. I gotta go see Mom."

"Oh, that's right." Halo tightened his fingers around mine. "Then maybe Tuesday?"

I wasn't sure if it was the fact it was nearly three in the morning, or because Halo was holding my hand and smelled so fucking good. But the next words I heard myself say were: "Why don't you come with me?"

Silence. Stillness. So much of it that I cracked one eye open to look down and see if Halo was still there and breathing. But I knew he was, I was holding his damn hand, and just as I was about to try and pull my fucking foot out of my mouth, Halo aimed a sleepy smile at me and said, "I'd love to."

THIRTY-THREE

Halo

IT WAS JUST after nine when I got home from Viper's, and as I let myself into my building, I shrugged my backpack up my shoulder. It was still quiet, everyone most likely already at work, but as I made my way up the stairs to my apartment, the door to my sister's place swung open, and then her voice rang out in the hallway.

"You've got some explaining to do," she said. When I turned around, she put her hands on her hips, her green eyes flashing.

"About?"

"Oh, don't play dumb with me," she said, climbing the stairs. "You think I haven't noticed you spend most of your nights away, but I've noticed."

"Creeper," I joked, but she glared at me.

"You've been home a month and you've never once said anything about a girlfriend."

"I don't have a girlfriend." I tried to smother a yawn, my lack of sleep catching up with me. "Can we talk about this later? I'm exhausted."

"From staying up all night?"

"Im—"

"You're not sleeping until I get answers."

I groaned, my head falling back. I'd successfully managed to avoid Imogen's questions when I first arrived back from Miami, and I'd been able to play off Viper's sexual comment on the beach as a joke to embarrass me in front of family, which she'd seemed to buy. But now? With her feet firmly planted, she lifted her chin in challenge, and blowing her off was *not* happening.

Running my hand through my hair, I resigned myself to my fate, though what I'd tell her, I had no clue. Certainly not the truth. "I need coffee."

"Coffee I can do. I'll even throw in breakfast."

"Patty's Diner or it's no deal."

She rolled her eyes. "Fine. Let me grab my purse."

PATTY'S DINER WAS a small twenty-four-hour place on our block, serving up cheap eats and strong coffee. Imogen at least waited until after I'd finished off my first cup of brew and we'd placed our orders to begin the inquisition, for which I was grateful.

"Spill," she said, wrapping her hands around her mug and blowing into it before taking a sip.

"I don't know what it is you want me to say."

"The truth."

I cocked my head to the side, giving her a look.

"Fine, I'll ask. Where have you been staying when you're not home?"

Shit, way to go for the jugular, Im. How was I supposed to answer this without lying to her? I tried for nonchalant, giving her a shrug. "At a friend's."

Imogen's brow quirked, and she tapped the side of her mug. "You know that vague shit isn't gonna fly with me, right?"

"Why does it matter?"

"Why are you being so defensive and hiding things? That's not like you at all." She batted away a stray piece of hair from her face. "You're not back with Phoebe, are you?"

"What?" The idea of Phoebe and me ever being anywhere near

each other was so far out of left field that I sputtered out a laugh. "No. Hell no."

"Then who is it?" Imogen asked, and then her mouth turned down and I knew which angle was coming next. The guilt angle. "You always tell me everything, and it hurts that you feel the need to hide something."

"I know."

"So? How is this any different?"

I lowered my gaze, staring way too intently at my coffee. "It just is."

She sighed, and then, thankfully for me, the waitress interrupted to bring out our food.

"A Belgian waffle with strawberry compote for the lady," the waitress said, setting down a plate in front of Imogen. "And Patty's Special for the gentleman. Can I get you two anything else?"

"No thanks"—I glanced at her nametag—"Lauren."

She winked at me. "Yell if you need anything." As she walked off, Imogen eyed my plate.

"Mmm, that looks good." She waited until I reached for the ketchup, and then she leaned across the table and swiped one of the sausage links off my plate before I could stop her.

"Jesus, what is it with you and Viper stealing shit off my plate?" I said, pouring out a healthy amount of ketchup to go with the hash browns.

"You talk about him a lot."

"Who?"

"Viper."

As I swallowed my food, I realized what I'd said, but it wasn't like I'd admitted he stole shit off my plate *in bed*.

With a shrug, I lifted my over-medium egg and placed it on top of my toast. "Yeah, well, it's bound to happen. I'm with the guys almost every day."

"No..." Imogen took a bite of her waffle, and as she chewed, she stared at me thoughtfully. "That's not it. You don't talk about the others as much."

I rolled my eyes and cut into the egg-toast combination. Sometimes my sister was too perceptive, but I'd been careful not to throw out any clues, so there was no way she could guess. Could she?

"So," she said, her tone turning casual as she cut into her waffle, "Viper eats off your plate, huh?"

I focused on my food. "He eats off everyone's plate," I lied. "He's an asshole like that." *No, you're the asshole*, I told myself. *Just fucking tell her.*

"Yeah, I guess a guy like Viper is used to getting what he wants." It was a simple comment, what could be an innocent observation, but I knew my sister, and her words made me lift my head and pin her with narrowed eyes.

"What's that supposed to mean?"

"Just that he's got a reputation for taking whatever strikes him. Food, sex, men..."

Goddamn the way my skin flushed so easily. I could feel the warmth flowing into my cheeks, and I tried to hide it by lifting my coffee to my lips with both hands.

"Halo." Imogen's voice was softer as she leaned over to cover my mug. As I lowered the coffee back to the table, her forehead creased. "Tell me. Tell me what's going on."

I stared at Im, wondering if I confessed, if I told her my secret, if she'd still look at me the same way she looked at me now. But the truth was that I was tired of hiding. She knew something was up, and eventually, she'd figure it all out. It was better to have it come from my lips than for her to find out some other way.

Setting down my fork, I let out a long rush of air, my skin scorching now. She waited patiently, and when I found my tongue, I said, "I'm involved with Viper."

From her lead-up to this moment, I could tell she'd been suspicious, but when I actually said the words, Imogen swallowed, the rest of her frozen.

"Define...involved," she said slowly.

God, where was the alcohol when I needed it? "I've been staying at his place most nights."

Imogen stared at me, and the shock written all over her face would've been funny if it hadn't been in response to what I'd told her. When minutes passed and she didn't blink or say anything, I waved a hand in front of her face.

"Im? You okay?"

"I... You..." She finally blinked. "I'm gonna need a minute." She held up a finger as she lifted her mug to her lips, finishing off the rest of the coffee, and when she set it down, she said, "Okay. I'm ready. Explain."

I started at the very beginning, when I'd walked into the audition and how Viper gave me a hard time. Even though she'd known that bit from my freak-out after the audition, now that I knew what Viper had actually been thinking, I had a different perspective on it. I told her about how he defended me after the disastrous show in Savannah. How we'd worked together to write the songs for the album, and how that slowly turned things into more, until it all exploded back in Miami. I glossed over the details, because my sister didn't need to know all that, but I explained the situation, how we'd agreed to keep our attraction strictly physical. Obviously I wasn't gonna tell her I'd started having feelings for Viper, because that was something that couldn't happen, but it was enough that she was in the know now.

When I'd finished spilling my guts, Imogen's mouth opened and shut a few times, like she had a million questions but couldn't decide where to start.

"But Halo, you're not... I mean, does this make you... Are you—"

"Gay?" I said. "Honestly? I've asked myself that, and I don't fucking know. Does being attracted to Viper automatically put me in that category? I don't know how this works, Im. I've never thought about it before, and I just..." I gripped the back of my neck. "I don't know."

"Hey." She reached for my free hand and squeezed. "You don't have to figure it all out right now."

I squeezed back. "I know."

Imogen rubbed her thumb over the back of my hand. "You really weren't going to tell me any of this, were you?"

I shook my head.

"Halo?" She waited until I looked up at her before saying, "I'm glad you did."

"Yeah?"

"Duh. We don't have secrets, you and me. And it's not like this changes anything. You're still the best person I know."

"Yeah, I am, aren't I?" I grinned, and she pulled her hand away, rolling her eyes.

"Let's not get cocky about it." She stopped herself and then laughed. "Oh God, the puns that are gonna present themselves now."

"Feel free to keep 'em to yourself."

"It's gonna be hard," she said, chuckling again, as she cut into her waffle, which had to be cold by now. As she chewed, she shook her head. "I told you Viper was fucking hot. Didn't I tell you?"

"You told me, all right."

"Damn. I feel like I deserve some recognition or something for putting the thought into your head."

"You didn't put the thought in my head." But then I remembered her telling me about how hot he was and the way I'd caught myself looking at him...and his lips. "Okay, maybe you did kind of push me in that direction."

Imogen grinned. "You're welcome. I'd ask how he is in bed, but I really don't wanna know about that anymore."

"I'm not telling you shit. Don't worry."

Sitting back, Imogen shook her head. "My brother has a hot boyfriend. Who would've thought."

"He's not my boyfriend," I said, pointing at her with my fork. "Just get that much outta your head."

"But he could be."

"Nah. Viper isn't a relationship kind of guy."

"Maybe not, but you are," she said, and my hand paused from where I'd piled hash browns onto my fork. She'd nailed it right on the head. I'd never been into the casual-fuck scene, and spending so much time with Viper only proved it.

Before I could say anything, she was talking again.

"You gonna tell Mom and Dad?"

"I don't see a reason to. Do you?"

Imogen frowned. "I guess not." Then she tilted her head to the side, seeming to think something over. "Do I get to meet him?"

"Nope."

"Aw, come on. You've gotta introduce me sometime. I'll pretend I don't know."

"Negative."

"Please? I'll do your laundry for a week."

I snorted. "Only a week? That's all a meet-and-greet with *the* Viper is worth? I'll have to tell him."

"Ugh." Imogen crossed her arms and sat back in the booth, pouting. "You're an asshole."

"Guess Viper's rubbed off on me after all."

Imogen began to laugh. "Oh God, the puns. I can't..." She laughed harder, wiping the corners of her eyes. My sister in hysterics was always contagious, and I found myself chuckling along with her, shaking my head at her ridiculousness. But inside, the knot in my stomach loosened, because I'd told my sister about Viper and my world didn't fall apart. She was making jokes and didn't seem bothered in the slightest by my revelation.

As her giggles began to subside, I reached across the table, and she put her hand in mine.

"Love you, Im," I said, grateful that I had this person in my corner, as my sister and my best friend.

"I love you too, Halo. Thanks for telling me."

"Thanks for forcing me to."

A brilliant smile lit up her face. "Anytime."

THIRTY-FOUR

Viper

"YOU'RE DOING WHAT?" Killian's voice echoed down the corridor of my condo, where he was waiting by the elevator for me to grab my shit so we could head to the pub down the street.

I poked my head around the corner. "What? It's not a big deal. You've met my mom. Slade and Jagger have met my mom."

"Uh, don't you think this is a little different?" he asked, his voice growing louder as he headed up the hall, and when he rounded the corner, I looked up at him. "You meeting his family too?"

I screwed my nose up and continued rummaging around through my drawers, searching for the drawing I'd done. "Fuck no."

"I don't know, V. I think you might be in over your head with the angel."

"And I think you might be a nosy motherfucker, but I don't call you out on it."

"Uh huh. So you're admitting it?"

"Jesus Christ." I slammed the drawer shut, what I was looking for obviously not in there, and headed toward my bedroom, Killian hot on my heels. I lifted the clothes piled on my nightstand that needed to be put away, and felt around for the sketch. Hopefully I hadn't left it sitting here where Halo could've seen it, but my brain had been scattered lately, so there was no telling.

Killian threw his hands up. "What *are* you looking for?"

I pushed aside another stack of clothes on the dresser, and Killian's eyes zeroed in on a sea-green shirt on top.

"Is that Halo's shirt?" he said.

Glancing to where he indicated, I shrugged. "Guess so."

He stooped down, grabbing something from off the floor, and when he stood back up, Halo's leather wrist wrap dangled from his fingers. "And this?"

"His too."

"So you guys leave your stuff at each other's places?"

"No," I said. "We don't stay at his place."

"Fuckin' hell." Killian squeezed the bridge of his nose, his eyes shut tight. "You're so stupid, V. I've told you that, right?"

"And if you say it again, I'll be tempted to wipe my floors with your face." I opened the top drawer, and sitting there was the sketch I'd been looking for. "Now we can go."

I didn't wait around for him to follow, and I was punching the button for the elevator before he finally caught up. He didn't say anything more on the walk to the pub, and for that, his face was lucky. I didn't need him giving me shit about Halo. So he'd left a couple of things over. Big fuckin' deal. It was probably my fault for stripping him out of his shit so often.

We entered the pub through the back, as we always did, and greeted the guys in the kitchen before stealing away to our usual booth away from everyone. If we'd gone through the front, we'd have been stopped about twenty times, and I wasn't in the mood to deal with drunk people today, fans or not.

After ordering a couple of beers, we got down to business. Since MGA had given the tour the go-ahead, Killian and I had decided to get a head start in designing the stage for what we were calling The Corruption Tour. It would be our biggest tour to date, and that meant a massive setup.

"I know we always do one stage, but what if we did two?"

Killian said, pulling out a binder and flipping it open. He also had rough drawings of ideas sketched out, which was the way we'd always worked. Coming together to combine ideas before presenting it to the guys for approval and any tweaks. Slade and Jagger had never held much interest in this side of things, and Halo said he'd like to see what we came up with before adding his two cents.

I flipped one of the pages around to get a good look at it. "So connect the main stage to one out in the audience?"

"Nah, not connected. Takes up too many paying seats."

"Then how the fuck do we get out there?"

Killian shrugged. "Run. Fly. Whatever."

With a snort, I looked back down at his drawing, and he showed me what he was thinking for the main stage. Not surprisingly, it fell right in line with what I'd come up with—with one exception.

I shoved my sketch in his direction. "What do you think about this? A play off the band name."

Killian's eyes roved over the page, and then he looked up at me. "What is it?"

"It's a fuckin' piano, genius."

He angled his head to the side, like he was trying to see it. "Doesn't look like one."

I snatched the paper back. "You're no artist yourself, asshole. These are wings," I said, pointing to the sides of the piano. "I figure they could rise, you know, like some massive angel wings, to frame Halo while he's playing."

"Ahh," Killian said, his mouth quirking as he sat back in the booth. "So this is a showstopper piece for Halo."

"Don't you think he'd look like a fallen angel sitting there center stage with the right lighting? Maybe some blues, some—" I stopped short at the grin on Killian's face. "What the fuck are you so smiley about?"

"You really don't get it, do you?"

"Get what?"

Killian chuckled, taking a long pull of his beer. "Look, I know you're gonna take this the wrong way, so try not to, but man... you are so far gone over this guy. I've never seen you like this before."

"Jesus Christ—"

"I know you're gonna try to deny it, but you forget I know you, V. You don't lose your head over anyone. But Halo? He's different. He makes *you* different."

I let out a low whistle and shook my head. "Is this where we talk about our feelings and shit? 'Cause I have to say, I don't plan to stick around if it is."

"It's obvious you like him. Hell, I think you actually care about him, which, trust me, blows my mind as much as it would yours if you would stop and look at what's in front of you."

"All I see in front of me is an asshole who's gone sappy as shit."

"Dude..." Killian rubbed his jaw before scooting forward to rest his elbows on the table. "What's the real issue here, huh? Is it because of what happened with Owen?"

"That was a long time ago."

"Then is it because Halo's our frontman and you don't wanna fuck shit up there?"

I hesitated, and then said, "No."

"Okay. Good. Because Halo's not Owen or Trent."

"You don't think I fuckin' know that?"

Killian lifted a shoulder and rolled his half-empty glass between his hands. "I saw him, you know. Trent. After the show in Savannah."

I blinked. That was months ago, and Killian had never said a word. "Uh, no, I didn't know."

"I'd been trying to get in touch with him for months, mend the fences, so to speak, but he wouldn't answer my calls."

"Because he's a shithead."

"V, please," he said.

"Fine. What about him?"

"Apparently he's been living down there for a while, on some island off the coast. South Haven, I think he said. He's writing again, working on his own stuff."

"Good for him," I said, bringing the beer to my lips.

"Yeah, he looked good. Happy." Killian hesitated, rolling his glass again. "I, uh, made a call to Marshall. Tried to get him back in with MGA—"

"You did *what?*"

Killian held his hand up. "Relax. Trent turned down their offer, which Marshall gave me a fuckin' earful about, but whatever. I guess he wants to do shit on his own terms."

"Huh," I said, digesting the news. I hadn't given much thought to what Trent was up to since he'd left, but...yeah, maybe he'd earned the tiniest bit of my respect back for fucking Gellar over. "There a reason you're bringin' this up now?"

"I don't know." Killian let out a heavy sigh, like he still carried the weight from all our internal band issues around. "I guess I just thought you should know. Things are going well with us, and I'd like it if we can all agree that Trent leaving worked out for the best."

"You think I don't know that?"

"Then why all the hate still, V?"

I tapped my fingers along the side of my glass, half annoyed to even be having this conversation, and half unsure why I couldn't stop my tongue from spouting off the shit I did when it came to Trent. Maybe it was a default reaction when someone brought him up now. Hell if I knew.

"Maybe it's time to remember we were all friends first, yeah?" Killian said.

"You want me to call Trent up and go all 'Kumbaya' on his ass? I don't think so."

"I'm not saying you have to *do* anything. But maybe stop with the shit talking, and if we happen to run into him, maybe you could be civil. Especially since we got Halo out of all this."

Just hearing Halo's name had my pulse kicking up a notch. It had only been a few hours since he'd left my bed, but it felt like years.

"One more thing, and I swear I'll shut my mouth," Killian said, as I groaned. "If you like the guy, stop with the 'it's just fucking' business, or you're gonna lose him. His stuff's at your place, you're with him almost every damn day, and I've seen the way you look at each other. Denial's an ugly beast, my friend."

"We done with the lecture now?" When Killian nodded, I lifted my hand to catch the attention of our waiter. "Thank fuck. My beer's gone bad."

Killian snorted and flipped through his sketches again while I placed our orders for another round, and while he didn't mention Halo again, I couldn't help but feel as though the angel was sitting at the table with us with the way I couldn't think of anything other than him.

THIRTY-FIVE

Viper

———————

"SO THIS IS where *the* Viper from TBD grew up, huh?" With his hands stuffed into the pockets of his jeans, Halo strolled down the sidewalk I used to take home from school each day and looked up at the old brick homes that sat side by side, taking in the neighborhood that had been my old stomping grounds.

"Yep. Me, Killian, and eventually Trent."

Halo looked at me where I was walking alongside him, my hands in the pockets of my leather motorcycle jacket. "Eventually?"

"Yeah, he moved here from Nashville," I said, glancing at the home with the fresh paint on the old porch railing, and I had a fleeting thought about my earlier conversation with Killian about Trent, and what he might be doing now. But as soon as it entered my mind, I shoved it aside. I'd promised Killian I'd try not to think shitty thoughts about Trent whenever his name came up now, but at the same time, I didn't have to actively think *nice* thoughts of him. Especially not tonight.

"Huh. I didn't know that."

"Some TBD stalker you are," I said, aiming a smirk his way, and when the angel's face lit up with amusement, my stomach did that new flip it seemed to do anytime Halo looked pleased with me.

"Well, in all fairness, I only listened to your music back then. It's only recently that I've turned into a stalker. Tracking down interviews, music clips, and magazine articles." Halo stopped walking and ran his eyes down to my mouth. "And I have to confess, none of my attention has been focused on Trent Knox."

"It better fucking not be."

Halo swayed closer to me, and as he tipped his face up, the streetlight caught on his beautiful skin, casting an iridescent glow around him. Never in my entire life had I wanted to touch a person more, yet as we stood there, I made myself keep my hands where they were, safely tucked away from the man in front of me. Safely tucked away from temptation.

If you like the guy, stop with the "it's just fucking" business, or you're gonna lose him. Killian's words from earlier crept in the periphery of my mind, and while I'd denied it at the time, I knew what was going on with Halo was more than fucking. That it was something that had the potential to end in disaster if we didn't pull back from it. If we didn't put a stop to it, and soon. But that was a problem for another time—not tonight.

"So, which house is yours?" Halo asked as he dragged his eyes away from mine and took a step back.

Damn, how did he do that? Know when to stop pushing me? When to give me my space? It was like he saw clear through me, and while most pushed until I snapped, Halo seemed to have this sixth sense when it came with how to deal with me.

I inclined my head toward the small semi-detached on the corner of the street and started walking again, reminding myself that this was no different than bringing the rest of the guys home to meet my mom. But as we got closer to the house and my hands began to sweat and my pulse sped up, I knew it for the lie it was. I was nervous, and that was what made this different.

Totally fucking different.

As always, Mom had left the light on for me, and as we walked up the cracked pavers to the steps leading to the porch, Halo hung back a couple of feet, letting me lead the way. When my feet hit the landing, the front door swung wide and Mom pushed open the security door.

Earlier this morning I'd called to ask if it was okay if I brought a "friend" to dinner, so she wouldn't get caught out in her robe and want to kill me, and as she stepped onto the porch to greet us, I could tell she'd dressed for company.

She'd curled her glossy black hair and "put her face on," as she would say, and was wearing a tailored pair of black slacks and a cream cowl-neck sweater. When her eyes found mine, they lit with pleasure as she put her hands on my arms and looked me over.

"David, don't you look handsome tonight," she said as she leaned up to kiss my cheek, and when I returned the gesture, she grinned, patted the left side of my face, and then looked past my shoulder. "But not as handsome as this young man."

When I turned around to see Halo had now moved up to stand on the porch, I couldn't have agreed with her more. He was fucking handsome. Beautiful, really, and when he flashed that heart-stopping smile our way, my mom whacked me in the chest with the back of her hand.

"Well, aren't you going to introduce me?" she said, jarring me out of my moment of stupid.

"Oh, right," I said, and cleared my throat. "Mom, this is Halo. Our new singer."

Halo took the two steps he needed so he could hold his hand out to my mom, and as she took it, my heart rate accelerated to the point I thought they both might look at me and ask me what that thumping noise was.

"Angel, isn't it?" At the use of my nickname for him, Halo looked in my direction, and I felt my cheeks heat. *Shit. Now* I'm *fucking blushing?* Okay, this was getting out of hand.

"Yes, that's right," Halo said, a smug grin curving his lips. "I mean, that's what Vi—*David* calls me."

Jesus, he was enjoying this a little too much. Not that I could blame him—I'd totally do the same thing, and he knew it. As he turned back to my mom, he continued on like the lovely young man he was no doubt raised to be.

"It's a pleasure to meet you, Ms.—" Halo cut his words off and started to chuckle. "I'm sorry. I just realized I don't know what to call you. Ms. Viper doesn't seem right."

My mom laughed along with him. "Oh, you are a total heart-breaker, aren't you? Our last name is Neil, but you can call me Wendy."

"Then thank you for having me over for dinner tonight, Wendy."

"It's my pleasure," she said, and as they dropped hands, she turned back to me and said, "I hope you're both hungry."

"Starving," I told her, and winked as she headed inside the house, leaving us to follow.

As I held the security door wide for Halo, he walked forward and then stopped before entering and said, "Thanks, David."

"Having fun with that?"

"Mhmm. Although, I have to admit, you definitely seem more like a Viper to me."

"Is that right?" We stepped inside and shrugged out of our jackets. I hung them on the hook in the foyer.

"Yeah. David seems too, I don't know, normal for you."

"And I'm not normal?"

Halo grinned, and it took every ounce of self-restraint I possessed not to grab him and kiss him. "No way. You're—"

"Careful," I said, and the expression in Halo's eyes went from mischievous to something much deeper in a split second.

"I think you're extraordinary."

I couldn't move. I could barely even breathe as I stared into a face I now knew by heart. And as we stood there in my mom's foyer, I realized what a monumentally stupid move it had been for me to bring the angel here.

What had I been thinking? But I already knew the answer to that. I *hadn't* been thinking. Not now. Not in Florida. It seemed I'd given up using my brain from the moment Halo walked in and auditioned for us months ago, and now I was neck deep in something I didn't completely understand. Something that had the potential to blow up in all our faces if Halo didn't stop looking at me and thinking of me as *extraordinary*.

No matter how much I liked it.

THIRTY-SIX

Halo

"DAVID TELLS ME your mother is Cheryl Olsen. She's such a lovely, talented musician. You must be so proud." Wendy smiled at me as she spooned another serving of some kind of sausage, peppers, and onions potato bake onto my plate. She was the ultimate hostess, refilling drinks and food before you could do it yourself, and though I was stuffed, I'd finish this off too. I wouldn't risk being rude in front of Viper's mom.

I thanked her and nodded. "Yes, ma'am, I am."

"And you're quite the musician as well. I've heard nothing but praises from David since you came along."

"Oh really?" I raised an eyebrow in Viper's direction, but his eyes were focused on his plate and he didn't respond.

"Yes, nothing but 'Angel this' and 'Angel that.' I was wondering if I'd ever get a chance to meet you. You've certainly made an impression on my boy." Wendy reached over and squeezed Viper's arm, and he finally looked up, giving her a tight smile.

What was going on with him? Ever since we'd sat down, he'd barely looked my way, and he'd had even less to say, only giving short, clipped answers whenever his mom addressed him. Had I done something to piss him off? Or maybe now that I was here, he was regretting inviting me over.

I scooped another mouthful of his mom's bake and tried not to let the change in Viper's mood bother me. But it seemed I wasn't the only one who'd noticed.

"You're so quiet tonight," Wendy said, giving Viper's arm another squeeze before pulling her hand away. "Is everything all right?"

"Mhmm."

That was all he managed, and as Wendy looked my way, I forced a smile. "This is delicious, Ms. Neil."

"It was nothing," she said, but she beamed and reached for the serving spoon again. "Can I get you more?"

"Oh, no—thank you, though. If I eat another bite, you'll have to roll me outta here."

"Well, hopefully you boys saved room for dessert. I made David's favorite, tres leches cake."

That should've gotten a response out of Viper, but his mouth stayed stubbornly shut, and I wondered again what the hell was going on.

Wanting to steal a couple of minutes alone, I told Wendy, "Tres leches cake sounds amazing."

"Let me go grab it out of the fridge and get some clean plates," she said, already pushing away from the table to rush into the kitchen. When she was out of earshot, I turned my attention to Viper.

"Hey." When that didn't get a response, I kicked him under the table, and his head shot up. "What's going on with you?"

"Nothin'."

"We both know that's not true. Did something happen?"

Viper's black eyes didn't hold the fire behind them that they usually did when he looked at me, and the blankness in them now made my stomach turn. I wasn't sure I wanted an answer after all, but I swallowed and asked anyway.

"Is it me?" I said. "Do you want me to go?"

"Course not." His gaze shifted toward the kitchen. "There's cake."

Another non-answer, and he was starting to piss *me* off. "You're acting like a real dick, you know that?"

"Nothin' unusual there."

"That *is* fucking unusual. You don't act like this with—" I almost said *me*, but Viper's eyes cut to mine.

"With *you*?" The way he said it sounded like an insult. Like it was the most preposterous thing he'd ever heard, and that felt like a punch in the gut.

"Dessert time!" Wendy announced as she entered the dining room holding a white cake decorated with berries and three small plates. She set the cake in the center of the table and then looked between us. "Who wants the first piece?"

Suddenly, the thought of having to sit here and small-talk over dessert with the tension radiating off Viper was too much to take. I wiped my mouth with my napkin and set it beside my empty plate before getting to my feet.

"I'm sorry, I'm afraid I need to get going," I said to Wendy, ignoring the way Viper's eyes bored into the side of my head.

"Already? But—"

"Thank you so much for dinner, and I'm sure the dessert is wonderful as well. More for Viper...David."

I didn't even wait around for Viper's reaction, and it didn't escape my notice that he hadn't exactly jumped up and asked me to stay. As I grabbed my jacket and shrugged into it, part of me waited for him to follow me out, to tell me he was sorry for being a jerk and that we needed to at least try his mom's cake or she'd be disappointed.

But when only the sound of Wendy's voice, still in the dining room met my ears, the only one disappointed tonight was me.

I reached for the doorknob and looked over my shoulder to confirm what I already knew—that no one was following me—and then I stepped out into the night, shutting the door quietly behind me.

My cheeks burned even as a cool breeze greeted me, my hurt at

Viper's obvious dismissal mixing with the anger that had decided to rear its ugly head.

What the *hell* was his problem tonight? Everything had been fine on the way over here. We'd been joking and laughing, and it'd been all we could do to keep our hands off each other. Hell, I'd even told him he was extraordinary, and—

My feet stopped moving. That. That had been the moment when I sensed a change. When something had passed over Viper's eyes, something I couldn't read, and I hadn't even gotten a chance to think on it, because Wendy had ushered me through the house to give me the full tour. But that was it. I'd bared the slightest bit of feeling, and Viper had freaked. He hadn't bothered to talk to me about it, just boarded up the windows and put a "closed" sign on the goddamn door.

Jesus, why was he so scared to admit I was any more to him than some casual fuck? He had to know that wasn't true, not anymore.

Cursing, I shoved my hands in my pockets and began to walk toward the subway, but halfway there I changed my mind and turned back. We needed to talk, and since he wasn't following me and I wasn't about to cause a scene in front of his mother, I'd wait.

I'd thought Viper was a lot of things over the time I'd known him: an intimidating rock god, a playboy with a sharp tongue, and an intensely passionate lover.

But I'd never, ever thought of him the way I did now.

As a coward.

THIRTY-SEVEN

Viper

FUCK.

FUCK. FUCK. Fuck. The soft click of the front door shutting might as well have been a slam, as Halo exited my mom's house and left without trying some of her famous tres leches cake.

I was such a fucking idiot. Wasn't that what Killian had been telling me? Yeah, well, tonight I had to agree with him, and not only that, I was a giant asshole to boot. As I sat there silently admonishing my shitty attitude, my mom's voice cut through.

"David?" When I didn't answer, or look at her, she put a hand on my shoulder and shook me. "David? What's going on? Why did Angel leave?"

"*Halo*, Mom," I said, and shoved my chair back from the table. "His name is Halo."

But even as I said it, the name got stuck on my tongue. It was so strange how a name made such a difference in how you viewed someone. Ever since I'd met Halo, I'd thought of him as Angel, and the only time that had changed was when I'd forced it. When I'd desperately been trying to create some distance, like now.

I think you're extraordinary...

I got to my feet and threw the napkin on the table, and my mom grabbed my arm and dug her fingers in, halting me.

"Don't you take that tone with me, young man. What's going on with you two? One minute you were laughing, joking around, and the next you're acting like a grizzly bear."

"*Nothing's* going on with us, and nothing can. Okay?" I pulled my arm free, and shoved a hand through my hair, frustrated. "Just leave it," I said as I brushed by her heading for my jacket and the pack of cigarettes that were in the pocket.

As I got hold of them, I pulled open the door, and at the last moment stopped and turned back to see her looking after me. Her expression was full of hurt and disappointment, the same one that used to make me feel guilty as a kid, and it still did the trick as an adult. But this time there was something else mixed in with that look, something that made me want to shout at the top of my lungs...pity.

I clenched my jaw and held up the cigarettes. "I'll be back in a few." She merely shook her head, hating this habit of mine, but there was no way I could sit there in the house now that Halo had left. *Yeah, because you made him, asshole.*

As I walked onto the porch, I lit up and shut the door behind me, then I looked out onto the street and my feet came to a stand-still. Halo was standing on the sidewalk under the streetlight staring up at the house. His hands were jammed in the pockets of his jeans, and the pissed-off expression on his face was one I'd never seen. His mouth was drawn taut, his body tense, and as I made myself move and walk down the stairs, his eyes zeroed in on me. Halo looked seconds away from exploding, and because I was the king of assholes tonight, I opened my mouth and hit the detonator.

"Decide to come back and apologize for being rude, huh?" As I stopped in front of him, I noticed the ticking in Halo's jaw and told myself that the smart thing to do here was to back the fuck off. But I'd never been really good at doing the *smart* thing.

"You've got some nerve," Halo finally said, and took a step toward me, and I wasn't sure if it was because I wanted to be close to him or because I figured he should have a fair shot at punching me if he wanted to, but I didn't back up.

I raised the cigarette to my lips and took a drag, and as I angled my head and exhaled, I said, "Oh yeah? How you figure?"

Halo's eyes narrowed as though he were trying to work out who the fuck I was, and where the man he'd known for the past few months had up and disappeared to. But fuck, with the album close to dropping and the band about to explode, it was time to lay all this shit out. Put into perspective what could and couldn't happen, and him thinking of me as extraordinary could *not* happen.

"Because you invited me out here tonight to meet your mom and then turned into a total dick. *That's* how I figure."

"A little bit touchy, aren't you?" I said, bringing the cigarette back to my lips. But before I could take a drag, Halo reached out, snatched it from my hand, and threw it on the ground. Then he got all up in my face.

"I'd rather be touchy than a fucking coward."

I reared back, the blow a low one, and as the impact of it slammed into me, I gritted my teeth and let my frustration at the situation rise to the surface.

I hadn't wanted this. I hadn't wanted all these complicated emotions pulling at me every time Halo was near. But as I stood there reeling from his blow, I did what I always did when someone backed me into a corner: I punched back with no thought other than landing a winning blow.

"I'm not a coward," I said, my voice low. "I'm just smart enough to know when things have run their course. And this is one of them."

"Is that right?" Halo let out a disgusted sound. Whether it was with himself for ever having touched me or me because I was being a piece of shit was anyone's guess.

"You know it is. Bringing you here tonight was no different than bringing Killian or Jagger here. But then you had to go and make it something more in your head. Sorry, Angel, it's just not like that for me. I told you. I don't do love. I don't do relationships—"

"You just do fucking."

"That's right."

"And that's all this was to you. That's all I was to you? A *fuck*?" Halo spat the word at me, and I made myself stand still and not react to his emotions, because if I did that, I would likely grab him. Grab him and kiss his snarling, pissed-off lips, and the whole point of this shitshow was to end things. I hadn't planned it to happen tonight, but we'd both known this thing had had a time limit, and Halo sure as fuck wouldn't be the one to end it—so okay, I'd be the asshole. It was a role I was familiar with.

"A really *hot* fuck," I said. "Don't forget that part."

Halo stumbled back a step, the anger now replaced with hurt from the blow I'd just landed, and he blinked several times and then slowly shook his head. I balled my fists by my sides and ordered myself to stay put. This was what had to happen—he knew it, and so did I.

"I'm such a fucking idiot," Halo said under his breath, and as he took another step away, he shook his head. "I thought... I..." When his words stopped, he looked up, and those light eyes were wide and full of disbelief and betrayal.

"You knew how this was going to end," I said, as though that would make things any better. "You're the frontman, Angel. Your career, *our* career is about to explode, and this can't be more than what it's been. So it needs to be done. I told you this already."

Halo's eyes flashed, and the anger from a second ago reignited. "And I told you I won't be someone I'm not."

I shrugged. "That's fine. But whoever you are has to be without me. I won't be the reason this band comes to a grinding halt."

Halo's mouth fell open as he walked back the couple of steps he needed so we were toe to toe.

"There it is," Halo said, his annoyance now spreading to his cheeks in a red flush. "The real reason here. It's got nothing to do with me. It's everything to do with you. You've been so closed off to anyone giving a shit about you that you don't know how to actually *trust* someone anymore. I'm not Owen. I'm not going to fuck you over or exploit you if this doesn't work out. And I'm not about to walk out on something I've been working my ass off for because I'm no longer allowed to fuck *the* Viper. So why don't you get the fuck over yourself already."

THIRTY-EIGHT

Halo

———

WOW. SO IT had come to this. I should've known better than to expect a warning before Viper decided he was done with me. The change in his mood had flipped on a dime, giving me whiplash, and worse, he'd done it in front of his mom.

And it was all because I'd told him I thought he was extraordinary? Was he fucking kidding with that shit? He was extraordinary, all right. An extraordinary jackass.

"What, nothing to say?" I asked when Viper shoved his hands in his pockets, looking entirely unaffected by what was happening, and *that* was fucking infuriating.

I knew better than to think I meant nothing to him. He could tell me I was just a fuck all day until he was blue in the face, but his actions spoke louder than his words, and it was the little things he did that showed me he cared more than he'd ever let on. So all this bullshit? This cement wall going back up around him? It was because he was scared. Viper was so scared of letting anyone in, because God forbid the man be vulnerable and put himself out there.

"Why can't you admit it, huh?" I said. "For one second why can't you admit this shit's got you running scared?"

Viper pulled his hands out of his pockets and spread his arms wide. "Look at me. You see me runnin'? Do I look scared to you?"

"Riiight. Big, bad Viper," I sneered. "Gotta maintain your image of not giving a shit about anyone or anything. What a miserable existence."

His eyes narrowed. "You done?"

Was I? No. Fuck no. I wanted him to fight back after he admitted he couldn't sleep in his own damn bed without me there. I wanted him to tell me he felt the same way I did—that this casual fling between us had changed over the last few months into something more.

"So this is it? It's over?" I said.

"You need more closure than this?"

Fuck me, he was being an asshole. He always told me he was, and I never listened, because he'd never shown that side of himself with me, but I sure as hell was seeing it now. The last thing I'd expected when he invited me to his mom's tonight was to get booted from Viper's life—and his bed.

"I wanna know one thing," I said. "Is the reason you're doing this because of the band? Because of what people would say about me if they knew about us?"

"It doesn't matter—"

"It matters to me," I yelled, shoving Viper in the chest, causing him to stumble back. "It fucking matters to *me*."

If he was surprised by my reaction, he didn't show it. Instead, he righted himself and pulled another cigarette out of his packet. After he lit up, he took a long inhale and then blew the stream of smoke away from me. "It's for the best. You'll see."

I shook my head and ignored the sting behind my eyes. "That's not a fucking answer."

"You know the answer," Viper roared, his indifference fading away as he finally snapped. "Stop pretending like we're something we're not, and move the fuck on."

His words were a slap in my face. Designed to hurt me so I'd back off—just the way he obviously wanted it.

"Look at me." My voice came out tight and full of gravel, because I'd been grinding my molars together so hard my jaw ached. When Viper didn't immediately comply, I raised my voice. *"Look at me."*

Hard, dark eyes met mine, and I couldn't stop myself from taking a step toward him.

I shoved my finger against his chest to punctuate my words. "You're making a mistake."

Viper wrapped his hand around my wrist to stop me, his hold firm to the point of pain. "My choice to make."

Right. How could I forget? It was Viper's choice. Viper's choice to chase after me, Viper's choice to fuck me for more than one night, and now it was Viper's choice to end things. I got no say. After all, who was I? Nothing more than a fuck in his eyes.

I ripped my arm away from his hold and walked backward away from him. Nothing else needed to be said right then, because if I didn't leave now, I would end up punching the shit out of that handsome face. The one he used to lure objects of his lust to his bed. To lure *me*.

He stared right back at me, unmoving, as I glared at him, my heart pounding in my chest and threatening to burst. When I couldn't stand to look at him anymore, I turned around, balled my hands into the pockets of my jacket, and walked off to the train.

I knew Viper wouldn't follow. He hadn't even come outside to see me; it'd just been happenstance that I'd been standing out there. God, what a fucking prick. But if truth be told, I was just as mad at myself for falling for the "casual fuck" bullshit as I was at him for spewing it in the first place.

Did he honestly think ending things would be a good thing for the band? Did he really believe that? Because as far as I was concerned, Viper flipping his "asshole" switch wasn't going to endear him to anyone, least of all me. Fuck, no wonder Trent left.

But I was different. I wasn't a quitter, and I wasn't about to be thrown out on my ass like a piece of garbage either. I was the lead singer of Fallen Angel, and I deserved better than that.

The train to my apartment dragged on forever, but the longer I sat, staring out the window into the black nothing, the more my anger began to dissipate. Taking its place was something much worse: disappointment. Something I was positive Viper wouldn't be feeling at all.

I leaned my head against the cool glass and closed my eyes, but when all I saw was the look of indifference on Viper's face when I left, I opened them again.

I thought I'd gotten through. I thought I'd cracked his shell. Hell, I was the one taking a risk here. Viper was the one out and proud, and my parents didn't even know about me. It was a good thing I'd never told them. Jesus.

When I finally reached my apartment, I unlocked the front door and braced myself for Imogen throwing herself out into the hallway at me. But when I saw the lights out at her place, I breathed a sigh of relief. I wouldn't have to deal with her questions right now. I needed to be alone to wrap my head around everything that happened tonight and then figure out how to do what Viper had suggested—"move the fuck on."

I put the key in the lock, but I didn't open the door. Shit, the last thing I wanted to do was sit on the couch or in the chair or on my bed, all places that would remind me of Viper.

No, I thought, tucking my key back into my pocket and continuing the climb up the stairs until I reached the emergency exit. *I need to be somewhere Viper hasn't touched.*

I pushed open the door—the alarm on it had never worked since I'd lived there—and took the stairs up to the roof. No one else seemed to come up here, which meant I was free to bring my guitar up and play without any of my neighbors beating on the wall to shut me up. I didn't feel much like playing tonight, though, which might've been the first time I'd ever felt so shitty and not reached for an instrument.

The air was chillier up here, the building one of the taller ones around these parts. A concrete wall surrounded the perimeter, giving it an enclosed feel, but that was what I liked about coming up here. I could sit in my folding lawn chair, look up at the sky, and pretend I could see the stars despite the bright lights of the city.

And that was what I did now.

I laid the chair out flat so I could stretch out on it and folded my arms behind my head. The anger that'd boiled so quick and fast inside me outside the Neils' house had simmered now, bringing only confusion and hurt to the forefront. I didn't want to feel any of those things. Why couldn't I be the kind of guy who didn't care so much? The kind that could have a longstanding acquaintance with someone else without it turning into more?

It all boiled down to one thing: I was guilty of caring too much, and Viper was guilty of not caring enough.

THIRTY-NINE

Viper

IF SOMEONE ASKED me how I ended up standing in front of Halo's apartment three hours after I'd watched him walk away from me, I wouldn't be able to tell them. But that was where I found myself, staring at the peeling paint on the left-hand corner of his apartment's door, trying to find the nerve to knock.

After our epic showdown in front of my mom's house, I'd forced myself to go back inside and eat some of the cake I knew she'd spent the afternoon making, figuring there was no reason to make everyone in my life hate me by the end of the night. Mom had been wise enough not to delve deeper into the surly mood that had only intensified after going out for my "smoke," and after I'd finally kissed her goodnight and headed down to the train station, I'd been tempted to stop at a liquor store and buy a bottle of cheap whiskey to drown out the words I could now hear on repeat in my head.

My words. Halo's words. *All* the ugly words that had been spewed between us in the heat of one of the most painful arguments I'd ever been a part of. Over the years, I'd become a master of not giving a shit. But from the moment the angel had pulled away from me at my mom's dinner table, to his final *you're making a mistake*, the cut had been made. I'd left it there to bleed, and now I was numb, in a state of shock over what the hell I'd just done to him, to me, to us, and I realized I didn't need alcohol, because without him, I didn't want to feel a fucking thing.

Raising my hand, I knocked and waited. I had no idea what I was going to say when he opened the door—*if* he opened the door —but I'd obviously caught the train here for a reason.

When there was no answer or movement from behind the door, I knocked again, louder this time, determined to see him or sleep on his welcome mat until he opened the damn door the next morning.

God, my chest ached something fierce, and if I hadn't ripped my heart out earlier and tossed it on the ground, I would've been worried I was having a heart attack as I stood there making a deal, with whoever might listen, that Halo open up his damn door.

When five, ten, fifteen fucking minutes passed and the door remained firmly shut, I cursed and whacked the heel of my palm against it. *Fuck.* What did I expect? That after every shitty thing I'd said in an attempt to push Halo away from me, he'd suddenly open up his door and invite me inside? Hell, at this stage I didn't even know why I was here. When we'd been going at it with one another, everything I'd been saying made sense, but now nothing made sense.

I took a step back to turn around and sit my ass down on the ground, and as I did, some movement over in the fire exit caught my attention. Halo had just pulled open the door to the stairwell, and as his eyes locked with mine, he froze in place. He gripped the door, his feet locked, and his shocked expression changed to one full of disgust. Then he took a step back and let go of the door, and before it fell shut, he turned and bolted up the stairs.

With no other thought than following him, seeing him, getting closer to him, I took off after Halo like the hounds of hell were chasing me. I shoved open the door, and as I burst into the stair-well and it thundered shut behind me, Halo stopped one flight up, his eyes clashing with mine from the landing above, his hands braced on the metal railing as he glared down at me. His breathing was heavy enough that I could hear it in the confined space even though we were a floor apart, and when my eyes shifted to the stairs and then back to his, my intention must've been clear, because the angel took off.

Halo darted up the next set of steps as I climbed the first, going two at a time in a race to reach him, and with my eyes firmly on him, I had the advantage. I could see the distance between us, he couldn't, and every time he glanced back to see where I was, he slowed, until we got to the final set and I closed in. He was almost home free and out the door, but just as his hand landed on the door handle, I reached for him and my fingers caught his wrist.

The contact sent an electric jolt through me, and him too, judging by the way his head whipped around, and I took full advantage of the distraction. I tightened my fingers until I had a firm hold of him, and when I was finally opposite him, I tugged on his hand, drawing him to me.

Halo clamped a hand down over my fingers and pried them off his wrist, but I turned my hand, caught hold of his, and pulled him toward me with so much force that he stumbled and put a hand up to brace himself. As his palm landed on my chest, right over my heart, I wondered if he could feel how hard it was pounding. I wondered if he knew it was for him and if he even cared. Then Halo angled his face up, his eyes flashing with fury as he dug his fingers into me as hard as he could and shoved me away from him. I was caught off guard; my grip on him loosened, and he yanked his arm free. Then he took a step back, his eyes trained on me with a *fuck you* look if ever I'd seen one, as he reached behind him for the door and shoved down on the handle.

Halo turned, pushed the door open, and stormed outside, a clear dismissal, but I followed after him. I must've been possessed or some shit, because I was not about to let him get away from me. I needed to touch him, talk to him, and somehow make him understand that every fucked-up thing I'd said to him tonight was for the best. I'd done this for him.

Halo stopped a couple of feet away from me, and as he stood

there with his back to me, looking out at the city lights, the message was clear: *go away*. That wasn't going to happen, though, and as I came up behind him, his shoulders tensed.

The words were on the tip of my tongue, the ones I never said to anyone, ever: *I'm sorry*. Two words, only seven letters, and yet they were the hardest to say in the entire English language.

Halo still had his back to me, though, so I moved up beside him, but even though I didn't touch him, he jerked away as though I had. Before he could move again, I grasped at his arm and spun him so that his back was against the concrete. I needed his attention, not for him to try to disappear, so I pushed my hips against his, locking him in place.

That move was one the angel would've liked had the past few hours never happened. But since I'd gone and fucked us to hell, Halo now strained against my hold, his chest rising and falling rapidly, like he couldn't get enough air with me this close. He wouldn't look at me. Almost nose to nose, and his eyes were everywhere except where I wanted them.

I held his chin and waited until he looked at me. At first he refused, but I told myself to be patient, and it wasn't long before those pale green eyes finally settled on mine. When they did, I opened my mouth to say those two words, those seven letters, but before they could come out, Halo pulled an arm free and clapped his hand over my lips.

Stunned, I could only stare at him as he shook his head, unwilling to hear me out, to listen to my apology. I'd said more than he wanted to hear tonight, and if I thought I'd felt like the biggest fucking asshole on the planet before, it was nothing like the feeling that seared me then. Because while Halo's eyes held all of the fury I'd expected to be directed my way, there was a more dominant emotion swirling in the fire: pain.

I inhaled through my nose sharply and dropped my hold on his chin. The look he aimed my way cut deep. God... I'd hurt him. I knew I'd pissed him off, but I'd done a hell of a lot more than that, and as I stared into the depths of all that emotion, I almost wished I'd never gotten a glimpse.

Halo held my gaze, baring it all for me. His palm continued to cover my mouth, his hold firm, but I could feel his fingers shaking slightly. From anger and disappointment? From the tension radiating through his body? From something else?

Shit, the last thing I'd wanted was to get feelings tied up between us, but there was no denying that whatever this was, it wasn't just a casual fuck, and I wasn't sure it ever had been. But that didn't matter—it still didn't mean anything more could happen. That was just the way it had to be, and maybe I should've cut this off sooner, but it was better to let the angel go now than make things even more complicated.

Like he could tell the way my thoughts had gone, Halo pushed me away suddenly, using the strength of his hand against my mouth and using the other one to shove at my chest. I wasn't letting him go so easily, though, and batted his hand away, grabbing for his hips. I curled my fingers around his belt loops and pulled him back toward me, but he gripped hard on my biceps, holding me at arm's length.

I didn't want to be at arm's length. I wanted him to be *in* my arms, which was the goddamn problem. Because more than anything in that moment, I wanted to kiss those angry lips until he opened up for me. I wanted to tangle my fingers in his hair and tug his head back so I could run my tongue down his neck to the hollow at the base of his throat. And then I wanted his body under mine, arching up against me as we connected in the deepest way I knew how.

But I didn't just want those things. I needed them. I needed *him*.

He still had a firm grip on my arms, but that didn't matter, because I unhooked my fingers from his belt loops and brought my hands up between us, holding his face between my palms as I dove in for the kiss I craved. The move took Halo by surprise, because he froze, and the thought crossed my mind that I might've gone too far, that he might well punch me, but fuck it. It'd be worth it, and I deserved worse.

When he finally realized what was happening, Halo ripped his mouth away from mine, his breathing coming hard as he looked at me with a mixture of confusion and outrage.

But he didn't throw a punch. He didn't walk away. So I reached for him again, entwining my fingers in his hair as I crashed my lips back on his, but he was ready for me this time, and he pushed me away before I got a good taste of him.

Halo took a couple of steps back and then wiped his mouth with the back of his hand, sending me a clear message that I didn't buy for a second. Why? Because the arousal in his jeans told me different.

I prowled forward as he backed up again, but because he kept his eyes on mine, he didn't notice the wall behind him until his ass bumped up against it.

He could've moved. He could've told me to stay the fuck away. He could've thrown that punch I was still waiting for. Instead, he watched me walk toward him, and when he was close enough for me to touch, Halo surprised me by grabbing two handfuls of my shirt, balling his fists in the material. He didn't push me away, but he didn't pull me forward either. I could sense his hesitation, the war being waged in his mind, so I did the only thing I could do. I forced his hand by licking my lower lip, and when his eyes dropped to the movement, something in him snapped.

Halo jerked me forward and attacked my mouth with surprising force, taking my lips in a brutal kiss that made my head spin.

This battle of wills had just begun.

FORTY

Halo

ANGER. HURT. LUST. As the three emotions battled for supremacy, I twisted my hands in Viper's shirt and scraped my teeth along his lower lip. The lip he'd taunted me with, knowing there'd be no way I could resist.

I twisted my fingers around the material and for one second imagined it was his skin I was sinking my nails into, that he could feel the bite of pain I was so desperately trying to inflict in that moment because...how fucking *dare* he do this to me.

How dare he come here after everything he'd said tonight and make me want him again. But he had, and I did. I wanted him so badly that I couldn't stop myself from reaching out and taking hold of him, even though I knew this was it. That this was our goodbye. I could read the apology in his eyes: *I'm sorry. I didn't mean for things to end this way.* But that didn't stop me from drawing him in.

Closer... Closer... I wanted him so close that Viper would never be able to forget the way it felt to have me touch him, kiss him, consume him the way he did me, and then? Then I'd let him go. Just the way he wanted it.

I shoved Viper back a step and pulled my mouth free, and as his chest heaved beneath my palm, I took in the wickedly hot visual he made standing there. The one that had made me fall for this bad boy in the first place.

Viper's lips were slick and swollen from my attack, his jet-black hair pushed behind one ear while strands on the other side had escaped to fall down and shadow those broody eyes, and there was no resisting him.

And that was the problem. I hadn't been able to resist Viper. From the very beginning I'd been intrigued, and ever since then I'd gotten in deeper and deeper with him, fooling myself that I could be as cool about this as he was. That I could be just as casual about sharing his bed, his life, his body, and then walk away—but no.

I had gone and done the unthinkable. I'd fallen for Viper even after he'd told me not to, and now here I was saying goodbye to a person I would forever be close to, but never again in the way I wanted to be. And I knew if I didn't take this moment, if I didn't allow myself this goodbye, I would regret it for the rest of my life.

I didn't want to talk. I didn't want to hear his *I'm sorry* or *this is how it has to be*. All of the words that needed to be said had been said, and those that hadn't were swirling in Viper's eyes for me to see. Apology. Regret. Desire and need. It was that last one that had me taking a step forward, so I could pull him back in and say goodbye *without* words.

Viper opened to me in an instant, just as he always had, allowing me to dive in and explore him in a way that no one had ever done in my life. I slid the hand on his neck up into his hair and tightened, and when he dug his fingers into my hips, I slammed my body up against his and tangled our tongues together.

Viper groaned and angled his head, deepening the kiss, as he began to walk forward and move me back to the concrete wall, where he pinned me in place and held my face steady. Then he fused our mouths together again in a kiss that felt like a battle, trying to see who could make the other give in first, and tonight I wasn't holding back.

I twisted my hand in Viper's hair and pulled hard, making him grunt and raise his head, and the fierce, untamed light in his eyes flipped some kind of switch in me. With my gaze locked on his, I was the one to torment this time. I slowly slid my other hand down to his jeans and began to rub, squeeze, and massage the erection I could feel pushing up against me, until a tortured groan rumbled from Viper's throat.

The sound was so damn sexy that I did it again, wanting to memorize it, and this time Viper's hips began to move against my palm until he was all but fucking my hand through the denim. He planted his hands on either side of my head against the wall, his eyes not leaving mine, and when that was no longer enough, I dropped my hand so Viper could move between my legs and press that hard cock of his up against me, then I took his lips in a savage kiss.

As he shoved his tongue between my lips, I moaned, the taste of him something I would never get enough of and never be able to forget. But all of this still wasn't enough for me. This wasn't how it was going to end.

Viper destroying me.

Viper making my knees weak.

Viper overwhelming every single one of my senses until I didn't know anything other than him—no. Tonight *I* wanted to be the one to destroy. The one to overwhelm.

I pushed off the wall, the adrenaline rushing through me now as I grabbed hold of Viper's shirt and tore my lips free. In an instant, I saw the question *stop?* enter his eyes, but that was the last thing I wanted.

Catching Viper off guard, I pivoted so our positions were reversed, but even that wasn't enough, because the truth was that I didn't want to stop tonight until I'd marked Viper the same way he'd marked me.

As I muscled him back to the wall, Viper's nostrils flared, my domineering actions inflaming his arousal in a way I'd never expected. His lips were pulled tight in a thin line, his jaw ticked, and his eyes were so dark they were practically black. He moved his hand to his jeans, and as he flicked them open and drew the zipper down, I did the same. But when he went to shove his hand inside, I reached out and wrapped my fingers around his wrist —tight.

Viper's eyes shifted to where I held his arm between us, and when he raised them back to me and arched an eyebrow, it was like the gunshot at the start of a race.

I yanked him off the wall and spun him around to face it, and this time when I crowded in behind him, I left no space between us. Viper let out a grunt as his front side came up flush against the concrete, and the sound that left me was a feral noise I'd never heard before.

I gripped Viper's hips and plastered myself against every hard inch of his strong backside, then I shut my eyes and took a deep inhale of his shampoo. The same shampoo I'd used just last night. But I shoved that thought aside, not allowing myself to think of then. Instead, staying firmly in the now, I wound an arm around Viper's waist and found his open jeans.

A hiss of air left Viper as I slid my fingers beneath his briefs and curled them around his stiff dick. I bucked forward in response, stroking him up and down as I ground up against his ass in an effort to get some relief. The thrill at having him in this position was as much of a rush as pulling that response from him.

I'd wanted Viper like this for a long time but never had the courage to act on it, because Viper had always been larger than life. He'd always been *the* Viper. A mystery I didn't understand. A legend no one could get close to. But here, up against this wall, Viper was just a man who wanted another man—*me*. The man he'd hurt and pushed away because he was so damn scared to care about another person, and now he'd hurt me to the point where I wanted to hurt him right back. Even more fucked up than that? I also wanted to love him. But since he wouldn't let me do that, I'd settle for something in between.

I released my hold of his cock and shoved my hand into the pocket of his jeans, and when Viper glanced over his shoulder at me, I wondered if he was about to tell *me* to stop. He didn't, though, merely eyed me in silence as I found what I was looking for and pulled his wallet free.

Viper swallowed as I flipped it open and got out what I knew was in there, and when I dropped his wallet to the ground and tugged his jeans and briefs down under his ass, I drove my hips forward, and Viper thrust back to meet me. That was all the permission I needed.

I brought the condom packet to my lips and tore it open with my teeth, our eyes connected and my intention clear as I freed my dick and suited up. Viper cursed and shut his eyes as I slicked my throbbing length with the lube he'd carried with him tonight—no doubt with the goal of using it on me, but he was in luck. Tonight he'd fucked me with no need for any of that, leaving them handy for himself.

Don't think about that, I told myself. *You'll have plenty of time to hate him and yourself later. Right now? Right now he's here...*

Take him.

I took in Viper's broad shoulders in his leather jacket, and the jeans pulled down under his bare ass, and it didn't escape me that he was now groaning and fisting his dick. His cheek was pressed to the wall, his eyes were shut, and he was about as vulnerable as a person could get in that moment, and I knew this was something he didn't give over easily, this trust—and that was what made his denial of this, us, so fucking infuriating.

Viper wanted me. He cared deeply about me. I knew it. He knew it. But the stubborn motherfucker would rather die than say it out loud. There was only one reason he'd followed me home tonight after our argument. One reason he was now standing on my rooftop letting me have whatever I wanted. Viper had needed to see me, needed to touch me, as much as I needed him—and damn him for that.

As my frustration at the situation once again roared to the surface, I stroked my slick fingers down Viper's heated channel and pressed the pads of my fingers to his entrance just as he did whenever he stretched me, and a throaty rumble of pleasure left Viper.

I squeezed my eyes shut, trying to block out the way that sound made my heart flip in my chest. But it was no use. No matter how mad I was at him, no matter how much I wanted to hurt him, I would never do it with my hands.

As I eased my finger inside him, the sensation of his body stretching around me made me imagine how that would feel around my dick. Then Viper shoved back, and I took that as a sign for more. I moved my hand, sliding my finger in and out before adding a second, and I knew the sounds coming from Viper would forever be ingrained in my mind.

When his hand landed on my thigh and squeezed, my eyes flew open and I saw Viper looking back at me, his eyes pleading for more, begging me to take him, to make him forget every shitty thing we'd said and done to each other tonight.

So I pulled my fingers free, and as the head of my cock bumped up against his entrance, Viper's jaw bunched, and he tore his eyes from mine. I glanced down at where our bodies were connected, and then I gripped the leather covering his shoulder and slowly eased my way inside him.

As the hot, tight fit of Viper's body surrounded me, I realized what a gigantic mistake this was. The pleasure was almost too much to take, and I had to shut my eyes to fight back the orgasm that was threatening to explode just from being granted entrance.

I dug my fingers into his shoulder and moved my other hand to the bare skin of his hip, and when I finally bottomed out, I couldn't hold back the groan of total ecstasy that racked my body. Viper felt incredible. I felt incredible. And I knew that when this was over, nothing was ever going to compare to how I felt right here in this moment, with him.

Viper groaned, and when I saw his arm move, working his dick, I braced my feet and pulled back, withdrawing my cock to the tip before I tunneled back inside. The ball-tingling pleasure I got from the way Viper took me had nothing on the loud shout as

Viper shoved back until his back was flush with my front and I held him there, wrapping my arm over his shoulder and across his chest.

Viper's head fell back as he started to feverishly jack himself off, and I began to move in time with him, giving sharp thrusts that had him cursing me, even as he turned his head in my direction.

His lust-filled eyes found mine, and the rampant desire there had my arousal hitting an all-time high, and I slammed our mouths together. We bit, licked, and sucked at one another as Viper fucked his fist and I fucked him, our onslaught of one another relentless. And as the pleasure became too intense and the emotions too much to bear, we both gave in to the battle. We surrendered with a litany of curses that soon faded into the night, leaving us standing there in silence, surrounded by the darkness that had come to hang over this relationship.

As the enormity of what I'd just done—what I'd allowed myself to do and feel after the way he'd treated me—slammed home, so did all the hurt and anger. It rushed in like a tidal wave as I pulled free of his body and rolled the condom off. I zipped my jeans and saw that Viper was doing the same, and when he turned around, I steeled myself against that face, those eyes, the body mine so desperately wanted in every way, and said goodbye the only way I knew Viper would understand.

"There. Now we're both just a fuck."

FORTY-ONE

Halo

"OH MY GOD, there's press waiting for you," Imogen said as the car slowed to a stop in front of the venue for Fallen Angel's *Corruption* pre-release party.

As I looked out the tinted windows of the Mercedes, I could see the red carpet that led up to the building, and on either side, a surprising number of photographers, reporters, and fans—none of which I'd expected, because shit, I'd never done this before. I knew there'd be industry people inside, but was I supposed to stop and talk to these guys too?

"Just smile and be your charming self," Imogen said, as if she could sense my sudden nerves. "You'll be fine. And I'll be right behind you."

"Shit, Im..." My hands grew sweaty, and I wiped them on my pants. Why hadn't the guys given me a heads-up? And why had MGA thought it'd be a good idea to have us all ride separately?

I didn't have time to dwell on that, because the driver was opening the door, and unless I wanted to spend the evening hiding in the back seat, I needed to make a move. I took a deep breath and let it out in a rush, and then I stepped out of the car and buttoned my suit jacket as camera flashes blinded me. It was all I could do not to squint under the assault on my eyes, and I somehow managed a smile and a wave before turning back to help Imogen out of the car.

We'd both dressed to the nines tonight—she wore a floor-length strapless emerald dress that matched her eyes, and I'd chosen an all-black suit, forgoing the tie and switching out the collared shirt for a black T-shirt so it didn't look too overdone and formal. It also happened to match my mood.

Imogen took hold of my arm, and off we went, stopping every few feet to pose for the cameras, pretending to know what the hell we were doing. As one of the reporters approached, Imogen gave me a gentle squeeze of reassurance, but there were no tough, hard-hitting questions tonight. They wanted to know what to expect from the album, how I felt about joining the band, and who the "lovely lady on my arm" was. It didn't escape me that once I introduced Imogen as my sister, the questions turned toward my personal life, if I was single, what my type was, and if I had a celebrity crush.

Yeah, I have a celebrity crush, all right, I thought, as another Mercedes stopped in front of the red carpet. When the door opened, I could see a dark head of hair, entirely too familiar, and the breath left my body.

Viper stepped out of the car, clearly not giving a fuck about the dress code, because he wore a pair of dark jeans and boots paired with a plain white tee and black leather jacket, and fuck, the memory of him paled to the real thing. It'd been days since I'd seen him—since I'd fucked him on the roof of my building—but it felt like years. God, seeing him in person now put me right back there, back to the way I'd sought to punish him the way he'd punished me. It'd clearly been a goodbye if ever there was one, which only became more apparent as the days passed and neither of us reached out to the other.

I hated it. I hated every second of hating him, because the truth was that I didn't hate him at all. He'd been upfront from the get-go, and I was the one who'd turned it into more, and though that didn't excuse his shitty behavior, the days apart had allowed me to see things a bit more clearly. So, no, it wasn't anger I felt toward Viper. It was heartache over losing what I never really had in the first place.

As if he felt my gaze on him, Viper's head turned in my direction, his eyes meeting mine, and my pulse sped up. For the briefest moment, I thought I saw the same longing in his expression that I felt, but he blinked and then it was gone.

Imogen tugged on my arm, her voice soft as she said, "Halo, we should probably go inside."

After spilling my guts to my sister, she'd taken on the protective mama-bear role, even insisting on coming with me tonight so I wouldn't have to face Viper alone. Thank God she'd seen through my protests that I was fine, because as I stood there with my legs feeling like they would go out any second, it helped to have her steady calm beside me.

When she tugged on me again, I tore my eyes away from Viper's and gave her a tight smile.

"Ready?" I said, and when she nodded, I led us into the building without stopping to speak with anyone else, and as soon as we were through those doors, I let out the breath I'd apparently held the rest of the way down the red carpet.

"Halo? You okay?"

"Yeah." My legs no longer wanted to collapse from underneath me, which was something, but I wasn't sure how I was supposed to be in the same room with Viper tonight and not feel like someone was stabbing me in the chest. One day it would pass and then all would be fine, surely. We'd be simply band members and nothing more, but right now? I wished I were anywhere but here.

"Maybe we should get a drink before we head up there?" Imogen suggested, and when I nodded, she steered us toward the bar and ordered a couple of vodkas on the rocks. I sat with my back to the entrance and noticed she kept looking past me, keeping a check on who entered the building.

I finished my drink off in a couple of long swallows, ready for the alcohol to numb some of my anxiety, but when I went to stand, Imogen put her hand on my arm.

"Wait," she said, her eyes focused over my shoulder, and she didn't have to say more for me to know Viper had made his way inside. A minute later, she dropped her hand. "Okay. You're good."

"Thanks, Im."

"Of course. Need another drink?" When I shook my head, she took a sip of hers. "PS, he looks like shit."

I snorted at her attempt to make me feel better. "He does not." Viper never could and never would look anything less than the gorgeous bastard he always was, no matter how I felt about him.

"Eh, maybe he's got some dark circle action goin' on."

"Good." I doubted it was true, but even if it was, it would probably only add to his appeal somehow.

Imogen finished off her drink, handed me a mint from her purse, and then we made our way to the elevator. The party was taking place in a ballroom on the top floor. The alcohol had started to kick in, easing the tension in my body as the elevator reached its destination and the doors opened.

The party was in full swing, people everywhere, and "Dark Angel" blasted through the speakers. As Imogen and I stepped inside, heads turned my way, and cheers and whistles rang out. I stopped, stunned that anyone even knew who I was—I'd probably never get used to that—and Imogen elbowed my ribs to get me moving.

I smiled and waved as we walked farther into the room, the crowd parting easily for us. Several people stuck their hands out as we passed, and I shook every one of them before Brian made his way over and shooed them away.

"Halo, finally. I've got a who's who of people for you to meet," he said, but when he caught sight of Imogen, he did a double take. "And who might your lovely date be?" Brian lifted Imogen's hand to his lips and planted what I was sure he thought was a charming kiss on the back of it.

"This is my sister, Imogen," I said.

"Sister?" Brian looked at me and dropped her hand as he straightened. "You couldn't find an actual date?"

As Imogen's mouth fell open, I said, "I'd rather have Im here than someone I have to pay."

Brian tsked and put his arm over my shoulders, leading me through the crowd, Imogen following. "You have so much to learn. You never have to pay a date. They'll pay to be seen with *you*."

The thought of someone using me to enhance their image turned my stomach, and I vowed right then that I'd never fall into that trap. "I don't think so," I said.

"It's the way this business works. You'll get used to it." Before I could respond, Brian tapped a woman on the shoulder, and when she turned around, he introduced me, ignoring Imogen completely.

Jesus, the guys were right. This guy *was* a total dick.

As the woman—the head of MGA's international department —engaged me in conversation, I reached back for Imogen and pulled her up to stand beside me, not wanting her to feel left out because our manager was a dick.

Brian stuck to my side like glue, unfortunately, taking me around for introductions with key members of MGA's team, and I did my part, giving them the agreeable version of myself that hadn't just gone through a shitfest of a week. I focused on the fact that the party tonight was for Fallen Angel, that we'd brought the music playing overhead into existence and everyone at the party was there to celebrate that fact.

If I hadn't been so distracted by keeping an eye out for Viper, I might've even said I was having fun.

After I made the rounds of industry execs, Brian ushered me toward a group of scantily clad women, a few of whom had on dresses—if you could call them that—that barely covered their asses.

"*That's* what he would've preferred for you?" Imogen said, the sour look on her face staying put as Brian presented me to the women and then stepped back, taking Imogen with him.

"You don't mind if I steal your dear sister away, do you? I've got someone I'd like her to meet." Brian was steering Imogen away before I had a chance to respond, and as she glanced over her shoulder at me, she shrugged as if to say, "It's fine."

Great. There goes my safety net, I thought, turning back to face the women who were circling me like vultures. It reminded me of the first night I'd gone out with the guys to Easy Street and had three groupies in my lap before I could blink. I wasn't about to put myself in that situation again, so before they could move in any closer, I held my hands up and said, "Ladies, thanks for coming. Enjoy the party and the album."

Then I was off, heading straight for the closest bar and praying they didn't follow me. There was only so much charm to pull outta my sleeve, and I wasn't wasting it on those girls, no offense to them.

When I reached the bar, I ordered a vodka soda, and when I had it in hand, I searched the room, looking for a quiet place to chill for a minute. I'd run into the guys as we got passed around the circles of execs, and I could see them now, still in separate corners of the room doing the meet-and-greet thing. I didn't see Viper anywhere, and I wasn't sure that was a good thing, since I didn't know where to avoid.

There were a couple of hallways that veered off the room, and without knowing where they led, I chose the one closest to me, hoping being out of view would give me a few minutes' respite.

My wish came true as I turned the corner to see a mostly empty hallway with only a couple of catering staff going in and out of the doors that must lead to the kitchen.

Good enough for me, I thought, leaning against the wall and taking a pull of my drink. I almost laughed at myself, because here I was, at my first official event, and I was lying low in a back hall-way. Ridiculous? Yes. But I needed a breather, and more than that, I needed a second to wrap my head around the emotions swirling through my brain.

I didn't care what Imogen said to make me feel better—Viper

looked good tonight. That perma-scowl and the don't-give-a-fuck attitude I'd been so attracted to until he'd used it on me...all that was still one seductive package.

Had it really been four days? I didn't think there had been a day that'd gone by since we met that we hadn't seen or spoken to each other. But sure enough, four long, miserable days had passed of wondering what he was doing, if he even cared what I was doing, and if any part of him thought I'd been right when I told him he was making a mistake. The look I'd seen flicker in his eyes on the red carpet earlier made me think maybe, just maybe, he was having a hard time without me too, but it had passed so fast that I wondered now if I'd made it up.

I dropped my head back against the wall and closed my eyes. Images of taking Viper on the roof, of using him the way I'd felt used, assaulted the peace I'd escaped the party to find, but I couldn't seem to open my eyes to make them stop. I still wanted to see the way he looked at me with his heart in his eyes even though he couldn't see it himself.

Forget him. Just fucking forget him.

Sighing, I brought the glass to my mouth and sucked an ice cube between my lips along with some of the vodka soda, and as I crunched on it, that was when I heard him.

"Hiding?" The deep rumble of Viper's voice had me snapping my head to where he stood a few feet away, his hands jammed in the pockets of his jeans. He gave me an uncharacteristically tentative smile. "Hey."

I swallowed the remaining ice but didn't move. "Hi."

Taking that as a sign he could come closer, he walked toward me, stopping a few feet away and letting his eyes roam over me.

"You look good, Angel," he said, and then, when it looked like he was going to move toward me again, I held up my hand.

"Don't. Just don't." I didn't need to hear him say that shit to me now, and I didn't need to be in a quiet hallway alone with him either. I didn't trust myself not to reach for him, even though I knew that would be a bad idea. A *very* bad idea.

Where the hell is Imogen when I need her?

An awkward silence descended as we stared at each other, neither of us saying a word, because what was there to say? We both knew where things stood, and that whatever had been between us couldn't and wouldn't ever happen again. It twisted my guts to think how easily I'd fallen for Viper, how I'd done it without even realizing. I never expected to want more. I never expected to want *him*.

As I looked at Viper, that was the one truth I couldn't deny. I wanted him. I *still* wanted him, and if he would only say the words now, tell me he was all in with me, then I'd be his in a heartbeat.

Say it. Just say it...

"Where the hell have you two been? Do you know how many people are looking for you?" Brian's voice thundered down the hall, startling us both out of our stare-down, as he marched over. "MGA hasn't spent tens of thousands of dollars on this party for the two of you to go MIA. Get out there and work the floor. That's what you're fucking here to do."

Viper ran his hand through his hair as he pinned Brian with narrowed eyes. "Give us a goddamn minute."

"Oh," Brian said. "I'm sorry, am I interrupting something? Guess what? I don't give a fuck. Get your asses out there before Marshall comes looking for you."

Viper took a step toward Brian, but before he could do something he'd regret, I said, "I'm going."

The look Viper gave me then told me he didn't want me to be the one to leave, but I wasn't going to stand around and play the staring game all night. If he didn't have anything to say to me, then I was out.

I made my way halfway down the hall before turning back in Brian's direction. "By the way, where the fuck's my sister?"

FORTY-TWO

Viper

MOTHERFUCKING BRIAN AND his motherfucking timing. The bastard always managed to stick his brown nose into shit he knew nothin' about, and as he pointed out Halo's sister and sent him on his way, I had the urge to rearrange his face.

"I've told you before not to fucking talk to me like that," I said, keeping my tone down to a low simmer so we wouldn't attract any attention—in case I *did* decide to give him an impromptu nose job. "And you sure as fuck don't need to speak to Halo with anything other than a 'yes, sir,' 'no, sir,' you feel me?"

I expected Brian's eyes to turn to slits and for him to mouth off the way he usually did. Instead, he crossed his arms and said, "What? Don't like the way I talk to your boyfriend?"

My face must've momentarily betrayed my surprise, because a smug smirk curled his lips.

"You think I don't know? I've seen you mooning the fuck over him all night."

"You've seen shit."

"Please. You haven't stopped watching him since you got here, and then you went and cornered him? What'd the kid do, turn you down and now your dick can't get over it?"

I growled and lunged at him, but Brian quickly jumped back a couple of steps, out of my reach and closer to the party.

"Whatever problem you have with me, leave Halo out of this," I said, teeth clenched.

"See, but that's the problem. *You* are the one dragging Halo down to your level. He doesn't need to be down with the likes of you—he needs to be out in the spotlight with a fucking supermodel."

Damn. That was it. That was fucking *it*.

I grabbed hold of his suit jacket and jerked him forward. "I warned you what would happen if you kept this shit up."

"What are you gonna do? Fire me?" He let out a strangled laugh. "You can't do that. You wouldn't be enjoying any of this"— he gestured behind him toward the party—"without me."

"I couldn't give two shits about what you think you've done or how long you've been with us. You're a fucking cunt, and if I have to look at your bitch-ass face for one more motherfucking second, I'll be tempted to rearrange it so you talk out of your asshole for the rest of your goddamn life."

Brian's eyes had gone so wide that I was shocked they didn't fall out onto his Gucci shoes. But it wasn't until I raised my arm, my fist balled tight, that fear entered his eyes.

"Wait, wait," he cried out, and I held my arm where it was. "I'm sorry."

"Damn right you are. You're a sorry sack of shit that's been a stain on our name for far too long. We're done. You're done. And you'll be lucky if you ever work in this business again—in the mail-room. Now, you can choose to leave quietly in the next five seconds, or I'll gladly have security toss your ass out. Do we under-stand each other?"

I punctuated my words by shoving him away so hard that he stumbled and fell back onto his ass. That slicked-back hair fell into his face, which had turned ten shades of crimson, and as I stepped past him, I said, "Oh, and Brian?"

I waited until his eyes met mine again, and then I gave him a savage smile.

"In case it's not crystal fucking clear—you're fired."

Brian scampered off like the cockroach he was, and as he disappeared from sight, he took with him the anger he'd ignited and left me with the original thoughts that had prompted me into the hallway, find the angel and talk to him—but Halo, of course, had vanished in the sea of people and was now nowhere to be found.

Christ. I'd known getting Halo to talk to me tonight would be an uphill battle, just as I'd known he would slam the door in my face if I dared set foot in front of his apartment after the way things ended on his rooftop. But when I followed him into the hallway and finally got my moment alone with him, I'd frozen, lost all my words, because Halo had looked at me with those gorgeous eyes of his, and I'd seen all of the pain and sorrow I felt reflected right back at me.

I'd really messed this thing up. No, not this thing—us. I'd really messed *us* up, and after copious amounts of alcohol, and four never-ending nights in an empty bed, I'd realized I had fucked up the best thing I'd ever had.

Not getting anywhere standing in an empty hallway, I shoved a hand through my hair and told myself to stop being the coward Halo had called me and go and find him. *Find him and tell him what you came here to tell him, or you might as well kiss him goodbye.*

I re-entered the party with about as much glee as someone at a funeral, and as I scanned the crowds of people, I couldn't see Halo anywhere. I wouldn't have been shocked to hear he had left, fled the scene so he wouldn't have to see me again. But I also knew how much this moment meant to the angel, and remembered his fierce stance on not quitting just because *we* no longer were.

"Looking for someone?" At the sound of Killian's voice, I turned to see him staring out in the same direction I was, and took in his styled hair, navy-blue suit, and the smug smirk on his mouth.

"Pretty sure you know who I'm looking for."

"Hmm," Killian said as he slipped his hands into his pockets and then finally looked in my direction. "Is he blond? About our height? Has a killer voice and the ability to make you fucking stupid?"

Ignoring him, I turned back to the people drinking, dancing, and mingling all around us, hoping Killian would get a clue—he didn't.

"Whatcha been up to this week?" he asked. "Haven't heard a peep out of you since you took Halo home to meet your mom."

"Haven't been up to anything."

"No?"

"No," I said, because a. it was the truth, and b. I wasn't about to tell him I'd spent the last four days in bed, sleeping with the shirt Halo had left behind.

"That's interesting."

"What is?"

"I asked Halo the same thing a minute ago, and he said almost exactly the same thing you just did."

Killian was staring at me with an eyebrow raised, and I knew there was no way I was walking away before he said whatever it was he had tracked me down to say.

"What did you do?" he said.

"Besides fire Brian? You're welcome, by the way."

That seemed to bring Killian's line of questioning to a grinding halt.

"You did *what*?"

"I fired that miserable cocksucker Brian. He's a piece of shit, and he pushed me too damn far tonight."

"Okaaay. We'll come back to that later. Now, what did you do to *Halo*?"

Acted like a total asshole. I had fucked over an angel. I was pretty sure that guaranteed me a special spot in hell. "I didn't do anything."

"Really? Because when I mentioned your name to Halo a second ago, his eyes took on this look. The same kind of look you get whenever someone mentions Trent. So I'm going to ask you again, what did you do, V?"

Shit. Shit, shit, *shit.*

I rubbed a hand over my mouth and shook my head. "I fucked up, okay? I fucked up the best thing that'll ever probably happen to me, and I'm trying to find Halo so I can tell him what a goddamn moron I am. So if you know where he is..."

Killian's lips twitched, as his eyes shifted over my shoulder. "He's across the room with his sister talking to Lori from *Entertainment Daily.*"

As soon as the words left Killian's mouth, I turned back to search Halo out, and sure enough, there he was standing opposite the curvaceous TV host, smiling politely.

Without any other thought in my head, bar getting to him before he disappeared again, I made a beeline through the crowd, my final destination clear. As my legs ate up the space between me and him, people moved aside, clearly sensing they should get the fuck out of my way and not bother trying to stop me. I was on a mission, and I was willing to walk over anyone to reach Halo.

As I closed in on him, his sister, Imogen, spotted me first, her eyes widening slightly—in alarm or surprise, I couldn't be sure. But before she could lean in and warn Halo of my imminent arrival, I opened my mouth and made sure he knew exactly who it was who had just stopped behind him.

"Angel." When Halo's head jerked in my direction, his lips parted, no doubt with a dismissal on them, but I beat him to the punch. "Can I speak to you for a minute?"

Halo's eyes narrowed, and as he stood there trying to work out what the hell I was up to, I could feel both his sister's and Lori's eyes boring into me.

"I'm busy right now," Halo said, polite as ever, and then went back to the conversation. But that wasn't going to work for me. I needed to talk to him. To tell him how wrong I'd been. How stupid, and that he was right: ending things had been the biggest fucking mistake of my life.

"Angel, I—"

"He's busy," Imogen said softly, but firmly, and when my eyes flicked to hers, I knew she was aware of everything that had gone down between me and her brother. She was aware and not fucking happy about it. Join the damn club. I don't think I could ever forget Halo's final words to me that night on his roof, and if he'd felt half as shitty as I had at hearing them, then I deserved every ounce of the disgust Imogen was aiming my way.

"I just want to—"

Halo turned on me, his eyes flashing as that fire from Monday night came to a head and he said between gritted teeth, "Not now, Viper."

But this time when he turned his back on me, Halo excused himself from Lori and went to leave. He got about two steps away, and before I knew what the hell I was doing, I said, "Well, then you let me know when you're ready, so I can tell you how much I fucking love you."

Halo came to an abrupt standstill, his entire body freezing in place, along with every other person in the near vicinity, and then he slowly circled back to face me. His eyes were wide, disbelief stamped all over his face, as his mouth opened and shut as though he were trying to speak but nothing would come out.

I didn't think it was possible to be standing in such a crowded room and have it fall silent, but the only sound I could hear was the music playing overhead mixing with the rush of blood in my ears. Everyone had stopped talking, because everyone was staring at the two of us, but the only person I could see was standing too far away from me.

I took the two steps needed to close the distance between us, and when I finally reached Halo, he blinked and shook his head.

"Wha...what are you doing?" he finally said, and for the first time in four of the longest days of my life, I reached out, took that exquisite face of his between my hands, and smoothed my thumb over his lower lip.

"I'm sorry," I said, and never had two words felt so right to say.

"I'm so fucking sorry for everything I said to you. Everything I did. None of it was true, Angel. You were right. I was scared. I *am* scared, because what I feel for you is more powerful than anything I've ever felt in my life. And the idea that I've lost you, that I've pushed you away—"

Halo reached up and gently touched his fingertips to my lips, halting my words, and all the pain and hurt that I'd seen earlier in his eyes melted away. "You wanna be with me?"

A heavy exhale left me. "You have no fucking idea how much."

Halo's eyes, those beautiful, luminous eyes of his, all but glowed as his lips curved into that charming smile I loved. "Then I'm ready."

It took me a second to realize what he was referring to, and then, without any hesitation at all, I said, "I love you, Angel. I love you more than I ever thought possible. And this week without you has been the most miserable fucking week of my life."

Halo slid his fingers through my hair, the grin on his lips growing impossibly wider as he rested his other hand over my thumping heart. "I love you too."

"You do?" I said as I reached for him, wrapping my arms around his waist.

"Of course I do. I'm a romantic, you cynical, jaded asshole. But if you ever pull this shit on me again—"

"I won't."

Halo chuckled as he wrapped both his arms around my neck and said against my mouth, "Good. Because every single person at this party is recording us right now. So I have proof of all of this."

"Wait, there are other people in this room?"

"Mhmm. For someone who didn't want to take this public, you aren't doing a real good job of keeping this a secret."

No, I wasn't. Was I? "That's your fault."

"How do you figure?"

"Because it's been too fucking long since I've kissed this mouth, and I'll be damned if I wait another minute."

As I leaned in to finally get my lips on the man smiling at me, the one who had consumed me from the moment I laid eyes on him, Halo curled his fingers in my hair, drawing me toward him. We met each other halfway, as equals, finally on the same damn page, and once his mouth met mine, I knew I was exactly where I was supposed to be. I was home. It may have taken me dragging us through hell to get there, but as I tightened my arms around Halo's waist and his mouth opened to me, I knew that now I had the angel right where I wanted him, there was no way I was ever letting go.

Thank You

Thank you for reading VIPER. We hope you enjoyed catching up with our smokin' hot rock stars!
Make sure to join us for the final book in Halo and Viper's journey, ANGEL, as they tackle their relationship and Fallen Angel's fame head-on.

You can pre-order ANGEL now!

Release Date: APRIL 25th, 2019

**Love VIPER? Leave a review!
Reviews are vital to authors, and all reviews, even just a couple of quick sentences, can help a reader decide whether to pick up our books.
If you enjoyed this book, please consider leaving a review on the site you purchased from. Halo and Viper may even give you a sneak peek of their new album if you do!**

Special Thanks

We've been wanting to dive into a rock star series for quite some time, and the stars finally aligned for us to bring you the guys of Fallen Angel! These sexy rockers are just getting started, so we hope you'll continue their journey in ANGEL.

We'd like to thank the following talented humans for helping us bring VIPER to life:

- Hang Le for the gorgeous Fallen Angel Series covers, banners, and teasers
- Sarah Jo Chreene for some fun surprises coming your way with this series (shhh we can't tell yet)!
- Arran for an always entertaining edit
- Judy's Proofreading for being our final eyes on HALO
- Charlie David for bringing these sexy men to life on audio.

A special thanks to the Naughty Brellas who named the guys of Fallen Angel!

Jay Ell ("Halo")

Jayne John ("Viper")
Brittany Cournoyer ("Killian")
Vandy Marie Bauer ("Jagger")
Sharna Morris ("Slade")

A huge thank you to the bloggers who support our work by taking time out of their busy lives to share our releases. You're the real rock stars. <3

Finally, if you're reading this, we'd also like to thank YOU for picking up this copy of VIPER. We're so grateful to be able to write these stories in our head for a living, and that is only possible with your continued support. A million thank you's and big bear hugs.

xoxoxox,
Brooke & Ella

About Brooke Blaine

About Brooke

Brooke Blaine is a *USA Today* Bestselling Author of contemporary and LGBT romance that ranges from comedy to suspense to erotic. The latter has scarred her conservative Southern family for life, bless their hearts.

If you'd like to get in touch with her, she's easy to find - just keep an ear out for the Rick Astley ringtone that's dominated her cell phone for years. Or you can reach her at www.BrookeBlaine.com.

Brooke's Links
Brooke's Newsletter
Brooke & Ella's Naughty Umbrella
Book + Main Bites

www.BrookeBlaine.com
brooke@brookeblaine.com

About Ella Frank

If you'd like to get to know Ella better, you can find her getting up to all kinds of shenanigans at:

The Naughty Umbrella

And if you would like to talk with other readers who love Ella's Chicago Universe, you can find them at:
Ella Frank's Temptation Series Facebook Group.

Ella Frank is the *USA Today* Bestselling author of the Temptation series, including Try, Take, and Trust and is the co-author of the fan-favorite contemporary romance, Sex Addict. Her Exquisite series has been praised as "scorching hot!" and "enticingly sexy!"

Printed in Great Britain
by Amazon

53275396R00147